CONVERSATIONS

WITH

LARRY XENOMORPH

Jay Cole

This is a work of fiction. Names, characters, places and incidents are the products of the author's imagination or are used fictitiously. Any resemblance to actual events, locals, or persons, living or dead, is entirely coincidental.

Published in the United States by Mach 1 Publishing, LLC.

1

I GOT IT STRAIGHT JACKET

If you've never spent a quiet evening in a padded cell, you haven't missed much. It's really quite boring.

Institutional living is new for me. A few days ago, I had a life—a challenging career, an active social life, a very high income and a Park Avenue address. Each new day was better than the last. Then I had a little nervous breakdown while strolling naked across the floor of the New York Stock Exchange. Surprisingly, everyone acted like this was an unusual occurrence.

The unexpected events of that particular day were altogether new to me in quite a few respects, but none were my fault. I had never before experienced a severe and completely overwhelming shock, nor did I know that a severe shock could turn me into a drooling, babbling idiot. In fact, I was completely unaware of both my surroundings and my nakedness as I attempted to explain to the rapidly responding police officers that I was speaking English and, in my mind at least, perfectly lucid. It probably didn't help that my confused ramblings were significantly louder than the fire alarm that I'd somehow managed to pull.

Living in New York City has some unique advantages. The police department here specializes in routinely handling weirdness. Two uniformed officers acted quickly and professionally. They carefully documented bits and pieces of the incoherent gibberish that I was spouting in the official arrest report, which also noted that my behavior was likely the result of either a genuine psychotic break or the use of some really primo illegal narcotics. The latter suspicion probably explains the body cavity search, and I can now state unequivocally that having a stranger stick a rubber-gloved finger into various orifices does not calm you down.

Since I have no living relatives, my case was presented to a judge from the Superior Court of the State of New York, who took all of thirty seconds to decide that I, Anthony Michael Sterling, needed to be hospitalized for a thirty-day psychiatric evaluation. Having never met the judge, I had no opportunity to plead my case. I can only assume the rule of thumb for judges is thirty seconds to sign the papers equals thirty days locked up in the nearest psychiatric hospital, which must of course be conveniently located anywhere but in the judge's home neighborhood.

The judge also appointed a conservator to look after my affairs. That's the legal euphemism for my money. Hopefully, there will be some of it left when I get out of here. I have twenty-three days to go. Twenty-three days to obsessively count and recount the days remaining in my sentence.

Sentence is actually the wrong word to use for a mental hospital, even if it feels right. I believe the correct term is involuntary commitment, but I'm not so much concerned with semantics as I am with my current living arrangements. I'm locked up with no parole, no reprieve, and no chance to appeal to the governor for clemency. The governor doesn't handle nut cases, which I also find surprising; I've seen the legislature.

For now, I sleep with a night light, a watchdog nursing staff, and relative to my behavior, the occasional straitjacket. At Sunny Park Hospital, they put everyone wearing a straitjacket into a padded cell. Arms contribute quite a bit to your balance, perhaps more than most people are aware. It's fairly easy to fall wearing this thing, and if you have to take a header into a wall, a padded wall is a huge benefit. Trust me.

Padded cells can actually be considered a modern invention. In ancient times, mental patients were taken care of by their families or simply left to aimlessly wander the streets and forage in the trash for food. Ancient Greek societies were particularly fond of the crazy. Many were called philosophers and the general public did their best to make sure they didn't starve, although the average, wandering street crazy was rarely invited into one's villa for a sit-down, home cooked dinner. Historians are split on whether this lack of dinner invitations is related to their mental illness or the fact that no one had yet invented bath soap.

Mankind soon progressed (?) to the Middle Ages when evil spirits, demons or the devil possessed the mentally ill. According to the most learned men of the time, exorcism and homicide were the recommended cures for people who were a little different. That is, until the even more learned men of the Spanish Inquisition developed an exciting new cure: slow and most vile torture, with burning at the stake becoming a very popular alternate.

Catholics have a holy day called Ash Wednesday. I wonder if that's related.

Regardless, burning the local witch or village wacko was considered great family entertainment in Medieval Europe. It was far cheaper than any Hollywood movie since you didn't have to purchase tickets to get a seat. There were no seats. And of course, the local vendors hadn't yet discovered that they could sell ridiculously priced tubs of hot buttered popcorn at a glass and chrome snack bar in the lobby. A medieval father could actually treat the whole family to a 3-D execution with live screaming for free. How can Hollywood possibly compete with that?

The highly enlightened times of medieval torture and death eventually gave way to our more modern, more enlightened age. Modern medicine took an entirely different approach to mental disorders. Freud brought out his cigar; Jung caught flack from everyone in his profession, and Dear Abby gave advice to those without health insurance.

Modern medical schools graduate modern learned men, highly trained in our newest religion, science. These learned men took over the duties of the village barber, the midwife, and of course, the exorcist and the inquisitor. Modern doctors no longer believe in demonic possession. Instead, they search for a pharmaceutical cure to mental disorders. Fresh, young medical students are routinely told that such a cure is a very realistic goal despite the fact that we do not fully understand human brain chemistry. They also ignore the other quite realistic view that most psycho-pharmaceuticals could just as easily have been mixed by a blind bartender.

It's important at this point to remember that, historically, psychiatrists have never been afraid of either a best guess or a genuine crapshoot when passing out pills in more colors than an extra-large box of crayons. Medical students are introduced to this bright, shiny, multi-colored future for psychiatric medicine during extensive overview lectures in their first year of medical school. It's one of the required prerequisite courses for young doctors along with Holier Than Thou 101, Ignoring Agony 302, and How to Biopsy a Wallet 207.

Naturally, modern times also require modern facilities. For the wealthy, private sanatoriums became the ideal place to hide the brother or cousin who was a little strange, or perhaps, more twisted than a corporate tax code lobbyist. State mental hospitals took care of everyone who couldn't afford better and had no relatives willing to hide them in the attic. The state hospital system worked for a while with varying degrees of success. It routinely weathered sensational front-page stories of abuse until various lawsuits and some very nasty political infighting killed the system.

Private sanatoriums were never an issue. The rich were permitted to hide their odd relatives wherever they liked. On the other hand, the state-run mental hospitals were very expensive to maintain and cutting the state budget always looks good at election time. More to the point, why waste public funds on caring for a bunch of loonies? This same money can be so easily embezzled or funneled into a congressman's pet pork barrel project. However, most politicians are astute enough to realize that publicly valuing money more than proper medical care for the unfortunate poor is suicidal during an election campaign. The voting public doesn't want that much truth! Therefore, you will never see a campaign slogan like, *Vote for me. I don't give a rat's ass about your crazy Uncle Harry.*

Our valiant political leadership developed an entirely different strategy. Civil rights issues play well in the press and make great sound bites for the six o'clock news. The Constitution guarantees every citizen the right to be as nutty as they please as long as they don't hurt anybody. (You can verify this with your nearest ACLU lawyer.) This philosophy evolved into our modern, politically correct solution to the sanity-challenged. All non-violent mental patients were released from the state mental hospitals and left to aimlessly wander the streets and forage in the trash for food.

If it worked for Aristotle. . .

As I mentioned, I have no family. However, I'm financially comfortable with fantastic health insurance, so I now have a padded cell instead of a heated sewer grate and my civil rights. After the above sophomoric history lesson, you'd think I would be happy to be in a nice warm hospital, but no, I'm pissed as hell.

I've actually been restrained in a straitjacket and padded cell only once. My behavior is generally very good, and despite rumors to the contrary, I'm perfectly capable of judging my own behavior. Trust me, my sanity is not at issue. My involuntary commitment to Sunny Park Hospital's mental health wing is purely a matter of circumstance. I'm not crazy. But feel free not to believe me. No one else around here does.

"Somebody come in here," I yelled. It took a while, but the sliding panel on my cell's padded door finally opened.

"What do you want, Tony?" The disembodied voice of the night nurse was aggravated at having his crossword puzzle and thermos of chicken noodle soup interrupted. I could tell from the heavily peppered aroma that the soup was homemade. Normally, I would have commented on how good it smelled, but I was distracted by the business at hand. "I need you to scratch my nose," I said.

"Scratch your own nose!"

"I can't, you idiot. You put me in a straitjacket."

The night nurse hesitated outside the door considering whether my calling him an idiot justified his ignoring my itch. Finally with a heavily labored sigh, he said, "Just rub it on the wall."

"I can't. The itch is right in the corner by my left nostril. I'd have to rub half my face off to reach it."

The nurse repeated his heavily labored sigh, which I believe was a commentary on his entire existence. "All right, Tony. But, this is the last time I'm coming over here tonight. After this, you get some sleep, you hear?"

"I promise."

"Bring your nose over to the door."

I hobbled towards the open panel. My ankle was still stiff from the sprain that I'd received when I fell in the cafeteria on a misplaced gob of potatoes and gravy while trying to prove that food fights are acceptable entertainment for the demented.

I think that pretty much screws my good behavior argument, doesn't it?

Anyway, the current administration of the hospital's mental health wing was not amused by a food fight in the cafeteria and hastily labeled it a riot. Worse, it seems I was identified as the instigator of the festivities. Not true, but I did admirably well considering my inexperience in edible warfare.

I did try half-heartedly to talk the hospital administrator out of confining me in this straitjacket and the padded cell, but a bureaucratic mentality and a sense of humor are the oil and water of the universe. It was a waste of breath.

The administrator, Arnold Pelekinako, was a big, brawny Hawaiian with a perpetual tan, pomaded black hair, and an unusually aggressive attitude about everything. The laid-back personality one normally associates with the wonderful people of the Pacific islands did not migrate to the mainland with Arnold. Hearing of the "riot" in the cafeteria, he charged in with an army of quickly conscripted doctors, nurses and orderlies. With the exception of a few extraordinarily dedicated food fighters, most of the patients and a few of the cafeteria staff froze in place when they saw Arnold's army arrive. The crowd's reaction reminded me of a large group of toddlers caught red-handed raiding a cookie jar.

Under Arnold's disapproving stare, the staff began gathering up the patients and herding them off to their assigned rooms. The more heavily food-encrusted had to be herded by way of the showers.

Now, I'll readily admit a food fight is incredibly juvenile, but most of the hospital's staff members were thoroughly amused. This was a break in routine.

People generally hold the impression that hospitals are exciting places to work. You've watched lots of television shows, which portray brave, incredibly handsome doctors fighting for someone's life in the emergency room, or bent over an operating table performing delicate miracles with ultra-sharp implements. In your living room, such programs fill the gap between commercials for new products that are built more cheaply than the ones you already own. However, television never broadcasts a show about the dedicated nurses and orderlies who change the same dressing on the same wound on the same patient on the same shift every four hours, day after day after day, sometimes for weeks. Sameness permeates most of hospital life. Outside of the emergency room, patient care is a lot of boring routine mixed with an equal lot of terribly tedious paperwork. The unexpected is most often feared due to the life and death nature of such events. However, when the unexpected is something as joyous and bloodless as a food fight, the hospital staff has every right to laugh, if only to relieve the tension from such incredibly long, incredibly dull workdays.

Regardless, Arnold Pelekinako wasn't laughing. He picked one of the patients, a small, timid young man in his late teens, and bellowed at him, "Who started this?"

The poor kid nearly collapsed in fright.

Now, I didn't know the young man's name or anything about him, but I did know two things: this young patient was afraid of the floorboards squeaking under his feet, and only a grade-A bastard shouts accusingly at an obviously terrified mental patient.

"Leave him alone," I said.

"So, you started it," yelled Arnold.

"No, I didn't."

"Then stay out of this." He turned back to the timid kid and started to open his overly large mouth.

"I said, leave him alone, Arnold. It doesn't matter who started it."

"My name is Mr. Pelekinako."

"Whatever you say, Arnold, now back off and leave the kid alone."

I figured the staff sided with me because one of the nurses hustled the frightened kid out of Arnold's reach while I had him distracted. "You did start it, didn't you," he continued as his face lit up with the satisfaction of finding the guilty party, or just as good, any available party to designate as guilty.

"This was a food fight, Arnold, not a murder. The damage can be cleaned up with a mop."

Now, he was bellowing at me. "This is a hospital!"

"That explains why there are no slot machines in the lobby. I swear that bus driver told me we were going to Atlantic City."

The nurses laughed, but quickly squelched it when Arnold's angry gaze moved in their direction. "You can't start a riot in a hospital," he said.

"This wasn't a riot and I already told you I didn't start it. If anything, this was good for patient morale, but if you want to blame me, feel free." I did my best to irritate him with my tone of voice and attitude, covering the frightened kid's escape. I slowed down a bit when I saw the day nurse lead the young man safely out a side door.

None of the other staff members or patients moved an inch. They all wanted to witness our ridiculous argument. Frankly, I didn't care if I won or lost. I figured irritating Arnold didn't have much of a downside. Understanding one's position in life is important in every circumstance but becomes critical during confrontations. I was a patient in a mental hospital. Arnold was the senior administrator in charge of the mental health wing. Despite his bluster, the worst he could do is screw up my paperwork.

Or, so I thought.

"Confine this patient to Ward Four until you're sure he's stable," said Arnold to Nurse Cassilio.

It's impossible to be a mental patient at Sunny Park for more than an hour without knowing that Ward Four was the designation for the hospital's padded cells (AKA rubber rooms; AKA isolation; AKA limbo; AKA Damn, you need a new decorator!). Word of fearful things like Ward Four—or Arnold—circulates lightning fast among the patients. The only thing that most mental patients fear more than solitary confinement in Ward Four is an involuntary trip to Electro-Convulsive Therapy (AKA shock therapy; AKA the world's worst buzz).

"That's not therapy, Arnold," I continued. "That's punishment for a crime I didn't commit, and very unprofessional."

"Ignore him," he said to Nurse Cassilio. "Take him to Ward Four."

I turned to Nurse Cassilio and modified the administrator's orders, "And see that Arnold here gets a change of clothing."

"What are you talking about," asked Arnold.

"Even a bastard like you shouldn't wear a suit that badly stained." I winged my last handful of potatoes and gravy at Arnold, nailing him dead center and ruining his cheap wool suit and the bland, blue silk tie, which he'd worn every day since graduating university with his master's degree in Ass Holiness.

"You. . .!" Arnold never did complete a coherent sentence. He was quite literally too angry for words.

"You can't blame me, Arnold. I'm a mental patient. I'm not responsible for my actions. Ain't life grand!"

The staff members held their sides as they tried to stifle their laughter. My immature antics made me a hero to everyone who had to work for this loud-mouthed prig. The patients remaining in the cafeteria were less concerned with hospital decorum and applauded over Arnold's overly loud demand that I be removed at once.

Nurse Cassilio led me along to Ward Four and apologized profusely for putting me in a straitjacket, but understandably she wanted to keep her job. I forgave her without a second thought. Nurse Cassilio is a sweetheart.

So now, I'm in an eight by twelve padded cell with a sore ankle, an itchy nose and a night nurse reluctant to address my minor nose itch problem because he's burdened with thoughts of an unfinished crossword and cooling-as-we-speak chicken soup. Fortunately for me and my itchy nose, the night nurse's dedication to his patients took precedence over hot soup and a seven letter word for a bunch of fruit (bananas).

"You're a saint, my nameless friend," I said as the hospital clean and neatly manicured hand reached through the door panel and scratched the corner of my nose. I suppressed a sudden, totally irrational urge to bite his Samaritan hand. After all, who knows when I might need it again? I thought it best to maintain nose scratching as a pleasant experience for all concerned.

"Is that better," he asked.

"That's wonderful. Just a little harder." The itch subsided, at least, the one on my nose. Directing my next question to the small portion of the nurse's mustachioed face that I could see through the open panel, I asked, "When do I see Dr. Busty again?"

"Dr. Bousteir will call for you when it's time." He feigned annoyance.

"You almost laughed that time. I saw it."

"She does have a great set of. . ." He stopped himself. His hand jerked back, disappearing on the other side of the door. "Tony, we can't talk like that. It's not good for you and I could get in trouble."

"Not good for me? Since when is it not good to talk about a fine looking woman? I'm not a eunuch. You just think I've lost a few of my marbles. And frankly, you haven't convinced me that I'm the one who's crazy."

"Go to sleep, Tony."

"Do you really think beautiful women don't notice drool? For crying out loud, the lady's got a Ph.D. or MD, or some other D. She's not stupid. Not to mention that she must look in her bathroom mirror in the morning. I just wish I could."

"Good night, Tony!"

The panel slammed closed. You just can't get a good, pointless discussion going at midnight anymore

I awoke when the breakfast cart clanked into the west wing and onto Ward Four through the extra-wide doors in the long, dreary, linoleum tiled corridor near my cell. I felt tired and stiff. The straitjacket I had somehow managed to handle, but sleeping with the lights on has always been difficult for me. Hospital policy lets the staff dim the lights a bit, but it's never quite dark. They're afraid one of the inmates is going to do a Houdini on the straitjacket and then try to kill themselves, or heaven forbid, someone important like a member of the staff.

Even in the regular rooms, small night lights are built into the walls just above the baseboards. They give off a constant dim glow. I figure I can forget about a good night's sleep until I convince my ever lovely doctor, Dr. Bousteir, that I'm not delusional, have no intention of doing myself or anyone else any harm, and that I really am telling the absolute, as-God-is-my-witness truth about what happened at the stock exchange.

I remained horizontal for another minute feeling sorry for myself and bemoaning my lousy night's sleep. It could have been worse. I could have been sleeping on the floor. The cot in my cell was a major concession from the staff. Most of the padded cells have no furnishings, again for fear of personal injury. However, Nurse Cassilio took pity on me and set up a cot with a cheesy little mattress in one corner. Hospital policy wouldn't allow her to give me sheets or a pillow, but I was genuinely grateful for her efforts to make me as comfortable as possible. I personally believe that the word nurse should be listed in the dictionary as a synonym for *all the really good stuff*. If it's a really hot nurse, feel free to use the same synonym.

Swinging my legs for leverage, I sat up, adjusting my rump on the thin, lumpy mattress hoping to find the spot with the smallest lumps. Before being strapped and buckled into this straitjacket, I never realized how important a good morning stretch is to me. Unconsciously, it's the first thing I do every morning. I tried flexing my shoulder and back muscles. It wasn't very effective, not the same thing at all. If this is what I have to put up with, the next time we have a food fight in the cafeteria, I'm going to throw more than potatoes and gravy at Arnold.

Using a little bounce on the cot, I managed to stand. I tried pacing my cell to loosen up a bit just as the door creaked open.

Breakfast!

Suddenly, I was ravenously hungry.

The nurse attending the breakfast cart is even larger than my new pal, Arnold. He's a friendly, black giant named Mohammed Ali Jones. "Mo" has a deep caramel complexion, a chrome dome, handsome features and a compassionate nature. At six-foot-five, two hundred and ninety-five pounds, Mo rarely has much trouble with the inmates, except for the ones who are truly crazy. The first time I noticed that his biceps are larger than my thigh, I decided not to be crazy around Mo.

He carried in my morning tray. The stainless steel cover over the plate had a hint of steam rising from the vent hole in the top. The kitchen staff went to great lengths here at Sunny Park to get your meal to you reasonably hot. Mo fed me today's special, scrambled eggs, hash browns and mildly spiced sausage links that weren't as greasy as I expected. There was no knife for obvious reasons, so Mo buttered my toasted

English muffin with the back of a spoon and set it on the side of the heavy ceramic plate.

Mo amazes me with how gentle he is. He helped me to sit back down on the edge of the cot and spooned the eggs, wiping my mouth with a napkin between bites. He told me what a great day I was going to have, how quickly I would get better, and how soon I would be out of the hospital and back in normal society. It was important to Mo to constantly encourage everyone. I didn't have the heart to tell him that I'm perfectly healthy and perfectly sane.

Mo fed me first on the morning that I ended up in the straitjacket. I think he likes easing into his daily routine so I was served before Little Richard, Winston Churchill and the other genuine wall-bouncers on the ward. And yes, they do indeed have the requisite Napoleon in residence, three cells down, next to Norman Rockwell.

Between the second bite of egg and the first bite of sausage, Mo started relaying the daily hospital news:

1. Patient Claudia Taron was being released today. The voice in her head was finally gone. It's rumored that it even said goodbye.
2. Nurse Dorothy's daughter had a baby girl, seven pounds-four ounces. Mother and baby are both doing fine.
3. The hospital administration is considering badminton for the non-violent, ambulatory patients and a possible field trip to the local candy factory. They'd give the staff a decision during next Wednesday's regular meeting.

While the hospital news is generally more interesting and has fewer commercial breaks than the sensationalized crap the networks broadcast at six and eleven, I had more important things on my mind. "When will I see Dr. Busty?"

"I imagine you'll see her this afternoon," Mo said. "I'll check the schedule for you if you like."

"I'd like that very much."

"No problem, Tony. I'll let you know as soon as I've finished feeding a few of the other patients."

"Thank you, Mo."

"You're very welcome, Tony."

Who says men don't have manners?

2

Honesty Is Optional

I felt the pull from the spaceship just after Mo left. It starts with a tingling, which quickly crawls through me until it sets my nerves to screaming. Not painful, mind you, but every sensation is heightened until I feel everything around me as if it were a part of my own mind and body.

Since the most ancient of times, mankind has tried to expand human consciousness. We've tried everything, sex, drugs, rock and roll, meditation and selective breeding. We've tried witchcraft and the so-called dark arts. We pray and starve and whip ourselves into frenzied states, only to be fooled into believing that we've achieved nirvana and oneness with our universe.

Mankind is a bunch of amateurs!

Yes, I know that sounds grossly egotistical, but I assure you no apology is needed. I stand alone in my padded cell as an alien pulls me away from my very existence. To say the feeling is strange is grievously inadequate. I could not have imagined this experience if I were skinny-dipping in a vat of LSD.

That's not my vat, officer. I read about it on the web, honest.

Actually, no one sells drugs this good.

No one blends scotch half as good.

No meditation is more than a smidgen as good.

No sensual woman. . . .Okay, I shouldn't go there if I ever expect to get another date on this planet.

My surroundings blend into consciousness as new limbs, new senses and new thoughts, even new emotions. The emotional parts are almost overwhelming.

Colors and textures evoke emotions most often. I feel the dull white from my cell's padded walls and wish immediately for something more vivid, exciting. Lime green would be nice today. Lime green feels like I'm a kid again, playing with a new puppy. It's all wonder, happiness and laughter, but warm and furry.

Just take my word for it.

The aluminum frame of my cot merges into my left side, forming a skeleton as the black-stenciled mattress wraps into flesh and skin around it, scratchy but muscular.

I'm aware that a few inquisitive ants have entered under the cell door. Their footsteps become mine. I feel the rush of breath through their spiracles and their antennae become my own, waving about, searching along the floor and wall. I experience moving with articulated legs and a burning desire to tell all my new ant friends where a few crumbs of toasted English muffin from my breakfast had fallen to the floor beside the cot. Having just eaten, I'm no longer hungry, but I can't speak for everyone in the nest. And of course, I know the queen, that greedy bitch, always needs a snack.

My straight jacket is a smothering cocoon, annoyingly part of me. The metal buckles weigh a ton. Then, it was gone.

The straight jacket can't make the journey with me. None of my clothing ever does. I guess aliens have a thing for studying their captives in the buff.

Then, it's light, pulsing, flickering, blinding white light.

Sensations amplify themselves tenfold when the light sucks me into a stream of energy and particles. All of my being joins the stream of rushing, swirling bits. I wonder once again why my consciousness doesn't just disappear when my brain is a trillion pieces of scattered flotsam. Think of more billiard balls than you've ever seen bouncing, jostling, careening off one another and the edge of the light beam, which forms a barrier or bumper of sorts. As my eyes are currently a mass of little floating bits, I can't see this swirling mess, but I'm somehow keenly aware of it. Then, very suddenly, it's gone.

I'm whole again, deposited ever so gently at my destination with a final little flicker and that peculiar tinkling sound that only light can make as it flows through your brain. Once again, I'm lying flat on my back on a very alien, very cold, metal examination table. The table is colder than usual this morning. I should file a complaint with the management.

I always land in the same room on the alien spaceship. At about twenty by thirty, it's fairly large, but just as sterile as Sunny Park Hospital. However, the pristine, hospital-white walls are now replaced with matte silver, punctuated by the occasional light fixture. The ceiling is crowded with equipment, wires and piping, forming an organized maze with unexplained purpose. Dull silver also covers the floor.

Apparently, alien culture has not embraced industrial linoleum, which I deem definitive proof that they're more advanced.

You have to see everything coated in this lusterless silver color to fully appreciate it. Try putting a large cast iron pot on your head. No matter which way you turn, everything has the same polished finish. Trite as it sounds, the best description is agonizingly dull. It's worse than Thanksgiving dinner with a dedicated accountant.

The equipment hanging on every wall and from the ceiling interested me on my first few trips. I asked numerous questions about the gear, but finally gave up. I realized the answers would always be extremely generalized or not answered at all. More than likely, many of these gadgets have no translatable name, or if they do, it's far outside my area of understanding. I should have taken more postgraduate courses in advanced aeronautics and alien spacecraft design. Although, I understand you can get the same information by logging onto Star Trek websites.

My alien kidnapper, Larry, hadn't arrived yet. He was a lousy host for which I was thankful. I was getting the mobility back in my limbs faster each time I went through the jump to the ship. I remember the paralysis scared the hell out of me the first time. I think it's somehow related to the sensory overload of my nervous system caused by the transport, but I think I'm getting used to it.

I concentrated on making my left foot move. By craning my head with a supreme amount of will, I saw my foot flopping around trying to follow my commands. I clenched my fists, wiggled fingers and toes, and was just trying to sit up when a portal opened in the wall to my left and my alien kidnapper, Larry, entered.

"Good morning, Tony."

While I admit to having a sarcastic streak a mile wide, I'm generally an even-tempered person and rarely am I intentionally nasty. My current situation is a justifiable exception. You have to understand that Larry took my life away—all of it. My involuntary jaunts to his spaceship managed to get me committed to a mental health facility. Without my consent, Larry had changed my career from Wall Street stock trader to incarcerated nutcase. Worse, I was expected to hold a part-time job on his ship serving as lab rat of the day. This is not the way to start a *Casablanca*-beautiful friendship.

I always met Larry with the same warm and fuzzy greeting, "Die, scum."

"Thank you. But, there's no reason to be formal at this point." I think Larry smiled, but I can't quite be sure. "We're becoming quite good friends, don't you think?"

"I never had a doubt. I've dearly loved each and every one of my kidnappers."

Larry hesitated. "You've had others?"

"The police in Podunk, Georgia held me and my Mercedes for ransom a few years back. It seems their speed trap took a dislike to my New York plates."

"Interesting. You'll have to tell me about that sometime."

Larry vocalized a string of shriek-whistle-click tones, which I must assume is his native language. He uses these tones to control the flat-screen monitor, which drops from the overhead on command. The monitor is paper-thin; there's no wiring and it floats freely in the air. If it were mounted on the wall, you could easily mistake it for a nice 36-inch, Earth-style television. Verbal command and some sort of proximity detection control the screen's placement in the room. I've seen it automatically move out of the way for Larry as he walks about the room. When not in use, the monitor floats back into its recess in the ceiling.

"Today, I want you to tell me about a new phenomenon," said Larry.

"Which one?"

The monitor started playing television commercials for some of the more popular health spas. Lots of good-looking, young men and women smile and sweat for the cameras in tight, skimpy outfits, displaying rock-hard bodies that normal people will never have. Then, the picture flipped to the six o'clock news from a local Midwest TV station that had a special report on the latest fitness craze that was sweeping the country. The reporter called it a 'phenomenon.'

"Oh, that one," I said to Larry.

"It seems your people expend time and energy without accomplishing any real work. And, they pay some of your money to other humans to do so."

"That's true."

Larry's questions were always monotone, never hinting at the sincere curiosity, which I've come to believe prompted him to become my kidnapper. "Can you explain?" he asked.

Here, I should mention one important caveat: You may notice that I'm never completely honest with Larry about the ins and outs of human culture. Keeping him confused is my primary goal and I believe I'm making good progress.

Can I explain health clubs? You betcha!

"Easy. Some of my people are addicted to pain and some are addicted to pleasure. It's a genetic predisposition. The ones that are addicted to pain pay money to so-called health spas and gyms so they can use their specialized pain equipment to work endlessly till they're sweaty, exhausted, pained, and possibly, genuinely injured. The ultimate accomplishment is to have pulled muscles and really wracking cramps while you puke in a metal bucket, but you have to pay extra for that.

"The people who are addicted to pleasure pay their money to certain barely legal business enterprises located in certain counties surrounding Las Vegas, Nevada, or to freelance entrepreneurs, who can be located anywhere. You have to pay a lot more to use specialized pleasure equipment, and generally, the pleasure people don't get to puke very often, but there are other compensations. They get just as sweaty as the pain people and they're permitted to wear a latex sheath on their genitals."

"This is fascinating," said Larry. "We didn't know anything about this." He set about making the usual copious notes, shriek-whistle-clicking away into the small handheld recorder that he always carries during our interviews.

"Is that all you wanted today," I asked?

"Just one more question. Your advertising seems to be aimed at the pain people. Don't the pleasure people compete for the money?"

"Absolutely! They advertise by word of mouth."

"Word of mouth?"

I nodded vigorously. "Every time you see two men together in a bar, you can bet one of them is telling the other about specialized pleasure equipment. And, every time you see two women together in a bar, there's a better than even chance they're doing the same thing. Unless one of them has found a fifty-percent off sale on a piece of clothing that the other woman hasn't seen yet. Then they'll be talking about where to buy it and where to get the best use out of it before they have to throw it away and replace it with some newer, brighter, slicker, faddy fashion, which is probably just as butt-ugly as it is uncomfortable."

I knew I was on a roll when the little hairy whatever-it-was on his forehead started to twitch a bit.

"Why would women discard usable clothing?"

"Are you kidding me? You've never heard of clothing mites. They breed in anything sold by a boutique. You can get a really severe rash if you wear something that's out of style."

"I see." That was Larry's favorite response, but I knew he didn't see squat. His little hairy bit went from twitching to dancing a drunken rumba. I haven't figured Larry out completely yet, but I think that means he's confused and trying to process the bull I was feeding him. My current goal is to get the little hairy on his forehead to pong all the way to the back of his neck someday. I figure if he could give me a nervous breakdown, I should have the right to return the favor.

"Why do the pleasure people only do this word of mouth advertising in bars?"

"Well, you can do it in other places, but in most countries, it's considered customary to advertise in a bar because of the close linguistic connection between *libido* and *libation*. And of course, libido and libation are also major factors in most countries' birth rates. In other countries, constitutional law requires the pleasure people to attend what's called Happy Hour. In that case, the advertising is just a matter of convenience since the people are required to be in their neighborhood bar anyway."

"I see." His little hairy was twitching overtime. "But, aren't the pain people allowed to advertise by word of mouth?"

"They were allowed to at one time, but it's now nearly universal, that is to say, it's customary on most of my little planet, to only endorse deep, seething aches and pains in locker rooms, ambulances and just after undergoing major surgery to correct your injuries. And most people stick with that. Unless you're a professional athlete, then your injuries have to be announced on the six o'clock news and they broadcast the replay of your injuries so everyone can enjoy the pain vicariously. It's the law, Larry. We respect the law."

Larry's little hairy was disco dancing up and down his forehead. I knew my next answer was going to require an extra dose of sincerity. It was time to pontificate.

"But," he sputtered, "why are all of the pain people in the advertising smiling?"

"It's because only the elite-class pain people are chosen to appear in the advertising. And, they're just incredibly happy that they finally made it into the elite category." My pores were oozing sincerity.

"What makes them elite?"

"We're talking serious pain here, Larry. Two, maybe three major groin injuries, at least one torn tendon, although some countries allow you to substitute a compound fracture, and at a minimum of weekly, everything you throw-up has to have come from a five star restaurant. It takes serious commitment and quite a bit of money to become elite."

Larry quickly updated his notes. "So, poor people have no hope of becoming elite?"

"Well, there's always hope, Larry. But, most poor people won't spend their money on a health spa. They get just as vigorous a workout by smoking a pack of cigarettes while pushing their broken-down car home."

He shriek-whistle-clicked a few more lines into the recorder. "I'm a little confused by this."

"Just relax. I'll explain it all in time. And, speaking of time, I have to be back for my appointment with Dr. Busty. Would you mind?"

"No problem, Tony. I'll talk to you again tomorrow after I've studied some more about this phenomenon."

It always creeped me out the way he could shriek-whistle-click and speak English at the same time. But usually, he only did that when he was saying good-bye and energizing the equipment to jump me back to Earth.

"Good-bye", said Larry.

"And, hemorrhoids to you, my friend," I said as the jump started.

Just for the record: During my jaunts to Larry's spaceship, I may have also commented on one or two other topics.

Larry Learns Money
"Money was invented for convenience. Originally, we traded women and horses, but both kept running away."

Larry Learns Economics
"Every country on Earth has its own economy, usually based on various concepts of fair competition. The trick is to make it unfair while avoiding uncomfortable chats with a grand jury."

Larry Learns Government
"Many countries had a king, who in most cases killed anyone who challenged him. Then we developed the dictator, who in most cases killed anyone who challenged him. This worked for a while, but people wanted something more formal. We then invented Fascism where the ruler killed anyone who challenged him *and* anyone who marched to a different drummer. This was very efficient, but the funeral costs were just outrageous."

Larry Learns Childcare
"If you can get away from your kids whining for a lousy twenty bucks, that's one of life's biggest bargains! Why? Do you have something against using mall cops as babysitters?"

Larry Learns Commodities Trading
"The price of gold is just ridiculous. Nothing should be that expensive per ounce when you can't put it up your nose."

Larry Learns Earth Science
"The Nobel Prize is awarded for discoveries and inventions that benefit all mankind, like the thong bikini."

Larry Learns Higher Education
"Japanese students who don't get accepted into college have been known to commit suicide, but American students who don't get accepted just continue living at home. They don't need to commit suicide. After a few years, mom and dad will kill them."

Larry Learns Food
"Eating chocolate releases endorphins that simulate the feeling of being in love. Current food researchers also hope to find a flavor that will simulate the feeling of a good one-night stand."

Larry Learns Bar Hopping
"Of course, there are some bars where even the cockroaches won't sit with their backs to the door."

Larry Learns Marketing
"The pope came to New York this past year. Commemorative souvenirs were selling on every street corner. I don't usually go for that sort of thing, but I got so caught up in it, I bought a nun."

More later. Right now, I have to get to my appointment.

3

DR. BUSTY'S FAMOUS BRAIN RECONSTRUCTION

Mo escorted me to Dr. Bousteir's office just before eleven o'clock. The walk to her office is one of my favorite pastimes even though the static scenery is rather bland. The sterile white walls display the usual bulletin boards crammed with announcements. These hang beside cheaply framed watercolors from local artists. While I truly sympathize with the plight of starving artists in today's quarterly statement challenged society, several of the paintings give me a distinct preference for the bulletin boards.

It seems that everyone who owns a watercolor set has to paint water—ocean waves, placid lakes, water going over a fall, water falling from a stormy sky, water with ducks, water with ducks swimming and flying, water with people in a boat scaring the ducks into swimming and flying. Endless blue water.

There is one painting of a classic clown face with a bright red nose, oversize smile and a single teardrop below the left eye. Except for the tear, there isn't a drop of water in sight. Assuming this local artist had access to the same water, water and more watercolor kit as everyone else, the only possible explanation is that he didn't read the directions.

Along our route, there are also two spots where the 1950's style, black and white floor tiles lay out an excellent hopscotch board. It isn't as much fun without a stone, but still genuinely challenging trying not to overbalance if you're wearing a straitjacket. I couldn't remember the correct rhyme for hopscotch, so I made up my own:

One, two, three, four,
Going to Dr. Busty's door.
Five, six, seven, eight,
Hope my breath don't smell like bait.

Okay, I'll never be Walt Whitman. Sue me.

Continuing down the corridor, the patient sideshows are the truly entertaining part of our walk.

- Mrs. Renardo is once again singing her aria from a bastardized version of Mozart's nightmares.
- Two orderlies are subduing a man, who is trying to eat an intern's shoe with the intern's foot still in it.
- Martin Something-or-other, the quintessential regular in the corridor, retouches all the artwork with an imaginary paintbrush.
- An Indian fellow with a bright yellow turban prays to the pay phone using a prayer mat and an incense burner that the staff will never allow him to light.
- Cute, freckle-faced Bonnie, one of the few resident teenagers, hands out toilet brushes, bristles up, as if they were long-stem roses. No one has yet figured out where she gets the brushes.
- Winston Churchill (I don't know his real name.) stops us briefly to seek our support for the lend-lease program and to ask if we want his autograph. He also has a bad habit of searching everyone's pockets, looking for his cigar.

I'm telling you, mental hospitals are the most unique version of *America's Got Talent* that you will ever see. If only some demented television producer would take notice, Sunny Park could become the best reality show ever.

Next along our route is a special treat, Nurse Tammy Sellers ambushes us to once again flirt with Mo. Nurse Tammy personifies cute. She's African-American, tall and slender but proportionally curvaceous, today wearing baby blue scrubs with sturdy nursing shoes. Her personality matches her perpetual smile, which is warm and sincere. There isn't a man alive who wouldn't judge Nurse Tammy an absolute knockout. My bet is that most of the unmarried males on staff have asked her out at least once, but Nurse Tammy has her sights set on Mo. She just about jumps into the big guy's arms every day while Mo blushes, stutters and desperately tries to find a reason to excuse himself and hurry away.

"Good morning, handsome," said Nurse Tammy.

"Yeah, uh. . . it's, uh. . . morning," stammers Mo.

Nurse Tammy touched the big guy's arm, gently squeezing his biceps. "I need you to lend me those big muscles this afternoon. I have to take Mrs. Henderson down for a CAT scan. She's convinced herself that she's paralyzed and won't get out of bed. We have to lift her and she's definitely a heavyweight."

"Lift, uh, okay."

Can Mo banter, or what?

Since Sunny Park is practically wallpapered with nurses and orderlies to handle patient care, it does make one wonder why Nurse Tammy needs Mo's help everyday.

"Shouldn't be a problem for a big, strong man like you," Nurse Tammy coos.

"Lift, uh, okay."

Believe it or not, Mo is intelligent, highly educated, and very articulate. Nurse Tammy just strips all the gears in the poor guy's head. I've actually seen a deer caught in my headlights. With Nurse Tammy in the vicinity, Mo is worse. Much worse.

"I'll page you when I'm ready," she said with an absolutely radiant smile as she leisurely turned and strolled back toward the nurse's station. Both Mo and I now had a ringside view of her truly magnificent butt, however that little extra sway in her hips was definitely aimed at him.

"Lift, uh, okay," said Mo. Mesmerized, he watched Nurse Tammy disappear around the corner, then he stared at his arm where she had touched him.

I've got to help this poor bastard. Anybody have a gun?

"It's called flirting, Mo. It's the best the poor girl can do without taking her clothes off."

"What?"

Obviously, the situation needed a more direct approach. "Why not ask Nurse Tammy out on a date?"

"Now, don't you go talking nonsense, Tony. I have to work here. I can't be fooling around with the other nurses."

"So, marry her. She'll be happy and you'll never have to speak to her again."

Okay, that trite effort wasn't exactly my best and I didn't get the laugh. When Mo laughs, it fills the corridors, booming and bouncing off the walls. It's really impressive. The trick is to hit the right bent for his sense of humor, and I'm getting better at setting him off. Today's attempt achieved a mid-level chuckle. Maybe six out of ten on the chuckle scale.

We finally arrived at Dr. Bousteir's office to pass muster with Ms. Emily Gearing, the receptionist\secretary\pit bull guarding the entrance. Ms. Emily is in her mid-fifties and wider than several New England states combined. She's only as pleasant as you are, no more, no less. I wonder if it would actually pain her to smile spontaneously while greeting someone. The onus to start the proceedings is always on the visiting team.

"Why, Ms. Emily, you've tinted your hair a slightly different shade from last time. It's most becoming," I said.

"Thank you, Tony. It's very nice of you to notice. You're two minutes late." She nodded to Mo that I could go in.

"I couldn't help being late. Once word got out about your new hair, your suitors were lining up outside and blocking the door. Mo and I had to wade through the crowd." I smiled my most charming, but she wasn't buying it.

"Get in there before I have to beat you out of my way to get to my suitors." Then, she smiled. She seemed particularly fond of any sentence that had the words *beat* and *you* in it.

Dr. Bousteir was writing at her oversize, cherry wood desk when I entered the inner sanctum. She held up one of her lovely fingers signaling to us that she'd need another minute. I drank her in while I waited. My lovely doctor has shoulder-length auburn hair, exquisite facial features, green eyes with gold fleck highlights, and in my humble opinion, the most terribly lush figure ever seen by mortal man. If I hadn't been locked in here because of Larry and his spaceship, I would have gladly committed myself voluntarily just to see her these few precious hours a week.

Yes, I know it's fairly common to fall in love with your therapist. But this was more than that. This was gut wrenching, nerve-jangling, sleepless night causing lust. Doc Bousteir tore the animal out of my soul, causing it to pounce and claw at the part of my brain that injects massive quantities of testosterone into my system. Give me a sword and I'll slay the fetid armies of hell for just a kiss. Hopefully, one of those long, warm, wet ones that, no matter what, makes everything in the world okay.

And yes, I know. I've got it bad!

~~*

"You have a relationship developing with this alien?" asked Dr. Bousteir.

"I guess you could call it that." I felt more relaxed since, at the doctor's instruction, Mo had removed the straitjacket.

"What do you feel this relationship is based on?"

"The most outrageous lies I can get him to swallow."

"Why do you lie to him?" She continually took notes on a yellow legal pad as we talked.

"Well, Larry says he's a graduate student in something that equates to sociology or anthropology for us, but I get the impression it's more like zoology. He's studying a lesser life form. To what ends, I don't know. Maybe it is for his term paper just like he said."

"He came to Earth to do a term paper?" She didn't believe it either.

"That's what he told me. Apparently, the graduate student course load is a real bitch back on Shriek-whistle-click World."

She stopped writing. "This alien told you directly that he's a student with his own spaceship?"

"Right. But, I don't know if I should believe him or not. You've heard, *I'm from the government and I'm here to help you*. Try believing, *I'm from outer space and I only want to study you*. I'm not buying it without substantial proof. Who knows? He could be a scout for the great invasion. So, I lie to him."

"You feel that lying is necessary because it's up to you to safeguard the human race?"

Nice try.

"Wrong delusion, doc. Believing I'm the savior of mankind would be a delusion of grandeur, a messiah complex, or something like that. My delusion is being kidnapped by an alien and forced into an involuntary career change."

She put her pen down for a moment to flex her soft, lovely hand. Neatly manicured nails frosted with a softly modest pink polish tipped her delicate fingers. "Explain this involuntary career change to me."

"I'm locked up in a mental hospital where I'm not allowed to have shoelaces, or a belt for my pants. Sharp objects of any type are definitely out of the question. The staff treats me with compassion and the proper professional distance. Most of the inmates are either taking medication, heavily wrapped up in their own problems or incapable of lucid conversation. Lately, the only one who talks to me like I might have something important to say is Larry, and I tell him nothing but lies. But then, you tell me that he's a delusion, so technically, those lies shouldn't count. If I don't find a way to laugh at all this, I really will go nuts, so I've made a temporary career change.

"To what," she asked.

"That would depend on who you talk to. If you ask the staff here or a certain Superior Court judge, I've gone from stock trader and broker to nut case. If you ask Larry, my delusion, I'm more of a lab rat. If you're asking for my personal preference, I'd have to choose professional wise ass."

"Pardon?"

"Professional wise ass," I repeated. "You know, class clown. There's no way out of this situation. I'm here for thirty days no matter what, so I've decided I'm going to have fun with it, especially when I'm lying to Larry."

"What do you lie about?"

"Everything. I told him that geographical boundaries were established in a board game like Monopoly. I told him the U.S. Navy was a cruise line for people who liked Spartan vacations. Our scientists have determined that man evolved from a particular type of sea slug. I can't count the lies I made up about our social and sexual habits. Oh, and I told him the United Nations has real power. That one just kills me."

"He believes you?"

"Apparently his culture doesn't understand the concept of lying. So far, he appears to be buying all of it. Although, I think he had trouble understanding some of the religious ceremonies I invented along the way, especially the ones using strawberry Jell-O molds as their sacrament. I don't think Larry believes you could feed all the people at the Sermon on the Mount with one four-ounce box. Larry's got no faith."

"And you're telling him all of this because you think he may be scouting for some sort of invasion force?"

I wondered if she was trying to fit me back into her savior of mankind theory. "There's no way to tell what his real intentions are, so like I said, I'm going to have some fun with him."

Psychiatrists must have a required class in medical school where they work on perfecting their body language and facial expressions. Dr. Bousteir didn't say one additional word, but everything about her was screaming *you're not telling me all of it.*

"Okay, I'm angry that he dragged me out of my life and made everyone think I'm a world class loon. The lies are part of my revenge on the little bastard for kidnapping me in the first place." I stretched out on the sofa. Too comfortable, I sat up again. Lying down just didn't suit the irritation I felt. "It's funny. I made up my mind to tell Larry nothing but lies and you nothing but the absolute truth. Now, he believes every word, and you think I'm crazy enough to be locked up in here. It's been an E-ticket ride from the first day."

"That's good? An E-ticket ride, I mean."

"Where'd you grow up, Doc? They were the best of the best. Ever been on the Whirly-gig?"

"No, but that's not what we're here to discuss." She shuffled through some of her older notes. "Tell me about the first time again."

"Not again."

"Please," she said.

"Her name was Sandra. We were on a date at this drive-in outside Atlantic City. She had. . ."

"I meant the first time you met Larry," Dr. Bousteir interrupted.

"Oh, that. I was working the floor of the stock exchange for Greebley and Grandy. Everyone calls them Greedy and Grabby, but they really are one of the more reputable brokerage firms. They haven't been charged with insider trading by the Securities and Exchange Commission in over a week.

"Anyway, I went to lunch about twelve-thirty. I remember it was a rather hot day. I walked out of Schweitzler's Delicatessen—great corned beef, very lean—and I saw a $100 bill lying on the pavement. No one else seemed to notice it. I leaned over to pick it up and the wind blew it down this little walkway beside the deli. So, I went after it. As soon as I was off the street, I felt the pull start."

"The pull?"

"That's what I call it," I said. "I was being pulled up to Larry's ship, but I didn't know that at the time. I was getting all tingly and lightheaded. At first, I remember thinking maybe I was wrong about Schweitzler's corned beef. Food poisoning, you know. But part of me was still focused on the money. Bending over to pick up the hundred, I honestly thought that I must be getting sick. I was beginning to hallucinate. I felt everything around me like it was part of me. Trust me, doc, you haven't lived till you've shared consciousness with the Dumpster behind Schweitzler's Deli."

"Go on."

"For some bizarre reason, it felt natural."

"Natural?" Doc Bousteir looked surprised.

"As opposed to normal. I thought I was getting sick. I certainly didn't think I was being kidnapped by an alien."

"Okay, continue." She penned another comment on her notepad.

What is she writing?

"Like I said, it felt natural right up to when this bright light hit me and I started to come apart. I'm pretty sure I was screaming when my mouth broke down into bits and flew into the light stream. I'm not sure since the top of my head was already streaming away somewhere. Anyway, I ended up in this drab silver room on a metal table, which I was sincerely hoping wasn't an autopsy table. I was paralyzed, so I wasn't screaming anymore, except in my head.

"I think you shrinks have several classifications for panic attacks. I developed a whole new one. Heart-stopping terror isn't descriptive enough for what I felt at that moment. The bloodiest, slasher horror film ever produced doesn't come close. It was a hundred times worse than a broken condom, and almost as bad as Tofurkey."

"I get the idea," she said. "What were you thinking at that moment?"

"Too much. All sorts of crazy thoughts were flying through my head. I wondered if I had died from bad corned beef. If so, I wanted someone to sue the deli for the wrongful death of a truly wonderful human being. I wanted to make a deal to put Jesus bumper stickers on my car if they'd just send me back. I wanted to kick someone's butt for scaring me like that. And I wanted my hair to lay back down. Every hair on my body was standing straight up. A thousand other thoughts went through my head way too fast to remember. It was too jumbled up to really grasp. Then, Larry showed up."

"Don't you feel it's a bit unusual for an alien to have the name Larry?"

"He doesn't. His real name sounds like a cat stepped on a hot waffle iron. I couldn't pronounce it, so I called him Larry."

"Can you describe him?"

"Sure. He's about five-nine, one hundred forty-five pounds, brown and brown, slightly balding, actually a rather good looking guy except for the hairy bit."

"The hairy bit?"

"He's got this small, triangular clump of hair right in the middle of his forehead. It jumps around all the time. I think that's an indication that he's excited or confused."

"Is it like fur?"

"No, just hair. A little depilatory in the right spot and he'd easily pass for human. He'd be a little on the anorexic side, but you wouldn't be able to pick him out of a lineup, I swear. You might see his forehead move a bit when he got excited, but lots of people have a tic. He'd pass."

"So, you believe in panspermia," she asked.

"Wait, I know that one. It's an evolutionary theory. Something about life on earth developing from life in outer space."

"You said Larry looks human."

Well, he does!

"That doesn't prove anything," I responded. "Most scientists think life on other planets may be bacteria or some sort of pond scum, but isn't that where we came from?"

"Isn't it also possible that growing up seeing humanoid aliens in movies and television shows that you subconsciously expect your alien to look human?"

I had to admit her suggestion was absolutely reasonable.

"I get it. Larry is supposed to be four-foot tall, green or gray with a big head and big eyes, right?"

"I don't know," she responded. "That's the point. No one knows what an alien race would look like, but it's mathematically improbable that they would look like us."

Gotcha!

"It's also mathematically improbable that we are the only intelligent life in our galaxy, much less the universe. It's also mathematically improbable that we are the most advanced race in the universe. Bottom line, Larry's existence is a near mathematical certainty."

"Perhaps so, but you said he looks human," she argued.

I have to give the doc credit; she's persistent. "Larry's looks are his parents' fault. I had nothing to do with it."

Doctor Bousteir made a rather long notation, probably not in my favor. In general, most people in authority write a book on you just before they throw that book at you. Maybe, I should quit telling her the truth and just tell her what she expects to hear.

No, tell her the truth.

After all, lots of sane people believe in aliens.

"How did you get back to Earth?" She almost said it like she believed it.

"The same way I left. Larry asked where I wanted to go and I said back to work. He screeched at his machine and zapped me back to the floor of the exchange. No one seemed to notice that I'd just appeared out of thin air, but they seemed to have a major problem with me standing there buck naked, screaming hysterically about being abducted by aliens."

"Why do you think your co-workers had a problem with that," she asked.

"First, they're not my coworkers. They're competitors. In a shark pool, there's no co-anything. Second, they had a problem with my story because they're morons. They won't believe an alien abduction story, but they'll believe Amalgamated Tire will hit thirty-five a share by June. I should know. I sold it to them."

"Larry sends you back to Earth naked every time?"

"Not anymore," I said. "I explained to him that public nudity was only socially acceptable at certain beaches, frat parties and at the US Mint where the employees like to roll around in the money. He agreed to put me back in my clothes on return trips and it's worked so far. I end up wearing whatever I had on before I left."

Dr. Bousteir paged through her previous notes. "The report from the emergency room states you were incoherent with some trauma-induced paralysis."

"I don't remember much about arriving in the emergency room, and even though I agree that first trip was traumatic, I thought I was pretty coherent once I calmed down. That intern who admitted me just wouldn't listen."

"You were in shock for quite a long time," she said.

"Look at the circumstances. I have a perfectly normal life one minute, and the next, my whole body is flying apart and I find myself lying naked on a metal table in an alien space ship. I'd say that's a bit of a shock."

"What did you talk to Larry about on the first trip?"

"I don't remember that conversation either. I just remember screaming a lot. But, I must be a pretty good source of information for him. He keeps bringing me back."

"How many trips have you made to Larry's ship?" Dr. Bousteir was very, very good! Her tone of voice wasn't the least bit condescending.

"I don't keep a count. In the beginning, Larry pulled me up just the one time, but lately, it's been everyday. Sometimes, two or three times a day."

Finally, something shocked her. "You're still going?"

"Everyday."

"And no one notices that you've left the hospital?" I think she tried not to sound skeptical, but failed miserably.

"No one noticed me disappear from the streets of New York. No one noticed me reappear in the middle of the stock exchange floor. Do you think anyone would notice me leaving and reappearing here?"

"What do you think about that?" she asked.

"I think psychiatrists answer too many questions with questions."

We talked for the rest of the session about what things I thought were rational, and why she thought alien abductions shouldn't be on the list. I didn't much care what we talked about as long as she talked to me. I was getting an occasional waft of her gentle but delightfully musky perfume coming my way. It was heaven. She was heaven. I finally worked up the nerve to compliment her on her perfume. Her response was graceful, feminine and incredibly enticing.

"Let's stick to the topic under discussion," she said.

Larry Learns the Traffic Laws

"Within New York City limits, putting on your turn signal announces your God-given right to cut off any three people of your choice."

Larry Learns Drug Addiction

"Withdraw symptoms vary from mild anxiety and a few hand tremors to an excruciatingly painful death, so most governments try to prosecute all the drug cartels except Starbucks."

Larry Learns Housekeeping

"It's really hard when you first move away from home. Mom or the good fairies took care of a lot of stuff. I never knew shower curtains could mildew, and mom never kept science projects in the back of the refrigerator at home. But you learn. At my first apartment, I used my broiler to cook a steak and forgot to clean it. A week later, I find this reeking, bacteria infested mess, and I made the decision right then to never open that again."

Larry Learns Nursery Rhymes

"No, you have to recite the words to the right rhythm. Listen again. *Jack and Jill went up the hill to film a sleazy porno...*"

Larry Learns Insults

"Normally, most people are pretty dull when it comes to insults, simply calling someone a pejorative name or ugly or rude. That's boring, boring, boring! Really slamming someone takes intelligence, subtlety, a certain amount of flair and genuine creativity, so it's unlikely you'll be good at it."

4

Doctor God and Patient Jerk

After our session, Dr. Bousteir released me from the padded cell and put me back on the Happy Ward. That's where they keep the DND's, Delusional but Not Dangerous patients. Staff members prefer working the Happy Ward because no one gets hurt when a patient gets into a fight with an imaginary opponent. The only injury I can recall on the Happy Ward is Nurse Cassilio slipping on a freshly mopped floor. Even then, it was only her well-cushioned and girdled pride that was hurt.

The Happy Ward is almost as large as a midsize high school's cafeteria and just as warmly furnished with long Formica covered tables and stackable plastic chairs. However, they do have several quasi-nook areas set up along the outer walls, each with a sofa, two or three lounge chairs and a coffee table. These nooks were intended for reading or watching TV, but the sofas are a favored spot for afternoon naps. Several flat screen LCD television sets are mounted high on the white walls where the controls are out of the patients' reach. Ugly industrial linoleum once again received two thumbs up from Sunny Park's architect or his budget, however the flooring is a soft blue-gray with varied size beige spots that remind me of paint splatter. It's regularly waxed to enhance its ugliness. Large fluorescent lighting fixtures dot the ceiling, but most are off during the day as the huge, unbreakable windows allow adequate sunlight. The Happy Ward just screams *Home Sweet Home* if you were raised in a Siberian orphanage.

There are numerous activities available, including many of the most popular board games. A fairly recent collection of magazines and a small collection of paperback books are available at the nurse's station, which is centered on the north wall. The patients do not have direct access to the bookshelves in order to keep agitated patients from dumping the contents onto the floor in the middle of the occasional psychotic break or medication mishap. It's entirely understandable that the nurses tired of restacking the books. Cleaning up after mental patients is a lot more work than cleaning up after a child or the family pet.

The patients are also permitted to bring various arts and crafts onto the Happy Ward as long as they don't make too much of a mess. I've met one or two painters, several avid knitters and needlepointers, and a variety of collectors. Stamps are the most common collector's item, although coins and baseball cards are also very popular. One gentleman began collecting insects, but his collection was confiscated when it was discovered that he was collecting them as a dietary supplement.

Nurse Cassilio distributes the daily dosages of prescribed medication for the patients. Lately, I'm given a placebo, two lovely blue sugar pills. I swallow, chasing them down my throat with a little Dixie cup of water. Out of curiosity, I once crushed a dose between my molars. It was sweet with no particular flavor and faintly reminded me of the numerous sugar candy dots that I'd consumed as a child. The dots came glued to a strip of paper, which from my adult perspective is in itself rather weird.

The story behind my placebo is related to how I originally ended up on the Happy Ward. When I first arrived at Sunny Park, I must admit that I was not in the best shape. Truth be told, the existence of Larry or any other extraterrestrial beings never figured into my plans for my life with any more weight than a lottery ticket. Meeting a friendly alien and contemplating winning the lottery are both nice as fleeting thoughts, but only an idiot invests a significant amount of time and money in such pursuits. The odds on both are literally astronomical, about the same as the odds on a Hollywood studio executive promoting an original idea.

While I vaguely remember screaming my head off on the floor of the stock exchange and hyperventilating like a fool in the ambulance, not much else during my breakdown seems to have registered. I remember walking into the emergency room with a paramedic leading and supporting me, but it turns out that was a genuine delusion, probably my mind's attempt at regaining control of my situation. In reality, I was rolled into the hospital strapped to a gurney like all of the other inmates. After that, the only thing I remember is following the normal procedure for a medical emergency at a big city hospital, which is putting your name on a list and waiting for someone to notice that you may be dying.

To further screw with my head, it turns out gurney rides are considered billable. I found it on my hospital bill under the innocuous heading of *ambulatory services*. In a hospital, anything that puts wheels under a patient is a billable service. However, my insurance company paid the bill without complaint, and I should probably considered myself fortunate that Sunny Park hasn't yet figured out how to charge me for walking on the hospital's floors.

Meanwhile, back on my gurney, I honestly believed that I was becoming more coherent.

Few people have a genuine understanding of shock. Why should they? In daily life, everyone follows some sort of structure. You go to work. You go home. You have a beer and watch the ballgame, play with the kids, or whatever. Friends and relatives come to visit. You slam a burger on the way to a movie. Taxes go up. Another bozo wins the election. Life goes on. Complacency becomes ingrained into everyone's system, and it's nearly impossible to imagine a car accident or some other physical or mental trauma interrupting your routine. Complacency is the norm of our happy or unhappy existence.

If every day for ten years, you come home and watch the evening news while sitting on a five-hundred-pound bomb and it finally detonates on the first day of the eleventh year, it would shock the hell out of you, although I admit, not for long.

While I was completely unaware, complacency had also become my norm. I believed I was in control of my life, period.

At the exchange, my daily routine is hectic, stressful and aggressive. I love every minute. I'm focused and always preparing myself for the next phase of my game plan. My client list is growing steadily. When the market booms, I boom. When the market tanks, I hone my nerves of steel and snap up the bargains as those who panic run for cover. It's hard work, but very satisfying.

I don't needlessly churn stocks and bonds in order to bill my clients' accounts large commissions for crap recommendations. I make money for my clients, quite a lot of it. In return, they give a very healthy percentage of those profits to me. When they succeed, I succeed. My clients love what I do for their portfolios. I love fat commissions and my own ever-fattening portfolio. Success *is* my life plan. All I have to do is stay the course and keep my focus.

Focus is everything.

I would never have described myself as complacent. I was constantly reaching, growing and expanding my talents. I was the best and getting better.

I had drive. I had flair. A styled wave in my hair.

I had no idea that Larry was going to screw me.

I also had no idea how many times that afternoon I was going to hear the phrase, "The doctor will be with you shortly," or even who said it. I had no idea about a lot of things that afternoon. My five-hundred-pound bomb exploded right in my face. Whether I was willing to admit it or not, I was in extreme shock. My nerves of steel deserted me. I am human after all.

Crap! Doesn't that just suck!

When I was finally rolled into an examining room, the intern handling that day's emergency admissions immediately prescribed a tranquilizer to ease my anxiety.

In fairness, I'll concede that anxiety was a very reasonable assessment of my condition. Being abducted into an orbiting spaceship, dumped naked in a public venue, and carted off to a mental hospital all in one afternoon will tend to make you a little anxious. Still, after spending more than two hours waiting in the corridor, I thought I'd had adequate time to recover my senses and didn't think I needed to be tranquilized. However, the admitting intern, an incredibly young looking kid, would not be talked out of using his prescription pad and his brand spanking new medical degree. He apparently went to a medical school that defined MD as an acronym for *Make Dosage*.

Normally, I'm very even tempered, and I try very hard to treat everybody with appropriate respect. When I act like a jerk, it's almost always intentional. However, while being admitted to Sunny Park, I was indeed a jerk and it was definitely beyond my control. Maybe I was still a little shaky despite two hours to calm down. Maybe fate just had it in for me that day. Maybe I was taking my anger at Larry out on Dr. Looks-Too-Young. Whatever the underlying cause, I refused to be pushed any further and this kid was pushing buttons I didn't even know I had.

I can't describe what happened next as a personality conflict. It was more like a personality holocaust. If we'd had weapons, we'd have used them.

"I'm going to give you something to calm you down," said the intern.

"No, you're not." I had a different plan. "I don't need to calm down. I need to get the hell out of here."

"You're in shock," he persisted.

"I realize that, but it's nothing I can't cure with a nice double dose of single malt scotch."

"This is just a sedative. It won't hurt a bit."

I wasn't worried about the pain. I just don't like needles. "You stick me with that and I'll stab you in the eye with it!"

Okay, that was probably not my best sales pitch, and I'd also have to say that any sense of common decency or courtesy had deserted me. My social skills, which I'd worked very hard to develop over the years, also disappeared.

I don't know why things worked out the way they did and I wish I had a reasonable explanation for what happened. I don't. Sometimes, if you put the right people in the wrong situation, things just happen. This young intern wasn't listening to me and I firmly believed that I was quite sane. However, everything I said and did was, to him, symptomatic of my disorder. According to Dr. Wet-Behind-the-Ears, the fact that I had very little recollection of the ambulance ride to the hospital and still exhibited some slight paralysis on my left side was absolute proof that I was still in shock. My very clear recollection of Larry was proof that I was delusional. Prancing around naked on the floor of the New York Stock Exchange was proof of abnormal behavior. He further tried to explain, "You're bad attitude is proof that. . ."

I'd had enough!

"You're wrong on that one, Doogie. My bad attitude is genetic. My father also hated putting up with geeky-looking little farts like you."

"There's no reason to be abusive."

"There's no reason for you to medicate me when I don't want to be medicated."

"I'm your doctor."

"No, you're not. You just happened to be on duty when I arrived. If you were my doctor, you'd have already gone through puberty."

"You're not rational, Mr. Sterling," he said.

"Absolutely, I'm rational." I was starting to yell. "And I'm well aware that on today's market, your services are as replaceable as socks!"

That didn't help, but railing the arrogant little bastard made me feel better. He made a notation on my hospital chart, upgrading my attitude from bad to belligerent, which apparently was also symptomatic of my disorder. At this point, I think drawing breath would have been symptomatic of my disorder. We continued our disagreement for several more minutes.

I had right on my side. I had not abdicated my freedom of choice, my right as a patient to decide which medications to ingest or inject. Although I doubt that was their original intention, our country's founding fathers fought and died for my right to sit in this emergency room and be as much of an un-medicated, belligerent jerk as I pleased.

Just because a young intern doesn't believe in alien abductions and naked prancing on Wall Street did not give him the right to suspend my free will, my personal freedoms, my constitutional rights. . . .yada, yada, yada.

My aggressive opponent was also well prepared for the fight. He had a medical degree and was standing in a hospital. That made him omnipotent, or so he believed. This kid's ego was as gilt-edged as his diploma from medical school. Since I was merely a lowly uneducated patient, he was right and I was wrong. His proof for this assumption was that my symptoms perfectly matched some mental disorder, which he'd no doubt studied in a fat obscure text with lots of Latin and pictures of dissected human brains. Mental patients are not rational ergo he wins.

In the few short minutes it took to complete our argument, this intern unilaterally declared himself the winner of our argument. There was no further need to listen to me, especially when he also had might on his side in the form of two very large orderlies. Strapped to the gurney, I couldn't put up much of a fight as they held me down and gave me an injection.

I should have fought one hell of a lot harder.

After being involuntarily medicated, I enjoyed a very relaxed and very tranquil introduction to the Happy Ward. In the midst of my pharmaceutical bliss, incoming nuclear missiles wouldn't have bothered me and I doubt I'd have been shocked to meet Satan himself. Likely, I would simply have wondered if he needed a good broker to handle his portfolio.

A good salesman sells 24-7, tranquilizers be damned!

Two delightfully dreamy days later, the nursing staff stopped my medication. I awoke to find myself involuntarily committed to Sunny Park under court order.

If that's not proof that drugs are dangerous, what is?

During my two-day medicinal vacation, there were several other incidents that I am again unable to fully recall. Apparently, my lawyer was informed (By whom, I don't know.) that I was incapacitated and stopped by for a visit. The following morning, someone from the court came to the hospital and interviewed me for the judge. I gave a court stenographer a rather less than lucid statement, which I've since had the opportunity to read. Apparently, my command of the English language was also tranquilized and I freely omitted various unnecessary speech components, like nouns and verbs. In hindsight, I'm also reasonably sure that the current President of the United States is not Sherlock Holmes.

Not everything ended up in the official transcript. I pieced together some of these events with a bit of help from a few members of the nursing staff, who were called to act as official witnesses. They told me that, in the middle of my statement, I stopped to ask the court stenographer for a date. I wanted her to see Larry's spaceship. The stenographer declined the invitation due to a previous engagement with her grandchildren, but then I apparently wouldn't take no for an answer. I really wanted her to see the ship since its walls were the same silver color as her hair. When she refused the fourth time, I asked her for a rain check while laughing hysterically and repeatedly singing "rain check, rain check" to the tune of *The Battle Hymn of the Republic*.

After recovering my senses, I found that last part particularly difficult to believe. I don't think I can sing that tune sober.

The stamped and witnessed court transcript was combined with various other documents to make my incarceration at Sunny Park official. The geeky-looking little fart intern signed my commitment papers as the doctor of record. I learned from the documents that his name was Dr. Vincent. I still wonder if his signing my commitment papers was his revenge for my giving him so much attitude.

Regardless, my commitment papers were processed the same day due to the emergency nature of my situation. Who exactly decided that pharmaceutical bliss was an emergency, I never found out. The Superior Court judge, based on the recommendation of her staff, signed off without reading my nonsensical statement. That's moot. Her reading it would not have accomplished anything, except perhaps to convince her to make my stay here permanent.

Once the judge signed on the dotted line, Sunny Park Hospital was legally my new address.

Being repeatedly injected with joy juice, I was oblivious to this entire proceeding. According to several witnesses, the only thing that concerned me during this period was the timing of my next injection, and could I have it now?

Dr. Bousteir was assigned my case by routine staff rotation for the resident psychiatrists. After her initial evaluation of my condition, she deemed further medication unnecessary. The nurses immediately stopped needling my buttocks with tranquilizers after every meal and at bedtime. I was sincerely disappointed, but it was some compensation that I quickly regained the ability to put my shoes on the right feet. I also stopped walking into walls, reacquired my verbal skills, and quit trying to spray all six urinals in the men's room when relieving myself.

Time for another shock!

This is the point when I realized that sobriety isn't everything it's cracked up to be. It depends largely on where you wake up.

Believe me, Sunny Park Hospital would not have been my first choice. However, sobriety led to yet another minor problem on the Happy Ward. When the tranquilizers stopped, several of the patients immediately noticed that I was no longer being given a needle or a little paper cup full of pills. They became agitated that I didn't have to take meds along with the rest of the residents. Why was I so special?

The other patient's twisted jealousy may seem childish, mainly because it is. Everything on a playground has to be shared equally to avoid tantrums, and apparently the Happy Ward utilizes that same rule. To ease the anxiety of the Happy Ward's unbalanced minds, the nursing staff asked for my cooperation and made arrangements for my placebo. I now take the sugar pills four times a day in front of the other residents to quell their consternation.

I am now their equal. I have to take meds.

This is reality?

I'm now officially certified nuts and they're feeding me candy. Don't you just love it?

Larry Learns Philosophy
"Ancient philosophers were mostly Greek, Roman or Chinese. Using nothing but pure reason, newly invented mathematics, and some basic observations, they were able to predict solar eclipses, a round Earth and the existence of the atom. The only modern day philosopher I know is a little Frenchman, who lives outside Grand Central Station. He predicts that the world is going to hell."

Larry Learns Facebook
"I'm sorry, Larry, but you don't have any friends."

Larry Learns the Bill of Rights
"The Second Amendment covers the right to bear arms and their use in regards to neighbors who park on your lawn."

Larry Learns Courtship

"Women love sincerity, so when you find yourself a hottie, you have to say it with just the right inflection. Now, repeat after me: *Let's go back to your place and I'll make you make noises only dogs can hear.*"

Larry Learns Great Cinema

"Movies have been in production for about a century. It's another art form and they're distributed worldwide. The true classics are all based on stories published by a company called Marvel."

Larry Learns American History

"The Revolutionary War was actually an accident. The British honestly didn't know that wearing red coats after Labor Day was a faux pas. Words were exchanged and things just escalated."

5

AROUND THE WARD IN 80 MINUTES

By now, you may have gotten the impression that I'm starting to have a good time here at Sunny Park. I really am.

After my first few days, I reevaluated my situation. Unless you live in Roswell, New Mexico, professing your belief in alien abduction is socially unacceptable. Showing up naked at work is also a little difficult to explain in polite society. I am therefore going to be incarcerated for the duration of the court ordered evaluation period. There's no legal way out of this hospital until I've served my thirty days. Once I accepted that fact, I had to let my anger go. Staying angry twenty-four hours a day is really only for people in divorce court.

I still have some doubts about my being released even when my time is up, but I'll face that situation if and when it arises. It's the only sane thing to do and I haven't given up my firm belief that my sanity is not in question. At least, it's not in question by the only true expert on the subject, me.

Deciding to accept my situation also gives me some time off work, which I desperately need. I haven't had a vacation in more than two years. The hospital's lack of a ski lodge filled with snow bunnies or a sandy beach filled with bikinis is not going to depress me. It's a mental ward ergo I'll take a mental vacation.

Objectively, this is really a very interesting dilemma. If I tell the truth about Larry, I'm locked away as a nutcase, possibly for good and possibly once again medicated into a near vegetative state. However if I lie like a rug, there's a slim chance that I'll released. Thinking about my situation consumed all of my time for several days. There is no obvious answer. Theoretically, if the truth is unacceptable, one has to lie. But then, I doubt I'm capable of lying well enough to convince a professionally trained psychiatrist that I'm "normal" once again. I'm pretty much screwed either way.

If you can't tell the truth and you can't lie, is there a third choice?

I finally figured out that my best bet is to convince Dr. Busty that my delusion is harmless. I once read a story about a fellow, who believed all of his life that he was a Russian prince, despite hard evidence to the contrary. He was never incarcerated, and people accepted him as just a little strange. Something similar could work for me. Perhaps.

Making Larry harmless shouldn't be too difficult. He's not some psychotic voice in my head that compels me to chase down hapless victims with a butcher knife. I haven't harmed anyone; and as far as I know, Larry has never harmed anyone either. I may be the only person on Earth who has had any contact with him, and realistically, there are thousands, perhaps millions of perfectly sane people who believe in aliens. Quite a few of them claim to have been abducted by UFOs and they're not locked up. In theory, my case is no different.

I hope.

In the meantime, I'm stuck here. I might as well enjoy myself. When your choices are laugh, cry or die, I choose laugh. If alien abduction is inevitable, relax and enjoy. It's all a matter of perspective and developing the proper attitude. Thickly layered sarcasm works best for me.

I'm perfectly serious about becoming a professional wise ass as I told my lovely Dr. Busty in our last session. Being sane among the crazy really can be a lot of fun. I'm also getting a real kick out of screwing with Larry's head.

Naturally, I'm more careful around the other patients. A few of them take every comment literally, no matter how ludicrous. Just to be safe, I rather heavily edit my conversations with the other inmates. The staff, however, is altogether different. Screwing with their heads is great entertainment, and it certainly helps pass the time.

"Nurse Cassilio, do you have a minute?" She's a sweetheart, so I knew that she'd find time to help me no matter what my problem was.

"Sure, Tony. What do you need?"

"I've noticed that Sunny Park Hospital is a very progressive institution."

"Thank you," she said. "We try to keep up with the very latest information and techniques."

"That's obvious. However, no one has told me which forms I need to fill out to arrange a conjugal visit."

Nurse Cassilio blushed to her toes. "There are no forms for that!"

"Are you sure? Why don't you meet me in the supply closet and we can look for them together?"

Nurse Cassilio playfully slapped me on the arm. I guess if the nurses are allowed to smack the patients, Sunny Park really is progressive.

Also on the Happy Ward, I've made several friends among the residents and my average day is pretty full. Mental patients are some of the most interesting people that I've ever met, but it can be exhausting keeping up with their slightly skewed world. Today started with a chess game.

My opponent, Carl Wallace, is a thirty-seven year old automotive engineer who likes to design cars with wings. The designs are very futuristic until he draws in the feathers. Carl is convinced that the future of engineering lies in making every machine part mammal, bird or reptile, with birds being his major preference. After performing some feathered modifications, Carl drove his car off a cliff. It shocked the hell out of him when it didn't fly. It shocked the hell out of everyone else that he survived the crash. He's been Sunny Park's resident engineer ever since.

Carl is sandy-haired, tall, and lanky as a stick man. If he were just a little thinner and had a hairy bit, he could pass for Larry's older brother. It's blatantly obvious that Carl has an IQ on the far, far, extremely far right edge of the bell curve, or perhaps he's completely off the charts. The guy may be nuts, but he's absolutely brilliant. He's an excellent bridge player and an outright wizard at chess. I haven't seen him lose once.

Carl's wife, Tina, visits him every day and brings in home-baked muffins in flavors that would choke the hardiest, scrub-eating mules in the forty-niners' gold rush. Today's tasty combination was artichoke and chocolate chip, which she called Arti-Choc. I won't tell you what we called it.

Tina is also tall and lanky, blonde with an overbite that's an orthodontist's dream. Other than her teeth, she has very little shape. Whoever passed their genes along to Tina forgot to give her a butt; and for her, wearing a bra is wishful thinking. Together, she and Carl look like the perfect couple. It's obvious that Tina really loves the guy. Unfortunately for the rest of us on the Happy Ward, Tina always brings enough muffins for everyone. It's not just the strange flavor combinations that turn people off. You could anchor an aircraft carrier with one of her muffins.

Back at our chess game, Carl had pinned my king's bishop and was moving in for the kill. I tried to sneak my queen back onto the board, but he caught me immediately. Carl always has the entire board in his head. Only, the one in his head has hooves and a tail.

Three moves later, I lost once again.

"Checkmate," said Carl.

"I agree. You got me." I tipped my king over, then began to reset the rest of the pieces back in proper starting order.

"Your game is improving."

"Why, thank you, Carl. That's very nice of you."

Carl setup his side of the board. "I can let you win on occasion if you like. I've done it before for people like you."

"People like me?"

"You know, people who have no chance because they're not very smart."

"I have a chance of winning!"

Carl laughed aloud. "That's a good one, Tony!"

Despite appearances, Carl was not deliberately aiming verbal spears at my ego. He simply has a tendency to state everything as empirical fact, which can be a little grating. However, he was correct on his assessment of the chess game. I have about as much chance of beating him at chess as I have of becoming Prom Queen at the local beautician's academy.

After one more game with Carl, I caught up on the latest magazines. According to the questionnaire in *Cosmopolitan*, I know a great deal about keeping my man happy in a committed relationship. I also learned "Ten Ways to Un-pucker Those Cottage Cheese Thighs", and *Reader's Digest* finally had a joke that I haven't heard before:

An elderly man contacted an attorney to prepare his estate. "Should I discuss the terms of my will with my wife, my mistress, my siblings, my six children and my fourteen grandchildren," he asked.

The attorney vigorously shook his head. "I don't recommend it, unless you want that to be your cause of death."

Time magazine had Thomas Findley, a senior vice-president from Greebley and Grandy, on the cover. Apparently, Findley was now one of the hottest movers and shakers in the financial world. The author of the article obviously didn't know that Findley's department is stacked with some of the best investment analysts in the country. They spend most of their waking hours covering up his mistakes. The best moving and shaking Findley does without help is at a little club in the village that caters to cross-dressers. He would have given a much better interview if they'd limited the discussion to taffeta.

After I finished reading, I lost five-for-five in the Happy Ward Table Tennis Championship of the World. The reigning champion, Monty, was unstoppable on Tuesday and any other day of the week that ends in Y. Even among professionals, it was widely known that Monty has a lethal overhand smash. And if they don't know, Monty will gladly tell them.

Monty is below-average height and Quasimodo-ugly. The hook on his nose was apparently stolen from the dogleg par five at some golf course. Deep acne scars cover his near perfectly round face under a tangled mane of flaming-red hair that is just beginning to show a touch of gray at the temples. The acne scars make him look like a small pox victim and Monty always needs a shave. However, if you aren't frightened by his looks, you'll find that he's really a pleasant person. You just have to ignore some of his more peculiar beliefs.

Monty may not be his real first name. He doesn't have a last name that anyone knows and he's not about to tell. If you knew his last name, you could steal his soul.

Monty was picked up in a police sweep on a bitterly cold day in February. The police were attempting to transport him to a shelter to prevent him from freezing to death in some back alley when Monty tried to steal their souls to add to his collection. Apparently, the procedure involved large quantities of excrement being thrown at the victim while speaking their last name. The police weren't amused and Monty ended up here on an overflow program for non-violent prisoners requiring mental health care.

Monty is very responsible when it comes to soul stealing. He follows an intricate and carefully designed set of rules that he hasn't modified since they were given to him by a dying wino on the railroad tracks outside the Chicago stockyards some years back. Most people are very safe around Monty. You have to get on his bad side before he will consider stealing your soul.

Meanwhile, back at the Happy Ward Table Tennis Championship of the World, I'd worked up a really good sweat defending my side of the table and thought for a minute that I had a chance to pull out the fifth game. Then, Monty let loose with his lethal overhand smash and shut me out. I may have a better chance tomorrow when the staff promises we can have a ball.

Monty was the only one to ask way I ended up at Sunny Park. "I was kidnapped by an alien," I said.

Monty nodded his head in stern understanding. "Don't you just hate that? I really hate it when I get kidnapped by aliens."

"I can't say I'm particularly fond of it at the moment." I offered Monty one of the Arti-Choc muffins that Carl's wife brought in this morning. Using his paddle, he wailed it into the nurses' station with his lethal overhand smash.

"They always did operations on me," said Monty. "They put strange instruments in my body that made me do things that I didn't want to do."

"Like what?"

"Like they'd make me get the cherry Slurpee instead of the Coca-Cola. I don't like the cherry, but there I'd be sitting on the curb sipping a cherry Slurpee. Aliens are really cruel."

"I can see how that could add unwanted stress to your life, Monty."

"I know." He looked down thoughtfully, then jerked his head back up with a big, I-wish-I-had-some-teeth-left smile. "Who's watching your television while you're in here?"

"I don't have a television."

"That's really sick!"

"I know. I've tried, Monty. I just can't get excited about anything but the sports channels and I watch the games on a big screen at my local bar."

He looked me in the eye, which is a bit difficult since his are rather crossed with one brown and one blue. He then gave me his ultimate litmus test for acceptability as one of his friends. "Do you watch the table tennis championships?"

"Wouldn't miss them."

"Fantastic!" Monty wailed another muffin into the nurses' station. It shattered into a thousand crumbs against an old workstation's black and white monitor. "See! See! Now it won't work in color anymore. I told you my overhand smash was lethal!"

"Truly amazing, Monty." I patted him on the back. "Let's go get some lunch."

During the week, lunch is served in the cafeteria on Monday, Wednesday and Friday. Tuesdays and Thursdays, they bus trays up to an enclosed patio near the ward. The patio has brightly-colored, cheerful picnic tables and chairs, mostly red, white and green. (Go figure.) Several of the tables sport equally bright umbrellas with a matching decorative fringe. The umbrellas are always open despite their uselessness in this indoor environment. Still, everybody rushes like school children to get a seat under one of the umbrellas. I've noted my fellow inmates have a distinct preference for meals on the patio. Some even claim the food tastes better when served here. If the weather is nice, the staff opens the jalousie windows to air out the patients.

Generally, the food at every meal is fairly good. The salads are always fresh and crisp. They actually steam the hot vegetables. That's a nice touch. On the other hand, the meat is either ground or cut into tiny pieces. No one needs a knife to eat at Sunny Park. The butchered-to-bits meat is always disguised in some sort of gravy or cream sauce. No one needs mustard to eat at Sunny Park either.

Desert is always a surprise. The hospital's pastry chef is a genuine artist. The cakes and pies are magnificent. I'm amazed that one of the better restaurants hasn't stolen him away and I hope the hospital is paying him a fortune. Before each of his days off, he makes something up in advance so that the patients won't have to settle for plain ice cream or pudding. Today, we had Black Forest cake loaded with real cherries! When I get out of here, I may try to steal this guy myself. As long as he keeps baking, I could keep him happy in a committed relationship. Just look at my *Cosmo* score.

In the afternoon, everyone takes a walk around the grounds with Mo. We follow an asphalt path that meanders across the broad lawn and around several clumps of maple and birch trees. The trees are practically littered with birdhouses that were probably made in the arts and crafts shop on the floor below the Happy Ward. Many of the little houses are occupied and we always stop to look and listen to the birds.

After a few minutes, Mo gets us moving again. We walk in a group and Mo always sets the pace to challenge us a bit. He wants us to have a good cardiovascular workout. Mo looks after bodies as well as minds and souls. There must be a special heaven for people like Mo.

Our dinner menu is interchangeable with the lunch menu and always served in the cafeteria. Generally, it's followed by some carefully screened television shows or a movie. I think the programming fits the

Happy Ward rather well—no sex, no violence, no reality. Thankfully, attendance at the television or movie screening isn't mandatory. I can't face sitting through another movie about a happy family struggling with too many happy kids. I have to fight the urge to yell, "Get a vasectomy!"

Skipping tonight's screening, I headed to the ward's central tables since I'd previously scheduled a fitting for a sweater.

Anna is the only patient on the ward who spends most of her time knitting. She's an expert at measuring you for a sweater. She's also the only one whose story makes me want to break down in tears.

Anna is silver-haired, cherub chubby and rosy, a sixty-some-year-old grandmother, who two years ago lost her daughter and four grandchildren in a house fire. She mails letters to them every day and waits by the door at visiting hours. When her husband, Roy, comes in alone, she's crushed by the horrible news about her daughter's family. Ten minutes after Roy leaves, she's writing one of her grandchildren a short note or knitting them a new sweater. The next day, she's crushed all over again.

And the next day.

And the next day.

Everyday at visiting hour, Anna's world falls apart with heartrending screams of almost unimaginable grief as she collapses in Roy's arms and a nurse injects her with a mild tranquilizer.

Some things really are too painful to watch.

Husband Roy comes everyday without fail to visit Anna and comfort her through her distress. He's another one who should be nominated for sainthood. Anna's son, Roy, Jr. teaches out west at Stanford University and rarely visits, but he calls his mother regularly. I have the impression that these calls are carefully scripted to avoid bad news since Anna is always cheerful after speaking to her son.

Having visited the hairdresser earlier in the day, Anna was sporting a new frosted perm. She always wears baggy, floral design haus-frau dresses that make her look like the perfect grandma for a vintage 1950's sitcom. Her extremely wide maternal streak causes her to look after everyone on the ward, me included.

"You look a little pale today, Tony," she said. "Are you eating your vegetables?"

"I had two helpings."

"Maybe you need some good red meat. Would you like me to fix you a steak?" The patients are not permitted to cook, but that never stops Anna from offering.

"I had one for dinner, Anna, but thank you."

"You have to look after your health, you know."

"I know."

After detailed fittings for each one, Anna made me two sweaters this week. If my chest measured three inches around, they'd fit perfectly. Lately, she's started playing checkers and will play with anyone who doesn't mind being measured for a sweater. I play with her fairly regularly, but I never play to win against Anna.

I just can't.

Larry Learns the Internet

"It was actually our pornography industry that figured out how to securely accept credit cards payments over the Internet. If you need a bunch of software geeks to be inventive and solve problems, nothing motivates quite as well as full frontal nudity."

Larry Learns Social Acceptance

"It starts with your parents, but most people branch out by making friends, and of course, reading. I remember reading a book entitled *I'm Okay, You're Okay* in high school. Then in college, I discovered one called *I'm Okay, Just Help Me to My Car*."

Larry Learns Religion

"We've got sacraments and rites and rituals and prayer mats. We've got angels, saints and martyrs. We've got priests, rabbis, ministers and imams. And just about everybody has a Good Book. It all gets very confusing at times, but no one has pulled it all together quite like the American South. They established the Church of Hellfire and Brimstone with Singin'."

Larry Learns Civil Service

"Under the new Civil Service Reform Act, managers can no longer hand out merit raises to employees who have died."

Larry Learns the National Parks

"I know you may find it hard to believe that the government can in fact mismanage dirt, but. . ."

Larry Learns Gentlemen's Clubs

"The male brain is visually-oriented and saturated with testosterone, the strongest sex hormone on the planet, so the desire to look at naked women is an entirely normal part of male psychology. The female brain is verbally-oriented, so it's an entirely normal part of female psychology to distract the male with a nice set of knockers while talking him out of a week's pay."

6

Who Need Sleep?

"Die scum."

Larry pulled me up to the ship just after I'd gone to bed. I thought I was having a really strange dream till I awoke mid-transit. I flopped around on the cold metal table for a few minutes, then managed to sit up just as he came into the room.

"You seem uncomfortable this evening, Tony," he said.

"This table is freezing and you woke me up. Don't they have common decency on your planet? You can't just pull people out of bed for no good reason."

"But, I have an excellent reason, Tony. I've learned some wonderful things today and require your assistance to understand them."

I think most people are inclined to help someone who is just trying to learn. Whether alien or human, there's something captivating about the eagerness of a student whose young mind is thirsting for knowledge and looking to you to quench that thirst. Some basic human instinct was telling me to be patient and help the poor guy.

I ignored it.

"You woke me up," I challenged.

"You seem to expect an apology. Will it help if I apologize," asked Larry.

"No."

"What would you like me to do, Tony?"

"Something anatomically impossible."

His little hairy started to bounce. "Is it important to you that we discuss that first?"

"No, Larry, just tell me what you want to know so I can get back to sleep."

"I researched your wars today. You seem to have a lot of them. It's a very bizarre concept, to kill one's own species. I think I understand. . ."

"Then, you're the first, "I interrupted.

"Really? That's very flattering." He took his recorder out of the pocket of the tan coveralls that he always wore. His coveralls have numerous front pockets starting on the torso and continuing all the way down to just above the knee. (I wonder what's in them?) His shoes are built into the coveralls, similar to a toddler's sleepwear, except Larry's have what appear to be fairly heavy rubber treads.

"I found some battles that seem to have no casualties," he said.

"You drag me out of bed to explain some obscure battles? And they think I'm nuts!"

"Only a few of them have me confused. Take for example, the Battle of the Bulge. It doesn't seem to be related to any particular war."

"Sure it is. That's World War II. A man named Adolf Hitler got a really high score in the fruitcake section of his high school aptitude test. He decided on world domination as a career choice."

"I don't think that's the one," said Larry.

Alien students and Earth students seem to have something in common. Obviously, Larry spent a lot his study time monitoring commercial television, radio and inane websites. The fact that he only picked up broadcast programming made sense. If his spaceship had cable, it would look like a very large version of tetherball. I also figured he was likely tapping the Internet from one of our communication satellites. Still, I was getting tired of explaining the drivel that the television networks' mindless executives and the equally mindless Madison Avenue advertising firms dump on us every day. I needed to broaden Larry's range of topics. "I'll explain the battles if you let me go back to sleep. And tomorrow, I want you to watch nothing but PBS," I said.

"Agreed. Who are they fighting in this Battle of the Bulge?"

"The Cellulites. They're an obscure mountain tribe from Tibet. You don't need weapons because it's a war of intimidation. If they see that you jog regularly and have smooth thighs, it scares the hell out of them and they leave you alone. If you eat lots of pasta and ice cream sundaes, they attack your butt without mercy."

I was really tired. That was the best I could do on short notice and his little hairy barely twitched. I either had to wake up or find a way to satisfy him with a couple of quick answers so he'd send me back to bed. The latter was my best option. I need sleep.

"I see." He shriek-whistle-clicked a batch of notes into his recorder. "The next one is the Battle of the Sexes. This is very strange. Male and female of the same species are not usually found to fight one another. Why do you have a battle between genders?"

"Oh God, Larry, I could feed you crap on that one for months," I said under my breath.

"Pardon?"

"Never mind. It's late and that's a really complex issue. What specifically do you want to know?"

Larry checked his recorder. "Do they use weapons?"

"Dull, rusty knives to cut your heart out."

This was the first time Larry appeared genuinely shocked. "That's barbaric!"

"That's unfair, Larry. I don't make judgmental comments about your species kidnapping people, do I? . . . All right, maybe I do. Bad example."

"But, you said they cut your heart out."

"Not all the time. Sometimes, it's just a pancreas or a small chunk of your liver. It depends on how serious the relationship was before she decided to throw all your stuff in the hallway and change the locks on your apartment."

"Why would a female throw all of your stuff out of your living quarters," he asked.

"Usually because they don't have enough upper body strength to throw out the actual male."

He made a few quick shriek-whistle-click notes into his recorder. "So, physical confrontation is part of your normal mating cycle?"

Jesus, I'm tired!

"No, Larry. Physical confrontation only occurs when the male is an asshole, or in some rare cases, when he needs to defend himself."

"Why would the male need a defense against a female?"

"Because they always want you to quit drinking."

"I assume you mean alcohol," said Larry.

"Of course, alcohol." I couldn't stop yawning. "A man can't stay married without alcohol. That would be cruel."

Larry's shock faded and his little hairy started to bounce. "I see."

"I doubt it. You have to have a heart to understand this one, Larry. You don't qualify."

"I have a heart!"

"Which planet did you leave it on?"

"If you're speaking of mates," said Larry, "my mate is on *Shriek-whistle-click*. She sends me messages quite often. We have a truly wonderful understanding."

"Oh please! Don't tell me that you understand women."

"Of course, I do."

"You must be from outer space, Larry."

"You know I am."

"I rest my case."

"I didn't see that you brought anything with you. Where is your case?"

"Aaaaaaah!"

Larry had perfect timing. I arrived back in my room and was just beginning to doze when Nurse Cassilio stuck her head in the door for bed checks. She must have worked a double shift today. It was easy to see that it was Nurse Cassilio because of the damn night lights. "I'm here," I said.

"Sorry to disturb you, Mr. Sterling." She started to tiptoe out the door.

"Call me, Tony." I matched her whisper.

"Good night, Tony."

"Not exactly. Would you like to hear about it?"

Shaking her head, she resumed her tiptoe and left. Smart woman.

Mo herded the Happy Ward group down to the cafeteria for breakfast. Along the way, I eavesdropped on his daily conversation with Monty.

"The night nurse told me that you slept on the floor again," said Mo.

"It feels better," Monty answered.

"You won't even try the bed. How do you know it feels better?"

"I'm used to sleeping on the sidewalk. I like what I'm used to."

"When was the last time you slept in a bed, Monty?"

"At the other hospital. They tied me to it." Monty tensed as he struggled with his feelings, then burst with anger. "They hog-tied me! I don't sleep good when they do that. I ache all over. It's not nice. They hog-tied me! When I get out of here, I'm gonna go back and steal their souls. You wait and see!"

Mo gave him a few seconds to calm his agitation. "No one here is going to tie you to the bed, Monty."

"That's what you say now. What about later?"

"The only reason I would tie someone to a bed would be to keep them from hurting themselves or someone else. You wouldn't hurt yourself or someone else, would you?"

"I never hurt anyone that didn't try to hurt me."

"There you go then!" Mo sounded really excited. "You can sleep in the bed now, Monty!"

"I can?"

"Sure you can. You know it's more comfortable than the floor and since you promise not to hurt anyone, no one here is going to tie you to the bed." Mo stopped and shook Monty's hand. "Congratulations, Monty! You get to sleep in a bed again!"

"I do?"

"You absolutely do."

"Wow! I get to sleep in a bed!"

It was a nice try, but by bedtime, Monty would forget. He would be found sleeping on the floor again that night.

The following morning, Mo would try again to convince him that beds were preferable and perfectly safe. I listened to numerous variations of this conversation nearly every morning. Mo never gave up, seeming to have an inexhaustible supply of encouragement and compelling reasons that Monty should sleep in his bed. Some of the more notable:

- People can avoid stepping on you in the dark.
- I made the bed for you with special, extra-comfortable sheets.
- Try it for an afternoon nap first. Let it grow on you.
- Everyone uses a bed. Join the club, Monty.
- You get a nicer breeze if you get off the floor.
- The nurses all think you look cute when you sleep in a bed.

That last one was definitely a lie, a white lie, but a lie all the same. Monty would never be cute, even with makeup, even with Spackle.

In truth, the best Monty could hope for on his better days was that people didn't run when they saw him. Mo still encouraged, cajoled and begged Monty to use the bed. He never lost patience and in the end, he succeeded in getting Monty off the floor and into a clean, comfortable hospital bed.

The winning argument: Table tennis champions only sleep in beds.

Despite relating this story about Monty and the bed, I don't normally eavesdrop on other people's conversations; at least, I never did intentionally until coming to the hospital. The tedium of the routine here makes you do rather strange things just to keep your mind occupied. At times, you have to find inventive ways to fight the boredom.

I was sitting near the nurses' station reading my latest mailing of financial journals when Nurse Tammy stopped in to see Mo and found Nurse Cassilio.

"He's bathing Mr. Turner down in Ward Six, you know, that fat old guy with the spinal injury. Mo's the only one who can lift him," Nurse Cassilio told her.

"Damn, I was hoping to catch Mo on my break. I only have a few minutes left." Nurse Tammy was clearly disappointed.

I heard Nurse Cassilio chuckle. "You may be wasting your time with that one, honey."

"Why do you say that? He's so nice and he's handsome, a big, handsome teddy bear."

"He's big alright. He's probably hung like a horse."

Women talk like that?

Frankly, I was shocked! Here were two lovely, highly educated women talking dirty about a friend of mine! Modesty prevents me from relating any more details, but fortunately it didn't prevent me from straining an ear to hear some more.

Cured my boredom.

Larry Learns Pillow Talk

"Women feel most vulnerable in bed. The ugliest woman on the planet still wants to be beautiful between the sheets, so you have to convince her that you're just being sexually adventurous when you ask her to lie face down."

Larry Learns Fine Art

"It started with Neolithic cave paintings, mostly in France, and a very talented young artist named Fred Flintstone. Then we went through various experimental periods, Renaissance, Romanesque, Gothic, Impressionist, etc. Cave walls gave way to painting on wood, canvas, metal plates, temple walls and Easter eggs. And some really progressive spray paint work is being done on the side of my local grocery store by an artist named Dribble Dawg."

Larry Learns Advertising

"Advertising is based on human psychology. For example, if you have a new product to sell and you just happen to know that most people have disposable income and lousy impulse control. . ."

Larry Learns Bureaucracy

"It's an important part of our social structure. Even the chronically dull deserve gainful employment."

Larry Learns the Federal Budget

"It always amuses me that women think they invented bloat."

7

REALITY, DON'T YOU MISS IT

Tough day, today.

I've figured out why farmers become accustomed to waking up to a cocky rooster every morning. They have no choice. Neither do I. The guy three doors down is crowing at the sunrise again.

"Check."

I hunched over the chessboard, viewing my king's imminent demise. My daily opponent, Carl, had me cold. Checkmate was four moves away and there was no escape. "Okay, you got me," I said. "Shall we go again?"

"What time is it?" Carl was no longer permitted to wear a watch because he'd glued the last one to his wrist.

"Ten-thirty."

"Tina should be here soon with muffins!" Unbelievably, he was genuinely excited about that. "We'll play till she arrives."

"Fair enough." I began setting up my side of the board once again.

"Tony?" Carl's voice abruptly developed a tremor, heavily laced with obvious fear. "Am I crazy?"

This one moment truly defined mixed emotions. Had I been anywhere but confined to a mental hospital, I would have let my professional wise ass persona out of its bag and zinged Carl fast and hard. After all, his question is the near perfect straight line. In reality, I am in a mental hospital; Carl is indeed crazy, and I'm not remotely qualified to handle his illness or his question.

A lot of people say they're compassionate, but that's seldom the case. More often, we succumb to our day-to-day frustrations, snapping and yelling at an innocent bank teller, cashier or some other helpless victim. We almost never walk a mile in our fellow man's shoes. We don't take a single step. Even if we keep our routine frustrations and anger in check, even if we're not from New York, we offer jokes, platitudes or polite and quite often diverting nonsense. It takes conscious effort to really feel for the other guy. At these moments that beg for a little kindness, pat phrases are so much less taxing.

True compassion is not ingrained in most people. It's not automatic. That's not mean. It's just human.

On the other hand, what if I say the wrong thing out of plain ordinary ignorance? I'm not trained in psychiatry. The basic psychology course that I took in college was mostly a history of psychology. Telling Carl about Pavlov's dogs and Mendel's peas isn't going to help. I also have a firm belief that Freud was lying about his cigar, but that won't help either. If I say the wrong thing, will it damage him further?

How the hell should I know?

Pitiful isn't it, to fear trying to help another human being?

I ducked Carl's question. "Wouldn't you rather talk to your doctor about that, Carl?"

"The doctors think I should stay here. They don't understand."

"You won the last game, Carl. You still want to play white?"

"I'm just trying to make things better for everyone. Engineers always make things better. Better cars. Better bridges. Even better plumbing."

"It's always nice to have good plumbing."

"Don't you see?" He was really agitated and getting louder. "Cars that fly are better for the environment. You don't need roads anymore and we'll have billions of highway dollars that we can spend on really important things, like avocado farms."

"Did I ever tell you what Freud said about his cigar?"

"It's genius, that's what it is," he said. "When you're a genius, people hate you."

"No one hates you, Carl. You're a great guy."

He started to shout, "They don't understand!"

"I think the hospital staff are nice people. They're trying to understand."

"No, they're not!" His yelling continued, rapidly gaining momentum. "They don't have my vision. They can't see nothing, anything, as it should be, everything. One. It's nature. Plants, animals, machines, they're the same. They're all part of the same design. I know because I draw designs. I'm the only one who can see. I'm the genius! Why don't they see that?

"The universe is one. It's one big machine. It takes an engineer to understand that. We design the machines. We build the machines. We're the only ones qualified to operate the machines." His rant paused for several ragged breaths, then his volume began rebuilding toward a new crescendo. "I'm an engineer, Tony! I'm qualified to operate the universe! I'm the genius who can show them the way! CAN'T YOU SEE THAT!"

I borrowed a lesson from Mo and let the air hang silent for a few moments, hoping Carl would calm down. I desperately looked around for a nurse while futilely trying to give Carl the impression that he had my full attention at the same time. Finally, I pointed to his side of the chessboard and simply kept my voice low and soothing. "It's your move, Carl."

In film and television, they can *wipe* the screen in a second, moving from one scene to another. Carl has that same ability. The straining muscles in his face and neck relaxed. The wild eyes regained their focus. His voice was instantly calm. "Can't right now, Tony," he said with a huge smile. "Tina's here with my muffins. I think she made asparagus-kiwi today."

As he ran to the door to meet Tina, I realized that I was more upset about Carl's rant than he was.

Is Carl crazy? Perhaps no more than asparagus-kiwi.

I found Nurse Cassilio plowing through the morning paperwork at the nurse's station. "I really can't talk about another patient," she said.

"Come on, I'm not asking for his medical history," I responded. "I'm just curious why none of the nurses responded when Carl blew a gasket, and I'd sort of like some advice on how to handle it if he goes off again."

She looked up from her work, pausing to determine how much to tell me. "You're a patient, too, Tony."

"And we both know that I'm as sane as you are, or you wouldn't be feeding me sugar pills."

She smiled, denoting agreement more than humor. "We watch Carl from a distance when he starts one of his rants. Confronting him increases his agitation, and he becomes even more disruptive and dissociative. When that happens, we usually have to tranquilize him. If we let him vent on his own for a minute, he generally calms himself. So, the best thing for you to do is just listen to him. We've got your back. You're safe, and Carl's safe. It's not something to worry about."

I'll be damned! They do know what they're doing!

I stood quietly at the faux-maple counter for a moment. Nurse Cassilio waited patiently for my response. "That's really very impressive," I said finally. "I have a whole new level of respect for nursing as a profession."

"Thank you, Tony."

"And I'm really hot for you right now."

Laughing, she pointed the direction with her index finger. "Back to the ward!"

It was my turn to help Anna with her spelling as she wrote another letter to a grandchild who would never receive it.

"Meticulous? Isn't that too big a word to use for a nine year old?" I asked.

"Perhaps you're right," she said, hesitating with her pen poised above the flowery, pink, designer stationery that she always used. "Let's use *fastidious*."

"Fastidious, F-A-S-T-I-D-I-O-U-S," I spelled aloud for her.

"Did I tell you that my granddaughter looks just like me?"

"Really?"

"She has the same beautiful, blond hair that I had as a child. Mine didn't turn brown till I was about twelve."

"I happen to like brunettes, Anna. I'll bet you had pretty brown hair, too."

She stopped writing and gave me a surprisingly mischievous grin. "In my day, I was a looker, Tony. I'd have knocked your socks off."

"What do you mean, in your day?" I laughed. "You're still gorgeous, Anna."

"That's another good word." She went back to her letter. "How do you spell *gorgeous*?"

"G-O-R-G-E-O-U-S."

"Nancy will like that. Can you believe she's starting to notice boys already? She'll like being g-o-r-g-e-o-u-s." She spelled out the word as she wrote it down. "I'm afraid I don't get to see her as much as I'd like. Ever since . . . ever since . . ." Her voice faded off to nothing, then returned. "Since I came here, I just don't get to see her much."

She paused the nib of her pen just above the paper for a long moment. Turning to me, a sheen of tears coated her eyes, threatening to burst forth. She dropped the pen on the table and frantically clutched my sleeve with both hands, nearly ripping the fabric. "I will get to see my grandchildren again, won't I, Tony? PLEASE GOD, let me see them again!"

I've never heard such naked desperation in a human voice. I think psychologists call this decompensation. All of Anna's mental defenses were collapsing right in front of me.

Help!

"Anna," I softly intoned, fighting back my own emotions, "I'm sure, no matter where she is, Nancy's waiting for your letter. We should finish it now. Nancy's waiting."

I wasn't sure Anna heard what I was saying until she slowly let go of my sleeve. She smoothed out the wrinkles in the fabric caused by her sudden, tortured grasp; ironing the cotton with the palm of her hand.

"Make sure you tell her," I continued, "that if her hair turns brown, not to worry. Brunettes are beautiful."

"That's right," she said, wiping her tears with the back of her hand and rediscovering the pen and paper in front of her. "I have to tell her. Does *brunette* have one 't' or two?"

"Two. B-R-U-N-E-T-T-E. Tell her brunette hair is very, very beautiful." I was becoming practiced at keeping my voice low and soothing. Watching her closely as Anna began to write again, I made a discovery of my own. Beautiful hair comes in many colors, even gray with frosted perm highlights.

"No more, Monty. You're killing me!"

Monty jumped up and down at his end of the table. "That's five games in a row that I kicked your butt! Another shutout for the World Table Tennis Champion!"

I lay my paddle on the table near the net. "That last game was embarrassing, twenty-one to three."

"Don't be embarrassed, Tony," he said almost meekly. "You have to remember there's no one can compete with me. I have a lethal overhand smash."

"I'll say."

We sat on the squeaky, rotting-peas-green vinyl sofa in the lounge to catch our breath and wipe the heat and sweat from our brows. Institutional furniture is apparently chosen with two criteria in mind. Comfort is not one of them. Ugly almost made the top two list, but came in third. The two primary requirements are simple: every sofa and chair has to be easy to clean and the budget-conscious accounting department can't gag when they see the price tag. Unless of course, the institution doing the purchasing is a branch of the federal government, which will only hire accountants with no gag reflex.

I lay my head back on the sofa cushion and breathed deeply while my heart rate returned to normal. Playing against Monty was a good aerobic workout. Without a ball in play to react to, your only choice is to react to the creative impulses of your opponent and your imagination. I've found that to be more strenuous than an actual game at times, and I'm certain that some of the moves we choreograph in pantomime are eminently more fantastic than would ever be seen in real play.

"I saw you helping Anna with a letter," said Monty.

"She's writing her granddaughter," I replied, momentarily revisiting the angst of that recently past moment.

Monty tossed his paddle in the air, flipping it end-over-end, always catching the handle. He switched hands, catching behind his back and still never missing the handle. After a minute, he stopped and with obvious hesitation, asked, "Would you write me a letter, Tony?"

"If you want me to."

"I never got a letter."

"Never?"

"Never."

How was this possible? I'm not particularly good at guessing people's ages, but Monty looked to be somewhere in his late twenties or early thirties. "Don't you have any relatives or friends that write to you?"

Monty intently examined the rubberized face of his paddle, checking for the slightest imperfection. "I don't have no family." He was unable to look at me. "My last friend died under the bridge we was living at last winter. An ice storm got him. He was like me. He didn't have no address. No one wrote to him either."

"I'd be happy to write to you, Monty. Is there anything special you want me to say in the letter?"

"Nah." He returned to flipping his paddle in the air. "Wait! Remind me to practice every day. You can't be a champion unless you practice every day."

"No problem."

"And tell me . . . tell me something nice. Something nice about me."

"There's lots of nice things about you. That'll be an awful big letter."

"Don't make fun of me, Tony!"

"I'm not! You're a nice guy, Monty. You really are. It's fun talking to you and I've learned a lot from the games we play."

"Really?"

"Honest, I've learned one hell of a lot. I'm sure just being able to play against a champion like you has improved my game tremendously."

"I did something good then."

I patted him on the back. "You certainly did!"

"Wow!"

"Why are you so surprised by that?" I asked.

Monty set down his paddle, something I'd never seen him do, but he placed it in his lap where he could quickly retrieve it. Looking around the lounge to make sure no one was around, he cupped his hands to my ear and whispered quietly.

"We don't have a ball," he said.

Larry Learns International Diplomacy

"The president negotiates all treaties with foreign governments and the US Senate approves all treaties after delaying the process long enough for the American public to believe they're actually doing some sort of work. We also have a Secretary of State, whose primary job is to meet with foreign heads of state and apologize for whatever the White House staff leaked to the press this week."

Larry Learns Pet Etiquette

I love pets, especially dogs, but this was for Larry. . .

"Men love good dogs, especially good hunting dogs. However, if you're not careful, you may get stuck with your girlfriend's nasty, whiny, yappy, little-shit lapdog. If your girlfriend is really, really hot, you have no choice. You have to let her bring her little rat-dog to your apartment, and you can't get upset when he takes a wizz on your new leather recliner that cost you big bucks and several pints of blood. But if your girlfriend is also a dog, you can generally risk completely losing it and tossing her little rat-bastard off your balcony.

"Now, relationships that come with a bird or a goldfish are a lot easier. Mostly, who cares? Birds you can cover with a blanket and fish don't bark. But if for some inane reason they annoy you, all you really need is an open window or a toilet and a well-practiced 'Honey, there was an accident' story."

Larry Learns Haute Cuisine
". . . On Tuesday, that's Michelob and a Wet Burrito Grande." On Wednesday. . ."

Larry Learns Cursing
"One of Earth's major art forms, which was perfected by Navy Chiefs and Marine Drill Instructors, true experts all. The secret is vivid imagery with a personal touch. For example, you don't simply call someone stupid; you ask how their mama managed to choose the dumbest sperm out of three hundred million."

Larry Learns Personal Grooming
"Ear hair must be either trimmed or braided. If you have red hair, a green ribbon is acceptable during the Christmas season. . ."

8

BLAME WHOMEVER'S HANDY

I wrote a long, encouraging letter to Monty. Mo checked the mailroom every morning (two days) until it arrived and made a special run, literally, to Monty's room for a hand delivery. Monty thanked me profusely, shaking my hand over and over again. Later, he asked me to read the letter to him. It was the first time he'd admitted to anyone on the ward that he couldn't read. My letter was that important to him!

Actually, that's not so surprising, if you think about it.

Hospital living (as opposed to life) revolves around the written word, prescriptions, charts and records. But for the patient in long-term resident care, plain ordinary mail—a simple but sincere letter, post card, or get-well card—is a major highlight of the day. Incoming and outgoing mail are both important, but incoming seems to be vital to the healing process. Think of it as postage-paid salve for the soul as thumb-worn pages are read and reread, and read again to friends. Outgoing mail is then a replacement for the conversations the patient would have had with loved ones if home.

Yes, I know that when you have a sick friend or relative in a long-term care facility, it's tempting to just pick up the phone, or not bother, since you intend an actual visit sometime next week or next month. I know longhand is dying and that you've been at your keyboard all day. I know you're busy, your show is coming on, or your basketball game just went into overtime. I know it's not a measure of your caring or compassion. I know, I know, I know!

Frankly, I've done the same thing for years, including rationalizing my own forgiveness, and forgetting that, whether you're applying an actual stamp or clicking the *send* button, mail is prescription-strength medication. Why should I withhold medicine from a sick friend?

I immediately wrote Monty a second letter. Mo walked me down to the gift shop and I purchased a get-well-soon card covered with flowers and songbirds for Anna and a postcard with a nicely detailed picture of the International Space Station for Carl. Then, I thought:

What the hell!

I purchased six dozen postcards and I've been spending a little free time sending get-well wishes to every patient I know here at Sunny Park.

I even sent one to Winston Churchill. I checked with his doctor, so it's entirely kosher at this point in his treatment that I signed it Franklin Delano Roosevelt.

I also sent a Just4Fun greeting card picturing a group of overly handsome, burly, shirtless firemen to Nurse Cassilio. The caption was, *Don't take fire prevention so seriously.*

A little personal mail made her day, too.

For the hospital staff, the written word is usually quite different. Writing is reports, records, memos and minutia. Mail is bills, insurance forms and records requests. It's a never-ending mire of bureaucracy. Incoming mail is more work to do. Outgoing mail is work completed, and almost nothing is signed *Warmest Regard*s or *With Love.*

Still, one can hope.

Dr. Bousteir has fine, even handwriting. Not scrunched or scratched or grandiose, not too many flourishes. (I'm beginning to question whether or not she actually went to medical school.) Her hand flows easily with firm, confident strokes of the pen caressing the paper. It's difficult to read upside-down, but I catch occasional glimpses of her notepad, especially when she sets it down to reach for the pitcher and water glass that always sit on the corner of her desk. One note in particular compelled me to comment.

"That's bull, doc, my parents had nothing to do with this."

I grew up in Philadelphia, just a hop, skip and a jump from some of our country's most wonderful playgrounds. New York, the Jersey Shore, Washington DC, New England and the mountains of Western Pennsylvania and West Virginia are all close enough for a weekend visit or a quick vacation. As a teen, my parents and I spent a lot of time in New York City.

In The Big Apple, I had access to Broadway shows, world-class museums, high fashion, fabulous jazz musicians, and street vendors or freak shows on every corner. With a teen's underage budget, I mostly enjoyed the freak shows and ate hot dogs from the colorful wheeled carts manned by immigrant cooks who spoke their own form of equally colorful English. More than half of New York City's stores claim to give you discounts or wholesale pricing, which is absolutely necessary because New York retail pricing is somewhat more painful than passing a kidney stone.

I also learned to love haunting New York's museums, particularly fine art. I developed a taste and sincere appreciation for sculpture in a variety of mediums. I don't know why sculpture appeals to me more than a fine painting by an old master. Maybe it's the three dimensional quality. Shape and form draw my attention more than bright color or deliberately altered perspective. Maybe I just prefer things solid, heavy and real. Who knows?

Central Park was also fascinating. It often had free concerts and entertainment, and of course myriad games, such as Frisbee, volleyball, chess, etc., during the day. At night, it has muggers, rapists, enterprising drug dealers and street gangs looking to expand their turf. A midnight stroll through the park is usually recommended only if you're able to bring your own SWAT team.

New York also has love at first sight. For me, that was the New York Stock Exchange. On my first visit, the vibrant energy of the exchange floor was simply overwhelming. What appears to be chaos is actually the pervasive scent of money flying through the air at light speed. The constant roar of commerce comes from traders who make money with their wits and a pocket calculator.

At the tender age of fourteen, I made my career choice, which I defined at that time as going to Wall Street with my own pocket calculator and making enough money to buy a car.

What a fabulous idea!

Below New York, the southern beaches of the New Jersey shore were a mere two-hour drive from Philadelphia. This was my summer haunt during most of my high school years. The attractions are cheap carnival games, arcades, Ferris wheel rides, saltwater taffy and Italian ices, which ease the way for a young man with a few dollars and a little patter to steal a kiss (and perhaps much more) under the boardwalk. Sunny days are fairly consistent, but the water is forever a murky brown. Ever since our earliest colonial days, the surrounding cities have continuously dumped industrial waste, trash, garbage and God-knows-what into the rivers and near-offshore ocean. However, this doesn't bother the millions of annual tourists, who come to sun themselves and wade into the surf, blithely testing their immune systems. Who cares about massive barges illegally dumping medical waste when the sand and the boardwalk beckon with girls in bikinis, which seemingly grow progressively smaller with each passing year?

Face facts, I can always commit to being environmentally conscious after I get laid.

I met my first love, Sandra Pinter, in a noisy, crowded arcade on the boardwalk in Ocean City. It was an overly thankful night for all concerned. Sandra was playing air hockey with her older sister, who was thankful for a reason to ditch Sandra and run off to meet her friends for an evening of loud music, marijuana smoke and smuggled beer. Sandra was thankful to have a night away from her overprotective parents. I was thankful that she wasn't wearing a bra. Sincerely thankful!

Sandra's cinnamon hair surrounded a cute, round face with bright, hazel eyes, a petite nose and glossy pink lips, which smiled easily. She had a nicely lush set of developing curves wrapped in the hippest beach fashion of the day, the shortest of short-shorts and a tube top. In reality, Sandra was your average girl-next-door. However to me, she was a radiant teen goddess with everything that I desired.

Did I mention that she wasn't wearing a bra?

My dad allowed me to borrow the car for our dates, and together Sandra and I explored South Jersey and various positions for unoriginal sin. Our relationship ended with the summer as we returned to our respective homes and high schools. Despite a series of overly passionate letters and phone calls, our hormones soon found new loves and eventually, our phone calls and protestations of true love transformed into sweet memories.

Bless you, Sandra Pinter. I wish you well.

Further south, I found Washington, DC. The trip was about three to four hours by either train or car, but absolutely worth it for educational value.

Okay, that may not be the truth, the whole truth, and nothing but the truth, but I had to tell my parents something.

I traveled to Washington with my parents several times to see the national fireworks display on the Fourth of July holiday. I visited all of the popular monuments, and haunted the Smithsonian Museum for long, leisurely strolls past vintage aircraft, fabulous gem collections and dinosaur bones. I remember climbing onto a massive steam engine with wide-eyed wonder and feeling the barely bridled power of this now cold steel.

Washington is also where I learned that it is just as easy to find interesting things in air conditioned spaces as it is to find them outside in the heat and humidity.

My dad took me to watch a session of congress from the gallery. They were debating an alteration to the esoteric laws governing interstate trucking. I was age ten at that time, and I didn't see any big trucks, so I found our political leaders less than impressive. My view has not changed since.

In my late teens, I would visit Washington on my own, staying in Silver Springs, Maryland with a favored aunt, who served spiced crabs, baked fresh cookies and slipped me a little extra cash so that I could enjoy my visit. Had she known that I was heavily entrenched in my *marijuana is cool* phase and that most of her cash went to purchase some excellent quality toke from a bearded leftover hippie on the campus of Catholic University, she would have withheld her generous gifts. However, I eased her conscious by conjuring memories from my earlier visits and daily informing her of the wonders that I had seen in the Smithsonian, one of the presidential monuments or the National Archives. Fables were much kinder than truthfully telling her that I'd spent the day getting baked and balling a kindhearted, incredibly stoned and incredibly horny university coed who thought I was "just the cutest".

Normally, I would have felt guilty about lying, but I strove to maintain my auntie's image of me as a hardworking young student more for her benefit than mine. She never would have believed our illustrious family could produce a stoner horn dog.

I eventually realized that being stoned causes one to miss out on the truly marvelous flavors of life. It's also a little stupid to smoke your entire entertainment budget. I gave up marijuana in my early twenties, but I didn't give up on spending lazy days with horny coeds.

I told you I wasn't crazy!

In another direction, I'd found the mountains to the west of Philadelphia while still in grade school. I confess that my dad did the driving to the Blue Ridge Mountains where we stayed in a slightly leaning, rustic cabin with significantly more charm than heat. I climbed across the open rafters of our cabin, exploring the monkey side of my boyish soul.

Western Pennsylvania and West Virginia comprise what is definitively some of the prettiest real estate in the nation. I hiked rough nature trails through the woods, chasing the resident deer and chipmunks with my camera. I helped cook meals over an open fire, and toasted marshmallows on a stick. We sang songs and told ghost stories till late in the evening, and closely supervised, dad let me help chop the wood for our fire. We had bunks in the cabin, but I was allowed to sleep on the floor in my Spiderman sleeping bag. Some things are more important than comfort and it was absolutely wonderful!

The real wonder of spending part of my formative years in the wild, wild woods is that I didn't die of tick-borne disease, a tragic accident, frostbite, predatory animals, snakebite or poison ivy. However, my parents were appropriately protective, saving me from the most obvious blunders that could be committed by my often-impulsive developing brain. What can I say? Look before you leap has never in human history been the preferred philosophy of a ten year old boy.

New England is equally beautiful, but with a very different flavor. I visited small seaside towns with fishing trawlers, sailboats, saltbox houses, and cafes serving grilled blueberry muffins with a steamy mug of hot chocolate, with whipped cream on top, please!

Many of the local restaurants had saltwater tanks with live lobster awaiting culinary execution. With the exception of cows, I had not often seen my food on the hoof. Watching the lobsters skittering over one another was fascinating. Their big claws looked viscous even with fat rubber bands holding them closed.

I found it hard to choose a lobster for my dinner because I liked them all, and I knew that picking one would condemn him to a pot with a decidedly different water temperature. I ended up giving one of the lobsters a temporary reprieve and ordered fish sticks, which should be considered a staple for American children.

New Englanders have a reputation for being down to earth, and perhaps somewhat too literal. However, I found that they are just as normal as everyone else in the country, and almost always pleasant. While I have no doubt that one must exist somewhere, I never personally met a mean New Englander. I liked everyone I met on these northern vacations. When my family spent my ninth Christmas in Bar Harbor, I received several additional presents from the locals, friends of my grandfather who retired there. Extra Christmas presents is a child's dream come true.

Granted, New England does not have a corner on the market for being nice to children. It's a nearly universal quality. People who are intentionally mean to small children are fairly rare in all locales, and I believe this small genetically defective minority should rightfully be covered under a special section of the Federal Disabilities Act. Not to give them any benefits of course, I just think it's a novel idea to encourage our government to keep a master list of grumpy people who are best avoided.

The disadvantage to New England is often assumed to be large quantities of snow in the winter. I disagree wholeheartedly. I love snow, and any young boy is eager and delighted to play in large billowing mounds of it. Many adults love it too, as long as they don't have to shovel it. The true disadvantage of New England was not apparent until I passed into my teen years. Any location that has its entire female population bundled like Eskimos for half the year is inherently less attractive when compared to warmer climates where the women have no need of layered insulation. However, I finally realized that the stoic New England male has an entirely different view. They never shy away from a pretty face, and see multiple sweaters, scarves and bulky parkas much like a box of mixed chocolates. When you finally get to open the box, there's always something sweet in there that matches your particular taste.

Coming home to Philadelphia was always exciting. I had numerous friends waiting to hear my sure-to-be-embellished tales of glorious adventure.

Glorious adventure sounds much better than summer vacation with my parents, doesn't it?

Philly itself has a ton of history. It was the original US capitol, the home of the Liberty Bell, and the site of the Continental Congress. Ben Franklin lived and worked here when he wasn't bedding some countess in France. Thomas Jefferson wrote the Declaration of Independence here. Although, Jefferson refused to do so until after his wife arrived. Apparently, he suffered from writer's block when he wasn't getting any.

Did you ever notice that the official versions of our history never describe our founding fathers as *randy*? Talk about a revision of history!

Philly is also the largest freshwater port in the world, accessed via the Delaware River. Like any port city, it offers the best and the worst, the harsh and drab docks as well as the designer coffee and silk fashions of Society Hill. It's also one of the few cities that can easily compete with Chicago for dirty politics. On occasion, the entire ticket of one of the major parties has been left off the voting machines in contentious districts. While this was a highly suspect occurrence since we have a two party political system, the upside is that the voting machines were fifty-percent correct.

These omissions were explained as an accidental oversight and buses were provided to take the missing party's voters to another district to complete their ballet. However, no promises were made concerning a bus ride home.

Democracy rules!

I grew up in Northeast Philly, which is a mixture of working class and upper middle-class neighborhoods. This section of the city abuts some even wealthier suburbs, and is dotted with large shopping malls, enclosed against the occasional winter storm.

Shopping malls were then a favorite teen haunt, as they are today. Even if I only had a pocketful of change, enough to buy a soda, the mall is where my friends gathered and (with luck) my next devastatingly beautiful girlfriend would suddenly appear with a heavy shopping bag, which I could offer to help her carry.

Here, I learned life's lesson that gentlemanly charm can be as effective as a fat wallet. I had to. When you're fifteen, unemployed, and nearly swimming in hormones, it just doesn't make sense to tell a pretty girl, *Wait here; I'll be back in ten years with a job.*

Where was I. . . .Philadelphia.

I went to private schools, so I didn't have to contend with teacher's strikes and out of date textbooks. My school years were a mixture of intense exploration of the subjects that I found interesting, and forcing myself to stay awake in all other classes. Mrs. Walsh, a jolly, motherly type, mentored me in high school, and daily encouraged my passion for all things mathematical. She always praised my academic accomplishments, and knew me well enough not to allow me to date her daughter.

In all, I had a great childhood. I traveled often. I eagerly explored the wonders in my little corner of our bountiful planet. I met truly wonderful people, and I received a fine education. I had no relatives who did not hug me. I was truly privileged.

Love you, mom and dad.

"Pardon?" Doctor Bousteir almost spilled her water.

"Your note about possible over-controlling parents. It won't wash. My parents were great."

"It's impolite to read someone's. . ."

"And, it's not impolite for you to make assumptions about two wonderful people that you never even knew. And never will, now that they're dead."

"What bothers you more, my note or that they're dead?" She had just a touch of superior in her voice, and it was the first mean comment that she'd made during our sessions.

"What do you think," I asked, my response shaded with a slight tinge of anger. "And isn't that a bit too much reality to throw at a recovering mental patient?"

"I'm sorry," she responded. "You reading my notes. . . it. . . I'm so sorry."

"It's okay. I shouldn't have been reading your notes, but it's hard to resist. They are about me, after all."

"Try to resist in future," she requested.

"Try to resist commenting on my parents in future."

As fights go, this one was pretty lame. It was more of an uncomfortable moment. It was also what keyed me into the fact that she was reaching for any reasonable, logical, medically sound reason for my breakdown. Since Larry couldn't possibly exist, he had nothing to do with my situation. My parents must somehow be at fault. Fate or just plain bad luck was out of the question. Dr. Bousteir didn't believe in fate, luck or Larry. She believed in thick books written by mind-dissecting philosophers, modern research, expensive pharmaceuticals and therapy customized to a patient's symptoms or assumed symptoms.

Overall, our sessions were becoming more intense lately as she pushed hard for me to face up to my delusion.

However, my lovely doctor was correct in one respect. I am delusional in thinking this is a relationship instead of therapy.

We stayed eye-to-eye through a long pause. I found myself getting lost again. She had such great eyes! They were the deepest, deep emerald green, perhaps just a slight shade darker. The flecks of gold were brilliant. They nearly sparkled. I was mesmerized. She blinked and looked away.

Crap!

She'd never believe that I was just admiring her eyes. Now, she'd be talking to her own analyst about the patient who stared her down. Maybe I should have apologized, but instead, I just returned to our sore subject. "My parents were killed in a car accident on the New Jersey Turnpike," I said.

"How did you react when they died?" Renewed professional empathy permeated her tone.

I took a moment to think before answering. "I was very businesslike in public. I handled the funeral arrangements and settled their estate very calmly. I did all my crying while alone in my apartment."

"You didn't want anyone to see your grief?"

"Not necessarily, I think it's perfectly normal to grieve. There was no shame involved. I just preferred privacy at the time."

"Is it possible your grief isn't as fully resolved as you believe?"

I didn't know whether to smile or sigh. "Doc, my parents were loving, caring people. They didn't beat me, abuse me or mistreat me in any way, physically or emotionally. They made mistakes along the way, but nothing that scarred me for life. I had a great childhood. They sent me to summer camp and took me to Disneyland. The loss of my parents was a tragedy, but neither my childhood nor their deaths is related to my current situation.

"You find it hard to blame Larry," I continued, "because you don't believe in him. You think of yourself as rational, and rational people don't believe in alien abductions. I fully understand your position." I poured a glass of water for myself from her pitcher. I looked her in the eye again for confidence sake, but avoided getting locked into another staring match. "I, on the other hand, know that Larry is as real as you or I. And since I'm perfectly sane, I know when I've been screwed."

"I never said I don't believe in aliens. The odds on life existing elsewhere in the universe are quite high. We discussed that."

"You don't believe in Larry."

"According to your description, Larry looks human."

"Except for the hairy bit," I interrupted.

"Except for the hairy bit," she continued. "He's visiting Earth to do a term paper."

"Zoology 101."

"Please, don't interrupt," she chided gently. "He's a student who came billions of miles to do some research and decided to kidnap a Wall Street trader from outside his favorite delicatessen so that he could explain human behavior as depicted in commercial television. He then returns you stark naked to the floor of the New York Stock Exchange."

She really must have thought I was making some progress if she was willing to confront "my delusion" so blatantly. I sipped my water.

She continued, "Using some sort of light beam, Larry kidnaps you at will in order to continue his research, but no one ever sees you leave or return, or notices your absence. During your conversations with Larry, you lie to him because you fear he might be scouting for the great invasion and to take revenge on him for ruining your life. Did I leave anything out?"

"No, that about covers it."

"Which part of this would you expect a rational person to believe?"

"Like I said, Doc, I know when I've been screwed."

My stay at Sunny Park wasn't all fun with the patients, dripping sarcasm on Larry, and teasing the hospital staff. There was a little bit of work involved. I was surprised when Mo told me I had a phone call at the nurses' station. Wilford Casey, one of my more aggressive clients somehow tracked me down for what he felt was critical investment advice.

Wilford is a computer programmer by default. He was an unpopular, geeky teenager who developed into an elite hacker until the FBI's computer crime squad decided to make him the focus of a get tough on computer crime campaign. They never did nail Wilford for anything particularly nasty. It seems Wilford was from the Hippocrates' school of professional hackers. His motto was always, *First, do no harm*. The feds eventually charged him with misdemeanor trespassing or some such nonsense, but made it stick. He received a fine and two years' probation. The publicity landed Wilford a great-paying job with the banking industry, beefing up their computer security. With his introduction to banks, Wilford developed an interest in money, specifically making more of his own. He was referred to me by one of his fellow hackers, who also happened to be a client of mine.

Wilford is not by any standard a bad guy, just a little limited. Aside from his interest in computers, his only other passions, inherited from his parents, were the 1960's, the Beatles and marijuana. He was determined to be a hippie even if he was born a generation too late. He married a stripper named Pinken Pretty (No, I'm not kidding.) and they live in West Chester County, opening their house routinely to a continuous flow of visitors with a similar hippie bent. Wilford and Pinken couldn't find a commune that was a convenient commute to his new, high-paying job, so they started their own right in the middle of New York suburbia.

Wilford's investment strategy is appalling. Over the years, he's ignored every bit of advice I've given him. Steady growth is not his style. He's always looking for the big score instead of the solid investment.

Now, I've got nothing against big scores. I like them a lot, but you swing them with your gambling money, not with this month's mortgage payment. That subtlety was something I could never get Wilford to understand.

Normally, I have tremendous patience with my clients. It's part of being a professional. You have to teach the beginners, keep the intermediates out of trouble, and hope the experts still need your advice. In that respect, trading securities is no different from being the owner of a garden supply store. Educate your consumers and they come back to buy more plants, mulch and fertilizer. However, in order to educate Wilford, I would have had to beat his thick skull with a hammer, which is hardly professional.

To be honest, Wilford is just one of those people who rubs the entire world a little bit the wrong way. He'll call you three times to ask advice on a sneeze, and then guaranteed, he'll ignore your advice and snort lemon cough drops instead. Sometimes, it really takes tremendous effort to be patient with Wilford.

"Tony, this is Wilford. It's really important. I need to talk to you."

"You are talking to me, Wilford."

"Right. How's the hospital?"

"Fine."

"What are you in for," he asked.

"Alien abduction."

"Bummer. So, what do you think of this new tech stock, Modem Whiz?"

I should have known Wilford was calling about another fad stock issue. "They're a mildly innovative software firm that has no hard assets, a mediocre management staff, soft R&D and a product that Microsoft could duplicate in their sleep. Modem Whiz basically developed a simple add-on utility that the marketplace happens to love at the moment. Something similar will probably be included in Microsoft's next release, *Windows - Time to Cough Up More Money*."

"Bummer. That doesn't sound like a buy recommendation."

"Not unless you want to throw your money away."

Wilford couldn't let it go so easily. "Any chance Microsoft will just buy them out?"

"Why bother? Even if Modem Whiz were to claim copyright infringement, they don't have the money to hang in there with Microsoft on a protracted law suit."

"You sure are a cynical bastard, Tony."

"I'm a realist. That's often confused with cynicism."

"Bummer. I guess I'll have to keep looking."

"Bummer," I said. "Why don't you use the money to invest in some good public utilities, Wilford? You probably have this month's electric bill right there on your desk."

My great escape from Sunny Park occurred on a Sunday afternoon. Mo caught up with me across the street from the hospital. I was in a little hole-in-the-wall tavern with older than old furnishings and trendy, new beer. I should have known it was Mo. He's one of the few people who could completely block all the late afternoon sunlight streaming in from the main door. I jumped a little as he put one of his meaty hands on my shoulder and said, "How's it going, Tony?"

"Fine, Mo." I continued sipping my lager, an offering from one of the city's newest microbreweries. It had good color and leaned mildly to the malty side. The only thing I didn't like about it was the name, Bart's Beefy Beer. I guess I'm not one who appreciates alliteration with my hops. I invited Mo to watch the football game with me.

"You slipped out a side door somehow?" The way he asked, I could tell the staff hadn't discovered my escape route yet.

"No." I raised my lager in a toast to freedom and ingenuity. "I removed the glass slats from the jalousie windows on the patio."

"I wouldn't have thought of that," Mo said as he settled onto the stool next to mine. We watched the game for a few minutes on the big screen behind the bar. It was an irrefutable rout. Philly's defense sacked the Giants' quarterback for the third time as we watched. However, this was a pre-season game, so it wouldn't matter much in the long run.

"I have to take you back," Mo said finally.

"How'd you find me?"

"Most everyone who escapes comes here. It's the closest bar. The bartenders call us whenever a customer walks in wearing pajamas."

I was wearing slacks and a sports shirt that I'd borrowed from an employee's locker. They shouldn't have been able to tag me. "Hey,

Mac," I called the bartender, "How'd you know I was from the hospital?"

The bartender looked up, but continued polishing the large stack of glasses at the other end of the bar. "No car and you're not local. You got no wallet and you're wearing hospital slippers. I guessed you might be from over there."

"Well, couldn't you at least have waited till after the game? This is going to seriously affect your tip." The bartender shrugged. I turned to Mo. "We're staying for the end of the game, aren't we?"

"You know I can't do that. I have other patients waiting."

"Well, at least stay for a beer."

"I'm on duty, Tony."

"Okay. Let's stay till I finish my beer?"

"Sure," he conceded. "I'll even pay for it since you've got no wallet."

"No need," I said as I pulled out my wallet-less plastic. "The mail came yesterday. American Express has great 24-hour service on lost cards."

Mo's laugh filled the bar. "I'm gonna have to confiscate that card, you know."

"Oh, well."

"You've been planning this escape for days haven't you, Tony?"

"I know the Giant's schedule. They won't let me watch football on the ward. I guess a three-hundred-ninety-pound tackle tap dancing on the quarterback's windpipe is a tad too violent for us fruitcakes."

"You're a card, Tony."

"No." I showed him my Amex. "This is a card. I'm a fruitcake, remember." I flagged the bartender again and bought Mo a Coke.

"You're not crazy and you know it," said Mo.

I looked him in the eye. He was dead serious. "So, how come you're the only one at the hospital who knows I'm not crazy?"

"My grandmother swore till the day she died that she met an alien in a spaceship. She wasn't crazy. She was one of the sanest people I ever knew."

"What'd her alien look like?"

Mo sipped his Coke. "Don't laugh. She said he looked like a skinny kid with a clump of hair in the middle of his forehead."

"No kidding!"

"I know it sounds strange, but she swore he was real."

"He was, Mo. Take my word for it."

Mo and I stayed and watched the game till the end of the second quarter. When we settled up, I left the bartender a good tip. Ratting me out to the hospital staff was just part of his job, and I can't see penalizing someone for just doing their job. I had enjoyed my taste of freedom and Mo had let me stay as long as he could.

Thanks, Mo.

Carl was seriously impressed that I had *engineered* an escape. Monty asked me to take him along next time. Anna wanted to know if I had taken a sweater to prevent catching a cold. Dr. Bousteir was amused, but went through the motions of trying to make me feel guilty for sneaking out like a sixteen-year-old with a hot date. "Don't you understand, you're here under a court order," she said.

"I'm here because no one believes the truth."

"Your little escape could be construed as contempt of court."

"Come off it, Doc. They can't hold me accountable. I'm nuts, remember. Besides, there are no sane people who don't have contempt for our courts."

I don't think Doc Bousteir was used to treating sane people. For a moment, she was at a loss for words. She made a pretense of checking her notes while she regrouped, desperately attempting to hide a smile that continually crept onto her lips with a will of its own. "You don't have any remorse at all over this, do you," she asked.

"Sure I do. I missed the last half of the game!"

After my reprimand by Doc Bousteir, I went back to my room. At Sunny Park, the patient's rooms are dormitory comfortable. I have a twin-size bed next to a Formica laminated nightstand. The dresser has the same lamination, a wood-grain pattern that is supposed to imitate a lightly stained maple. To the front of the room, there's a small closet with hangers that can't be removed without a hacksaw and no clothing hooks that might (God knows how) cause an injury.

Music is piped in on wall mounted speakers hooked to a simple on-off control. The curtains on the unbreakable windows remind me of a country kitchen, pastel blue with lots of frilly lace and flowers. I imagine that was the decorator's idea of giving the patients some slight touch of home.

For ventilation, the windows open four inches before being mechanically stopped. The walls are the same hospital white that covers the rest of the building and the light fixtures are flush-mounted in the ceiling tiles. Table lamps, picture frames and other breakables are not permitted. A stiff-back chair sits in front of the small writing desk. The desk doubles as a bookshelf, populated with a collection of classics that must have been purchased in bulk from a wholesaler. The books all have the same red and gold binding. *Moby Dick* is among the selections, which is probably therapeutic for obsessive patients.

Lying on my bed, I managed to do little more than count ceiling tiles. A nap was apparently not in my immediate future, so I tried reading. Monty's yelps and groans as he practiced his lethal overhand smash out on the ward kept breaking my concentration.

I tried exercise. After ten minutes of calisthenics on the floor beside my bed, my major accomplishment was a clean spot on the floor. So, I trudged back to the Happy Ward, which at the moment was also CSPAN boring. Nothing interested me today.

Another Table Tennis Championship of the World with Monty wasn't in the works. He was playing both sides of the table in his own little world and didn't even hear me call his name.

I tried to find Carl for a game of chess. He was napping. At least, someone could sleep.

I wondered if Mo would take me out for a walk around the grounds, but he was busy helping to sedate an agitated patient on another floor.

Anna was in the middle of knitting a large sweater order for one of the nurses, who had a large doll collection in need of accessories. No help from Anna.

What to do?

I felt the pull from the spaceship begin. Perfect! What better way to pass some time than to screw with Larry's head?

Larry and I discussed my great escape briefly. He had a few questions about the great lager from the microbrewery, but was primarily interested in the football game. Since I was having such an exceptionally fine day, I explained the rules to him with suitable sincerity.

"A football field is one hundred yards long, marked off in ten yard increments. The idea is to move the ball down the field and into the end zone, which is the goal and marked with a goal post and a lot of white lines painted on the ground. Once you move the ball into the end zone, you have to dance like a lunatic in front of sixty to eighty thousand people. You dance completely around the goal post without stepping on any of the white lines if you want to get six points. If you step on a white line, they can take points away or penalize you with yardage. Yardage is usually a nice pinwale corduroy or a hand-woven muslin.

"Moving the ball into the end zone is called a touchdown, and I can't stress strongly enough how important it is that your celebration dance be original. Players pull out all the stops, act the fool, and really try to be a crowd pleaser. If you can't dance, seek help immediately. Your coach will generally recommend a good ballet teacher or put a dab of Tiger Balm in your jockstrap."

"The players carry the ball or throw it," he asked.

"No. You have to carry the ball or catch it. You can't throw it until after you're in the end zone and then, you have to throw it into the ground. It's called spiking the ball. Normally, the only one who can throw the ball on the field is the quarterback and he'll only do that if he's looking for serious yardage or he's running for his life."

Larry was shocked again. "People get killed in this game?"

"Of course not! Well, very rarely. Mostly they just get bruised a little. Remember, you're talking about some really big guys playing this game."

"Your females don't play?"

"Sure they do. They play on the sidelines in short little dresses or hot pants with lots of sparkles on them. They get extra points for showing lots of cleavage and they all try to score with the quarterback. If they don't, it won't matter. The quarterback will usually tell everyone he scored with them anyway." Larry's little hairy was bouncing quite nicely today. For the briefest moment, I actually thought I saw it do a back flip. Maybe all this crap was making me as delusional as Dr. Busty claimed I was.

"This seems to be a very complex game, Tony."

"It is. A lot of people spend their whole lives studying it. We even have a school for the blind that teaches football. Their graduates are called referees."

"What happens after you spike the ball in the end zone," he asked.

"After spiking, you kick for the extra point. Now, kicking is an ancient and extremely fine art, which brings us to a team called the Rockettes. . ."

Larry Learns About the Vatican

"Vatican City has an area of roughly 110 acres, and is the only absolute monarchy left in Europe. It's widely known for its tourist attractions, most notably the only ATM in the world with instructions in Latin."

Larry Learns English Literature

"Shakespeare's plays are still performed for people who need to pretend they fully understand the nuance of archaic language. Don't get me wrong, his plays are great stories, but no one has the guts to update the language and make them popular again, so the people the plays were written for, the common people, never get to see them unless their daughter is cast as Juliet. And frankly, they don't want to see the play if their son is cast as Juliet."

Larry Learns Family Planning

"Modern birth control has completely changed the dynamic. People no longer name their baby Oops."

Larry Learns Golf

"After hitting the ball, which is called teeing off, you chase after it and hit it again until you knock it into a hole in the ground on what's now called the green. It used to be called the red because of the faces of the people who kept missing the hole."

Larry Learns the Pentagon Budget

"You may actually have a chance on this one, Larry, because the truth is no one on Earth understands it."

9

INCARCERATED, WHITE, PROFESSIONAL
MALE NEEDS LOVE

"Psssst! Psssst!"

"What can I do for you, Monty?"

"I need to ask you something real important."

"Sure. Go ahead."

"You have to promise to keep it just between us. It's top secret."

"I promise," I replied.

"They still haven't found the ball. I think the nurses are hiding it on purpose. They're afraid to play against me." He tossed his paddle into the air and caught it behind his back. "They don't want to lose."

"No one likes to lose, Monty. You said you have a question."

He slammed an air ball with his lethal overhand smash. "When do you think the lady with the muffins will get here?"

A little after ten, Mo escorted me to Dr. Bousteir's office. My appointment was scheduled earlier than normal because she had to attend a conference of some sort in the afternoon. I was still exhausted from another midnight visit with Larry and my generally poor sleep because of the night-lights.

I was almost too tired to enjoy the patient sideshows today. Mrs. Renardo was still singing her aria, but repeating the same passage over and over. She was either trying to hit high C or imitate a mortally wounded seagull. It sounded somewhat similar to Larry's real name. I'll have to ask him if Shriek-whistle-click world has music. Mrs. Renardo could be a superstar.

Most of the other corridor regulars were involved in their usual less than sane activities. However, the guy with the prayer mat appears to have given up on the telephone, shifting his turban, mat and incense thirty feet down the hall. He was now worshipping the water fountain. Apparently, AT&T hasn't answered his prayers. Not surprising, since they haven't answered mine either. Their stock lost three points a share in just the last two days.

Nurse Tammy ambushed Mo as we passed the nurses' lounge. It's embarrassing watching the big guy's discomfort. Nurse Tammy gushes.

Mo stammers and looks at his feet. She preens. Mo blushes. She gushes some more. Mo mispronounces one and two syllable words.

I pretended intense interest in a watercolor on the corridor wall, another pond with ducks, so as not to intrude on their romantic moment. Still, I watched Mo's unbelievably awkward reflection in the Plexiglas that covered the painting. I think he's developing a twitch!

Finally, I cleared my throat, giving Mo an excuse to escape. It was the merciful thing to do. I can't let Mo stand there, caught squarely in the middle of Nurse Tammy's ever so unsubtle pass while my CPR certification is expired. What if his blood pressure shoots through the roof and the poor guy's heart gives out? I'd have to remember. . . .what is it, two breaths, five pumps and repeat? Something like that.

Hey! Sunny Park probably has a CPR refresher course. I should get re-certified while I'm here.

I talked with Mo about the Nurse Tammy situation as we made our way down the hall. Realizing this was a somewhat sensitive subject for Mo, I started gently.

"You stupid SOB! Can't you see that woman wants to jump you with sneakers on! The woman's practically throwing her panties at you!"

"She's a nurse here. I'm a nurse here," he stammered.

"Great. Take her to a movie. Choke on the popcorn, then let her practice the Heimlich maneuver on you."

"It's not good to be dating people where you work."

"Says who?"

"I don't know. They just say that."

"I've heard a lot of advice from *they*, my friend. If any of it was worth a damn, *they* would have signed their names to it."

"I don't think it's a good idea, Tony."

"Normally, it's probably not," I said, "but there are exceptions to every rule. What do you want the girl to do, quit her job just to get a date with you?"

"Don't be silly."

"Look, Mo, take some advice from the only sane inmate in this place, ask her for a date, just some dinner. What's the worst that can happen? You end up having an evening of wild, unbridled sex and the restaurant calls the cops."

Mo's laugh filled the corridor. His guffaw was a deep, rich baritone that drew several patients out of their rooms to see what was going on. Frankly, I'd have looked, too. Baritone guffaws are pretty rare.

"I'll think about it," said Mo.

"Good. We're making progress here. There's a chance that Nurse Tammy won't end up an old maid after all."

"She won't end up an old maid just because I don't ask her out."

"It's not worth the risk, Mo. Ask her out. Do it, today."

We arrived at Dr. Bousteir's office. The reception area was empty. Ms. Emily wasn't at her usual guard post. "She'll be back in a minute," said Mo. "She probably just went to the ladies' room."

"She's probably..."

Self-preservation made me swallow my remark as Ms. Emily stepped into the reception area from Dr. Bousteir's office. Until you know what kind of mood they're in, it's best not to make jokes about women who frighten Sumo wrestlers.

"Good morning, Ms. Emily."

"What are you doing here? Your appointment's been rescheduled. The doctor left early for the conference."

O Juliet, Juliet! Wherefore art thou, Juliet!
You stood me up again, damn it!

I must have looked like someone kicked me. Even the titanic Ms. Emily softened. "Are you all right, Tony," she asked.

"I'm fine. Uh... When is the doctor coming back? That is, when is my next appointment?"

"If the conference doesn't run too late, she may try to see some patients late this afternoon. But it will probably be tomorrow. I think I have you scheduled at three."

"Come on, Tony," said Mo, leading me to the door.

"Thank you, Ms. Emily," I said.

She gave me a look that reeked of pity as we left. Maybe Ms. Emily guessed what I was feeling. Maybe she just thought I was nuts. After all, that's fairly common among mental patients.

"We'll take the long way back to the ward," said Mo, "so you have time to get your color back."

"I'm fine."

"That's what you say. But, I'm thinking you won't be happy till some restaurant asks you not to come back, too."

I really like Mo.

I took an "emergency" phone call from Wilford at the nurses' station once again. I had the feeling that, once he'd located me here at the hospital, this was going to be a daily occurrence. I don't know Wilford's ethnic background, but I have a suspicion that he's part Bull Terrier.

"Tony, Wilford here. I need to talk to you."

"You are talking to me, Wilford."

"Right. How's the hospital."

"They've diagnosed me as terminal."

"Bummer. So, what do you think about Mary Hallesten's Miracle, Inc.?"

"I think it's a miracle that they're letting her go public. Basically, it's a personality cult. She's a Martha Stewart wannabe with a lot of hype behind a mediocre mail order catalog business and a daytime TV show customized for the bored housewife. Up until a few months ago, the company's income statement was a joke and there's almost no prospect for future growth. Mary's cashing in on her fifteen minutes of fame. Period."

"Bummer. That doesn't sound like a buy recommendation."

"Not necessarily. Jump in on the IPO while she's hot and suck a little cash out of it the first day or two, then dump it before the housewives who have pictures of Mary in their living rooms figure out they spent a week's pay on potpourri. Just make sure you get out fast. That stock will tank faster than IQ's at a meth party."

"Bummer."

"Bummer for anyone who still owns Mary's stock at the end of the week."

"You should stop being so cynical, Tony."

"You should stop picking stocks while you're baked, Wilford."

I filled in the rest of my morning with another sweater fitting from Anna and a game of chess with Carl. My mood was lousy and I was barely competition for Carl, not that I was much competition for him when I was feeling good. He wiped me off the board three times in a row. Even the pigeon feathers Carl had glued to my king and queen weren't much help. Apparently, his engineering skills were expanding across the ward. There were now feathers glued on all the light switches also. I wonder where he got the glue. So does the nursing staff.

"Maybe you'll play better tomorrow," said Carl.

"We'll see."

"I'll put some extra feathers on your rooks. Then they can make a flying tackle when they capture another piece."

"Uh-huh," I said. My conversation skills were sparkling this morning.

I pretended to read the Happy Ward's rumpled and dog-eared magazines for the third time just before lunch.

This mild depression has me concerned. It's much too close to a genuine touch of insanity. Doc Busty hasn't said one word to me that was other than professional. She gives no indication that she's the least bit interested in me other than in a clinical sense. And yet, missing my appointment has me feeling so down, I can't even think of a decent wisecrack to make about Carl's queens with pigeon feathers. Not that that matters particularly; Carl wouldn't have understood my comments anyway. Carl is a marvel at non-linear equations, but a little weak on non-linear punchlines.

Maybe a little exercise will help my mood. I got up and began jogging in place. No one noticed. It's one of the major benefits of being crazy.

Monty won another game of table tennis against his imaginary opponent. No one noticed.

Carl glued yet more feathers on the rooks, knights and bishops. No one noticed.

Anna knitted another miniature sweater. No one noticed.

After about ten minutes, I switched to jumping jacks. No one noticed.

A few minutes later, I gave up. The only thing worse than being depressed is being sweaty and depressed. As I collapsed onto the sofa, Larry pulled me up to the spaceship.

No one noticed.

Larry Learns Estate Law
"There are also a few very rich people who die with no will and a lot of greedy, bickering relatives. The American Bar Association refers to this as hitting the lottery."

Larry Learns Online Video
"You're just not getting it, Larry. Watching your one thousandth video of a cute puppy chasing his tail or a kitten attacking a shoe is personally and culturally significant. Do the math. An average three minutes per viewing times one thousand equals three thousand minutes or fifty hours. That's an entire workweek! No one wastes that much time unless. . . uh. . . uh. . . Let me think. . . uh. . . Hang on, there has to be a reason. . ."

Larry Learns Optimism
"It doesn't really matter if the glass is half-full or half-empty as long as you don't spill your Martini."

Larry Learns About the Governor
"The state takes great pride in giving the people honest leadership. The governor's name is often preceded by the word, Honorable; just ask his father, Geppetto."

Larry Learns About the CIA
"The *New York Times* and the *Washington Post* need scandalous headlines, including fresh international news, in order to stay in business, so they lobbied the government to create the CIA, an intelligence agency, the sole purpose of which is to do incredibly stupid things in foreign countries and get caught red-handed."

10

BUMMER IN LOW-EARTH ORBIT

One thing in life you can always count on: When you're feeling like crap about one thing, something worse will happen. It's a fatalistic philosophy that I've developed since being locked away here at Loony Central. Nothing quite compliments a bad mood so nicely as being held prisoner while lying naked on a cold metal lab table in a spaceship that everyone but you believes is imaginary.

"Hello, Tony."

"Die scum."

Larry's little hairy was off to an early start today. It bounced up and down in an erratic rhythm as he shriek-whistle-clicked to his instruments. At least, he was in a good mood.

"I gave a great deal of thought to what you said the other night about your gender conflicts," he said. "This is such an interesting area of study. There is only one other planet in our records that displays behavior that is quite so baffling. On that planet, G-477, the female will kill and eat the male after mating."

"Black widows."

"You know of this? It occurs on your planet also?"

"Only on very rare occasions when they need to sell a lot of newspapers."

Larry stared at me for a few moments that, in my morose state, seemed incredibly long. "What's wrong, Tony?"

"Look, I'm already in a mental hospital. I don't need you to psychoanalyze me, too."

"Maybe I can help. I've programmed my analyzer with a detailed breakdown of human physical and mental characteristics. There is much that I don't understand, so it's not complete yet, but the information entered so far is probably more accurate than anything you'll find on Earth, especially concerning human physiology. Your science is incredibly primitive."

"And what does your analyzer think my problem is?"

Larry shriek-whistle-clicked to his monitor and examined several pages of cryptic characters that appeared sequentially on the screen. "Your immune system is slightly depressed. Your hormone levels are elevated and your endorphin levels are extraordinarily disturbed. The analyzer suggests unrequited love. And you've been jogging."

"I hate you, Larry."

"Really? The analyzer doesn't show that."

"It also missed the jumping jacks."

"I only set the analyzer to examine you," he said. "This readout doesn't cover your friend, Jack."

I didn't bother to explain it to him.

"Who are you in love with," he asked.

"It's not really love. It's infatuation. There's a difference."

"I see."

"No, you don't. You can't run everything through your analyzer, Larry. There are some things you just have to be human to understand. Or, even misunderstand."

"Emotions are not exclusive to your world. We also have love and hate."

"Well, on my planet, the opposite of love is not hate. It's indifference."

"Interesting. What's the opposite of hate?"

"A turbo-charged Porsche and fifty miles of highway with no speed traps."

Larry's little hairy gave a shimmy to the left. "I think your emotional issues are more complex than I initially thought. Perhaps it would help me to understand if you could explain your infatuation with Dr. Bousteir."

"If you knew it was Dr. Bousteir, why did you ask?"

"I thought you might feel better about it if you told me yourself. Love seems to be a private issue for humans. You tend to resent intrusions into what you consider your personal lives."

It never occurred to me that Larry could be sensitive. He was still a bastard for kidnapping me and ruining my life, but maybe he had a good side. Aliens always seem to be portrayed as viscous killing machines in late night B-movies, but Larry had never tried to harm me. The damage he'd done to my life was unintentional. It's hard to fault someone for being stupid, especially when their IQ is higher than any that has ever been measured on our entire planet. I tried to explain a little bit about the human condition.

"Infatuation occurs when your initial impression of someone of the opposite sex is idealized. They come to represent the perfect mate in your mind."

"And this pains you," asked Larry.

"Only when they don't respond to the signals you give them."

"What signals did you give Dr. Bousteir?"

"Good point. Getting admitted as an in-patient at a mental hospital and spending your time talking about alien abduction is probably not the best way to impress a woman."

"What does impress your females?"

I shifted my butt on the table. It was still cold. "That's hard to say. It depends on the female. Sometimes making a lot of money and driving a nice car impresses them. Sometimes it's just being a little different or having a good sense of humor. Sometimes, it's as simple as just saying I like you. And of course, being a member of the British royal family also helps."

Larry's little hairy bounced again as he made notes on his recorder. "So, the problem is that you've given Dr. Bousteir the wrong signals."

"No, you idiot!" I hadn't meant to shout. "The problem is that we met under such bizarre circumstances that she'll never consider me anything but a nut case. I like to think otherwise. That's my real delusion in this whole mess. I can't fool myself forever."

"It's possible that she likes you also."

"I doubt it. I'm just another hospital chart to fill out. And I have you to blame for ruining what could have been the love of my life."

I suddenly realized that I would never have met Dr. Bousteir if it hadn't been for Larry abducting me in the first place. Catch-22? No, that's a different kind of crazy. Mine had spaceships not bombers.

"It's a paradox," I said. "If you hadn't kidnapped me, I never would have met her. And, now that I've met her, she'll never take me seriously because you kidnapped me. That's a paradox, right?"

"Well, it has a definite element of truth to it, but by definition a paradox is..."

"Great! My heart's bleeding all over this stinking metal floor and you want formal definitions."

Larry gave the monitor another look, apparently to confirm that my crappy mood hadn't improved. He shrieked the monitor back into its overhead storage bay, then offered me a tab of what I assume was medication from a corner storage compartment.

"No thank you," I said.

"It should make you feel better and I can assure you it's completely harmless for your species."

"No, thanks. I just need to. . . Hell, I don't know what I need." Actually, I did, but I doubt Dr. Bousteir had any current plans to tour Europe with me as her lover.

"My mate and I found ourselves with a similar dilemma," said Larry, interrupting my self-pity. "When I was chosen to take this voyage, it was because of the prestige of being chosen that her parents agreed to our bonding. Yet, because of the duration of the trip, our bonding was postponed."

"So, you're not really married, bonded or whatever?"

"Not yet. After my return, the bonding ceremony will be performed."

"What's her name?"

"*SHRIEK!!-whistle-whistle-whistle*. I call her, *Whistle*."

I decided not to mention that I used to call my dog much the same way. "What's she look like," I asked.

With a chirping verbal command, Larry returned the monitor to viewing level, turning the screen toward me. He shriek-whistle-clicked and a picture of his mate appeared. She was tall and thin with long, straight, blonde hair, a beaming smile, and soft yet strikingly beautiful features. Her fingers had polished nails, a passionate red that one would see regularly on Earth. She could easily qualify as a top fashion model in New York or Paris. I had to admit Larry's mate was exceptionally attractive except for the hairy bit on her forehead, but I figure that particular feature wouldn't cause Larry much concern.

The pictures rolled through a series of poses: *Whistle* smiling, *Whistle* pensive, *Whistle* teasing, *Whistle* frolicking in a park with strange flowers, *Whistle* at the beach in what was apparently the shriek-whistle-click world's version of a topless bikini.

"Very nice! Good going, Larry."

"Thank you. And we have two children." He shriek-whistle-clicked again and two little Larry-clones appeared on the screen.

"Wait a minute! You're not bonded and you have two children?"

"I know. We were hoping for more, but my studies have taken up a lot of my time. We're planning several more after I return. This one is *Shriek*. And, this one is *SHRIEK!*"

"Nothing personal, Larry, but could we not talk about your kids. Their names hurt my ears."

"I'm very sorry about your ears, Tony. But, I'm very proud of my children."

"I'm proud of my car horn. I don't hold it against my ear and lean on it."

"I don't think that's quite the same thing."

"Probably not. But, how come you have two children before you've bonded?"

Larry thought for a moment. "I see. You're curious about our social differences. My home world's bonding is not like your marriage ceremonies. We're mated by contract between the families. Then, after ten orbits, our solar years, the families and the couple must decide if the relationship is to be permanent. Then comes the bonding."

"You have ten years to decide if you want to get married?"

"It would be about fifty of your years. My planet's orbit is longer and, well, there are several other factors."

"That system wouldn't work for humans, Larry."

"Why not?"

"Earth's average male finds a mate in his twenties. If he took fifty years to decide if it was permanent, most of them would be dead before they made up their mind. Our government generally frowns on marrying dead people."

"You will have to marry Dr. Bousteir earlier in your lifespan."

"It's not that simple. Consider the roadblocks. Not the least of which is that she thinks I'm crazy."

"That explains why you're depressed."

"I'm not really depressed," I replied.

Larry pointed to his monitor which, on command, flipped back to a screen of cryptic figures which I assume was the scan he'd performed on me earlier.

"Okay, I'm depressed, but mainly I'm just disappointed that I didn't get to see her today."

"Would you like to see her?"

"You can do that?"

Larry shriek-whistle-clicked again and Dr. Bousteir appeared on the screen. She was sitting at a large, crowded conference table arguing rather heatedly with the man seated at the head of the table.

"She seems angry," said Larry.

"That's called spirit. She's not really angry yet."

"How can you tell?"

"The men aren't running out of the room."

"I see."

"No, you don't. But, who cares."

Watching Dr. Bousteir on the monitor was an interesting experience, alien reality TV. She really was angry. The man at the head of the table was apparently trying to defend his position. His body language told me that he was losing the argument. After a few minutes, there was a show of hands, a vote. Dr. Bousteir smiled broadly. She'd won her point, whatever it was.

"How can you do this, Larry?"

"It's a technology that your planet has not yet discovered. I can pinpoint anyone whose bio readout has been programmed into the *whistle-click-click.*"

"Why'd you program Dr. Bousteir," I asked.

"She's close to you. I programmed everyone who has contact with you at the hospital. It's necessary so that I can examine, document and try to understand human interaction. Your interaction with others is an important part of my study."

"You're a peeping Tom!"

"Tom? Does this mean you don't want to call me Larry anymore?"

Somehow, I felt a lot better after talking to Larry. Maybe I just needed to talk about my confused feelings. I couldn't talk to my doctor for obvious reasons.

Dr. Bousteir, I'd like to talk to you about my infatuation with Dr. Bousteir.

That would surely make an interesting therapy session.

Strangely, Larry's impromptu, enforced visits tended to pick me up lately. My depressed state made today an exception, but this visit was really the first time our talk had been personal. Doc Bousteir may be right; maybe Larry and I were developing a relationship. He really wasn't a bad guy for an alien kidnapper. At times, Larry was quite interesting. How often do you get to discuss the human race with someone who really does have an outsider's perspective?

I finished up the rest of my day on the ward. Anna gave me another recently completed sweater, pea green with a big, baby blue diamond on the front. I thanked her profusely. She measured me for another while she told me additional stories about her grandchildren. They were smart. They were funny. They did well in school. They were great kids.

Knowing Anna would never see her grandchildren again made me even more depressed. I couldn't help it.

Mo, checking up on me, brought me an extra slice of cake after dinner and before he went off shift. He was concerned that I was still upset and probably figured a few extra calories would help. My mother had practiced the same curative philosophy throughout her life. She would feed a stubbed toe.

While I thanked Mo for both the cake and his thoughtfulness, after he left, I gave the cake to Monty to celebrate his daily win at the table tennis championships.

As the evening progressed, I was actually feeling a little better. I stayed for the movie, an old, old copy of *Yours, Mine and Ours* with Lucille Ball and Henry Fonda. I enjoyed it, too many kids, happy ending and all. After the show, I went to bed early. I wanted to get some extra sleep in case Larry was planning another midnight visit.

Larry Learns Fashion
"It's really simple, Larry. Normally, both men and women keep two separate wardrobes.

"Women keep clothing that fits and clothing that they hope will fit after they eat nothing but lettuce for six months.

"Men keep clothing to wear on a date, and also stained, ripped, nasty, ugly, most-likely-laundered-within-the-last-decade-or-two, seams-unraveling-but-please-don't-fall-apart-yet clothing because it's their favorite and so very, very comfortable.

"Women dispose of old clothing to make room in their closet for new stuff. A man will throw out a beloved, old, beer and blood-stained hockey jersey only if his girlfriend sees it and he decides to keep her."

Larry Learns Grocery Shopping
"Most people try to buy natural foods, like fresh fruits and vegetables. Buying meat is a crapshoot and you can only hope that it has fewer active hormones than your senior prom."

Larry Learns Charity

"Private charity usually supports a cause that you personally care about, like churches, food banks and various national and international relief organizations. Government charity provides minimal disaster relief for taxpaying families in case of flood, earthquake or tornado, and massive disaster relief for large banks and corporations in case of fraud and criminal negligence."

Larry Learns Compromise

"Many compromises are unspoken. For example, take a young, married couple living in an apartment with only one bathroom. They're deeply in love, so the husband never asks his wife why she ties up the bathroom until his bladder is about to burst, and in turn, the wife never asks her husband how many times he's taken a wizz off the balcony."

Larry Learns Gender Equality

"That refers to equality of rights under the law. In the US, a woman has the right to file suit, even against her husband. In Saudi Arabia, a woman has the right to make her husband a suit."

11

GURGLE, GURGLE, EEK, MY LOVE

For such a large man, Mo can move very quickly. He was leaving the cafeteria when I saw him run back around the corner and duck into the staff entrance for the kitchen. Moments later, Nurse Tammy came around the corner, leaving a trail of cuteness in her wake. I gave her a little wave, which she returned with a dimpled smile as she entered the cafeteria.

Crossing the corridor, I stood beside the kitchen entrance and waited. The door slowly crept open. Mo cautiously stuck his head out to check the corridor. "It's okay," I said. "She's gone."

Mo turned towards my voice. Seeing me, he immediately tried to bluff, "Who?"

I just laughed.

"Don't you say nothin', Tony." He started off down the hall. "Just don't you say nothin'."

Most people think they face a lot of insanity at their jobs, but it takes special people with special qualities to handle real insanity forty to sixty hours a week, fifty weeks a year.

The new instructor for the Arts and Crafts Shop was obviously fresh out of college and probably wasn't being paid enough to justify owning a goldfish. Miss Gualter was a sweet, politically correct kid, who should have been teaching elementary school in a nice, SUV-cluttered, suburban neighborhood. Like most of the staff here at Sunny Park, she was genuinely interested in doing her part to help the patients' progress. She was liberated enough not to mind being called miss and could generate enough enthusiasm for a hand-woven potholder to make a patient think he had constructed Michelangelo's Pieta. However, she was having a particularly rough time, today.

Our assigned project was rice painting, which was probably not the best choice for the Happy Ward inmates. It involves taking individual grains of colored rice and gluing them with good, old-fashioned, (non-toxic, totally safe to handle or even eat, and cleans up with soap and water) Elmer's Glue to pieces of construction paper. The end result, of course, is supposed to resemble a picture.

Nice in theory.

Miss Gualter ran from one patient to the next, trying mightily to give individual instruction and encouragement. Naturally, the fates of insanity intervened. I listened to her comments as she tried to cope with her students.

"Monty, please stop hitting the rice all over the room. Put the paddle away.

"I'd be happy to call you, Winston, Mr. Churchill, but don't you have a real name?

"Carl, if you've glued your fingers together, just go to the sink.

"Mrs. Renardo, would you mind not singing for just a little while. It's giving Winston a migraine.

"Let's put the prayer mat and incense aside for a little while. You can pray to me later.

"Uh, sure. If you want to glue your picture on a sweater, Anna, I guess that's okay.

"Carl, why does the faucet have pigeon feathers glued to it?

"Mrs. Renardo, please stop sing . . . Monty! Stop hitting me with rice!

"Thank you, Bonnie, I already have a toilet brush. Oh, don't cry! I meant to say flower, honey. Honest, I meant to say flower. Please, don't cry.

"Where's the food coloring, and why is your hair green and orange?

"You are not praying to me! You're looking up my skirt!

"I'm sorry. I didn't make any Siamese-cat-colored rice today. MONTY! STOP!

"Carl! You've glued your toes together!

"Thank you, Winston, but I don't think I need another autograph. You already gave me three. . . No, I am not a Nazi!

"Everyone! Everyone! Can I have your attention? Please don't eat the rice. You won't be able to finish your paintings if you eat all the rice."

I'm proud to say that my picture had a real three-dimensional quality to it. The center was plain white rice. I used the rice with the blue food coloring for the edges and shaded the background with pink. It came out quite nicely. Miss Gualter finally managed a moment to check on me. I handed her the rice painting.

"That's very nice, Tony. What is it," she asked.

"An aspirin tablet. You looked like you needed one."

It was good to see the kid smile, which she did until she was once again pelted in the back of the head by flying rice. "MONTY!"

Miss Gualter resigned at the end of her first week.

God bless the ones who stay.

If you're wondering what I miss most about the outside world, it's not some special cappuccino or snobbish wine. It's the press of the crowd on the floor of the exchange as some bit of news breaks and the feeding frenzy begins. You ride this intensely frantic wave of humanity, timing your shot at the brass ring, and the brass ring is always a moving target. As the ring moves, the wave of traders scurries after it. The trick is to climb over the falling bodies till you're at the top of the wave.

I know. It sounds pretty pathetic.

After the excitement dies down, the wounded limp away. If you're good, you're not one of them. Then with your brass ring in your pocket, you go off to enjoy your cappuccino.

I'm very good and I love getting the brass ring.

Money's a cold business. I don't know why I like it so much. Probably because I'll only have to work two or three more years before I'm set for life. I've set the goal for my personal portfolio at twenty million dollars. Currently, I'm just a hair over seventeen point five million. When I hit twenty mil, I'll never have to work again, except at things I really want to do. That's freedom.

When you've been involuntarily incarcerated, a lot of your thinking revolves around freedom.

I was in my room, vicariously planning my next financial killing when Mo arrived. He came to escort me to my daily therapy appointment. Nurse Tammy was missing from today's walk to Dr. Bousteir's office. It was her day off. Mo seemed relieved.

We talked politics along the way. Mo was a Democrat. I offered to help him with his investments so he could become a Republican. He said he'd think it over as we arrived in the reception area.

"Why, Ms. Emily, that's a new dress," I said.

"No, it's not. You're late. Go in. I'm busy." She barely even looked up. I'll bet Ms. Emily graduated at the top of her charm school class, just before she ate her classmates.

"Larry and I seem to be having more personal discussions lately," I told Dr. Bousteir.

"Are you still lying to him?"

"Not as much. I still throw in something outrageous now and then, just to keep him off balance. He seems to be opening up a lot more, too. He showed me pictures of his wife and kids."

Now that I had convinced myself Dr. Bousteir would never view me with any more affection than a lab rat, it seemed easier to relate somehow, but looking at her was still killing me. Every time I saw her, it was a jolt to my nervous system. She was just so very lovely. Even her voice had just the right sweetness.

Figures! Just when I meet someone who really rings my bell, the bell tower collapses on my head. But there was no point in railing against my miserable fate.

"He carries photographs," she asked.

"On his computer monitor, or whatever you call the alien equivalent."

"What does Larry talk about?" She made a note about the photos, which I read upside-down again.

"His family, life back on Shriek-whistle-click World. He's the only one on his ship for the duration of his mission. He's lonely."

"What makes you believe he's all alone on the ship?"

"He told me he was," I replied.

"Does that make sense to you? An alien culture that is sending a spaceship on a long voyage would surely send a larger crew, don't you think?"

"So, I imagine that Larry is all alone because it would be too complex a delusion if the ship had a large crew."

"Do you think that's possible," she asked.

"Sure. It's also possible that Larry is from an advanced society where automation does everything but wipe their butts. His ship doesn't need a large crew."

"That's very convenient. Don't you think an advanced society would be concerned about their astronauts' psychological health? Wouldn't they put other crew members aboard to help ease the loneliness of a long voyage?"

"Maybe their psychology is also alien."

"Exactly!" Her exclamation punctuated what was apparently an important point, but I wasn't catching on, so she continued, "You say

Larry looks human. He speaks English. He has a wife and children just like an Earth family. He's social. He's a good conversationalist. He's curious. He's alone and lonely. Larry does not have an alien psychology. There's very little that's alien about this alien of yours."

I searched for a good defensive point. "He whistles for his wife like she's a dog. No, wait, some people down here do that, too."

"You've certainly ascribed a great many human traits to your alien friend."

She had a point. Larry was very human, or at least, very similar to human. "I gather you think my delusion isn't alien enough to be a genuine alien."

"The only thing that you've mentioned that makes him significantly different from us is what you called," she checked her notes, "his hairy bit."

"What about the spaceship? What about the light beam transport?"

"Nearly every science-fiction program has one," she said.

"What about your meeting the other day when you were angry with the guy at the head of the table?"

Dr. Bousteir hesitated. "How did you know I was angry at the conference?"

"Larry and I watched you from his ship. You were arguing, then took a vote. Apparently, you won whatever it was."

She was shocked. I could see the wheels turning in her head trying to figure out how I'd managed to escape the hospital and watch her meeting. Or, maybe I'd heard second-hand what had happened. "That you somehow know what happened at the conference does not prove aliens had anything to do with it."

"Look, we're just at odds here, Doc. You're convinced I'm caught up in a grand delusion and I'm convinced that Larry. . ." A light tingling sensation started to creep along the nerves in my extremities. ". . .that Larry is as real as you or I."

The sensation started to crawl up my arms and legs. Larry was pulling me out of my therapy session! I had to hurry. "He's a genuinely harmless delusion. Let's just agree to disagree. Come on, shake on it."

"I can't condone delusional behavior, Tony."

"I don't care what reason you use. Just to make me feel better, shake my hand."

Dr. Bousteir held out her hand. I shook it gently but quickly firmed my grip and didn't let go. The panicky look on her face told me that she felt the tingling, too. She tried to take her hand away. I held on. The tingling overwhelmed us.

I could feel parts of the room and the furniture melding into our consciousness. Her large, polished-cherry desk was most intrusive. I forced myself to shut out the surroundings in order to concentrate on her. She was terribly frightened. I could feel it. She wanted to scream.

"It's okay," I said. "It's just Larry." I'm not certain she heard me, but I did try. My mouth was moving; I just don't know if I made any sound, but Dr. Bousteir seemed calmer as she sensed that I wasn't at all frightened.

We blended into one another as the intensity increased. The quickly waning fear was but a small part of her being. She was soft and warm. Her soul was joyous and caring. I could feel how highly intelligent she was. Her pride, her spirit, I could feel them as if they were my own. I felt a range of emotions that I would not have guessed. Her needs and desires became clear, became my needs and my desires. Her thoughts were my thoughts. Her breath was my breath. Her heartbeat, mine also.

The sensations amplified as we flew into the light stream together. As a trillion flying bits, I knew all of her like I know myself. She must be feeling the depths of my soul also. Still, it was comfortable. There was no sense of personal violation, just an inquisitive sharing, willingly so. That was the sweetest revelation, she willingly shared. Dr. Bousteir wanted to know me.

Then, for both of us, it became a thirst to know more, to feel more, to not let go. I did not want to let go! We did not want to let go! I needed her. She needed me.

Her consciousness held onto mine. It made her feel secure. Somehow, that made me feel incredibly manly.

And she did like me!

I was whole again, lying on the table in Larry's ship. I could feel Dr. Bousteir beside me, but couldn't move yet. I was completely drained; it felt like hours before I could sit up. I've heard many people claim that various activities were better than sex. This really was better.

Take my word for it.

I looked over at her lying naked beside me and was again amazed. Doc Bousteir was beautifully formed the way Venus must have wished she were; and while I'm an avid reader of *Playboy's* trendy, insightful and challenging interviews and articles (Ahem!), I never once saw a centerfold so exquisite. "Doc, I never imagined! Well, of course I imagined, but Oh My God, you're gorgeous! Top to bottom, you're absolutely, totally, lusciously gorgeous!"

She opened her mouth to speak. All that came out was, "Gurgle, gurgle, eek!"

"It's okay," I said. "The paralysis goes away in a few minutes. It may take a little longer for you because this is your first time."

"Gurgle, gurgle, eek!"

Larry entered with his recorder. He stopped mid-stride when he saw Dr. Bousteir on the table beside me.

"Hi, Larry!" I'm sure I sounded intoxicated.

"Hello, Tony. Is this Dr. Bousteir?"

"She's beautiful! My doctor is beautiful, isn't she?"

"Are you okay, Tony?"

"I'm great! I never felt this good before!"

Larry walked over to the table. "How are you feeling, Doctor?"

"Gurgle, gurgle, eek!"

"She can't move yet because it's her first time," I said.

"It's the passive restraints," said Larry. "They're automatically more intense for first trips."

"Gurgle, gurgle, eek!"

"Well, turn them off. Can't you see she's distressed?"

Larry thought for a long moment. "It's against policy, but I think I can trust you. You've never tried to harm me. I don't think you would."

"Harm you! After what I just experienced, Larry, I could kiss you!"

"Gurgle, gurgle, eek!"

I leaned over, holding my face where Dr. Bousteir could see me. "I'm working on it, Doc. Just give me a minute while I talk Larry into turning off the restraints."

Larry shriek-whistle-clicked at his equipment. "The restraints are off," he said.

I held my face over Dr. Bousteir again. "Is that better?"

"Gurgle, gurgle, eek!"

"I thought you said the restraints were off."

"They are," said Larry. "She's in shock. It happens quite often on first trips."

"Can't you do something?"

"It's best to wait. She should come out of it naturally in a few minutes."

I leaned over her face again. "It's going to be okay, Doc. It's just Larry's spaceship."

"Gurgle, gurgle, eek!"

I just love those sweet nothings!

Larry Learns to Be Politically Correct

"Race and religion mostly. And gender. Sometimes, changing one word can make a huge difference. It's acceptable for a man to tell his wife that she's got a sweet ass, but a woman can't tell her husband that he's a candy ass."

Larry Learns Modern Warfare

"Let's say you're a terrorist who puts a bomb on a bus full of schoolchildren. Your goal is to get media attention, and the modern military is willing to assist. Drone pilots, Seal Teams, Delta Force, NATO, they all want to see your obituary in the newspaper."

Larry Learns Mardi Gras

". . .parades, floats, music, dancing, costumes, fancy balls, lots of overeating and alcohol. Mardi Gras also has a reputation for public nudity and women flashing their breasts, but that's just propaganda to boost the multimillion dollar tourist economy. The real Mardi Gras tradition can be traced all the way back to medieval Christian Europe, where women weren't allowed to have breasts."

Larry Learns Product Liability Law

"If a product is truly dangerous, the consumer has a right to know. However, if the consumer is a freakin' moron who drank a can of paint, giving him a multimillion dollar settlement is not going to protect society nearly as much as neutering him."

12

THIS IS MY DELUSION, LARRY

Dr. Bousteir was still in her transport stupor. Larry hovered around her taking readings with his recording instrument. Of course, that's an assumption on my part. For all I know, he could have been taking photographs to show his buddies back home. I wonder if Shriek-whistle-click world has *Playboy*?

While we waited for her to come around, I explained modesty to Larry and convinced him to retrieve a blanket, which was the same drab silver color as the rest of alien culture. I took one last look at Dr. Bousteir's lush form and gently wrapped the blanket around her. Sometimes being a gentleman is an unbelievably oppressive burden.

A few minutes later, my lovely doctor sat up. Larry and I took turns encouraging her and she was eventually coherent. I did the introductions.

"Larry, this is Dr. Bousteir, my psychiatrist. Dr. Bousteir, this is Larry, my delusion."

"He's real!" she exclaimed.

"I noticed that, but no one seemed to believe me."

"Greetings, Doctor," said Larry. He has a way with words!

She repeated, "He's real," a few more times to convince herself.

I remembered the trouble that I had believing in Larry on my first trip and waited for her to grasp the truth.

Whether they believe in aliens or not, most human beings are programmed to believe that they will never meet one. However, Dr. Bousteir was a trained scientist. In addition to her extensive biological training, she had the advantage of our therapy sessions, during which I had discussed my delusion, Larry, at length. With this fortuitous preconditioning, meeting an alien was not quite so shocking for my lovely doctor. Her grasp of reality may have been shaken, but she recovered quickly.

"Larry won't hurt us," I said. "He's just here to study us, remember."

"He speaks English," she said.

"Good thing, too. We'd have a better chance of talking to dolphins than learning his native language."

"That's not entirely true, Tony," Larry explained. "Human vocal chords could not cover the full range of sounds required to speak *Shriek-whistle-click*, but you could easily learn the basics. Of course, your accent would be horrible, but you could be understood."

"You said he's all alone in the ship?" Dr. Bousteir asked me. She was hesitant to talk directly to Larry, the same mannerism a lot of people adopt with the very young, the very old and the handicapped. They talk about them and around them, but not to them.

"Doc, he's right here. Just ask him."

"Yes, Doctor, I'm all alone on my ship," said Larry.

"What are you doing here," she asked.

"I'm a student, Doctor. The study of emerging species is part of my training."

"We're an emerging species?"

"That is how you are classified."

Dr. Bousteir had the same confused thoughts that I had the first time Larry pulled me up to his ship.

I should qualify that.

The first time Larry pulled me up, I was overcome by the shock of the experience. When he later pulled me up un-shocked, I had an entirely different reaction. The temptation to spit out every stupid question that comes to mind is tremendous and waiting for answers between questions doesn't seem terribly important. Then, you hesitate. You decide to choose your questions carefully, as you self-consciously begin to fear giving away too much information about Earth, your home team.

"I'm pretty sure he's telling the truth, Doc," I said. "He's a student."

"You said we're part of your training. What is your particular area of study," she asked.

"*Shriek-whistle-click-whistle* is the technical name. It does not translate well to your language."

"Come on, Larry, give it a try," I said.

He spoke to his monitor and viewed several screens of characters before venturing a guess. "This is not a literal translation, but it should be fairly close considering the disparity in our linguistic abilities, the restrictive nature of Earth languages and the lack of a formal key to translation. Of course, you must also account for the computer's interpolation, an estimated error percentage and. . ."

"Okay! Okay! Spit it out," I interrupted his overly lengthy explanation.

"The best translation that I can currently determine for my field of study is Probable Losers in the Natural Selection Process."

Dr. Bousteir and I looked at one another for a moment without speaking. "Should we kick his butt?" I asked.

Unknowingly, Larry had thrown down the gauntlet to Dr. Bousteir and the great debate was instantly off and running. Larry quoted experiential data from a hundred species we knew nothing about and Dr. Bousteir countered with her belief in the human race's will to survive, our indomitable spirit, and the dignity of mankind.

Larry spoke of factionalism. Dr. Bousteir cited numerous instances of man pulling together in times of crisis.

Larry argued misuse of planetary resources. Dr. Bousteir returned fire with pollution control legislation, recycling and specific programs designed to equitably distribute wealth.

Naturally, I rooted for Team Earth, but stocks, bonds and options are not much of a reference when you're trying to justify the long-term survival of your species. Then again, the floor of the New York Stock Exchange is a great place to learn about survival on an instinctive level. Ask anyone who's been on the floor when they announce the results of a Federal Reserve Board meeting when the board does something unexpected. It's eat or be eaten.

Not a bad idea actually, I am rather hungry.

After debating for a while, the only point Dr. Bousteir and Larry agreed on was that probabilities were not a guarantee of anything. I agreed to stay out of further discussion if Larry would find me something to eat.

My lovely Dr. Bousteir continued to adamantly fight for the dignity of humankind. "You're studying the subject from too great a distance and basing your research on theories postulated from data collected on unrelated species."

"Absolutely," I said. "Let's shorten the distance between us and Schweitzler's Deli. We can postulate a grilled Reuben."

"Doctor, life is born of a natural, universal commonality; no species is completely unrelated to all others," said Larry. "And distance is a factor that must be integrated into the interpretation of numerous observations, but it does not necessarily discount the relevance of data."

"I agree. What do you say we integrate an observation of some potato salad on the side?" I tried not to salivate too heavily.

"I disagree." Dr. Bousteir wasn't giving an inch. "Distance has a direct impact on the relevance of the data and can easily cause the interpretation of observations to lose all relevance."

"She's got you there, Larry. Potato salad may look good from orbit, but until you taste it. . ."

"I assure you that I am a well-trained observer," continued Larry. "A trained observer will easily be able to determine an acceptable percentage of error in any basic study. The purity of the data remains untouched."

"Just some chips? Any chips around here, Larry? Maybe, some Doritos?"

Dr. Bousteir leaned forward, sensing the weakness in Larry's argument. "Acceptable percentage of error! If the data collected by the observer is slanted by both distance and his unrelated experiential studies, the data is hardly pure. The entire study could be in error. Your data. . ."

I warmed to my own debate, loudly. "To hell with data! Let's collect some food!"

They both suddenly realized I was still in the room and both responded as one. "Are you hungry, Tony?"

I'm firmly convinced that, by nature, people with a superior IQ may be experts in their particular field of study, but still have an inordinate number of moments when their grasp of the blatantly obvious fails miserably. Over the years, I've also met a few geniuses who likely need someone to tie their shoes for them in the morning. Larry and Dr. Bousteir weren't nearly that bad, but their intense focus on a theoretical argument had allowed them to momentarily ignore my very existence. I might as well have been speaking *Shriek-whistle-click*.

"Are you hungry, Tony?" they'd asked.

"I'm about to eat Dr. Bousteir's blanket!"

Dr. Bousteir tucked her blanket tighter around her lovely form. "This blanket is in use right now," she said.

"I can assure you, that blanket has very little nutritional value," Larry added.

Like I said, geniuses!

"Which way is the kitchen?" I asked.

Larry took us to the dining area of the ship. It was a cramped little room with a bench and a table that grew out of the wall on command. Dr. Bousteir had toga-wrapped the thin blanket around her, holding it in place between her lovely breasts with a female tuck or whatever you call that thing that men can't seem to master. She and I had a seat on the bench while Larry cooked.

Well, it was something like cooking.

"I hope you'll forgive me for making your selections," said Larry, "but, neither of you is familiar with the ship's menu." He took several place mats from a small compartment on the wall and set them on the table in front of us. Apparently, this was going to be a formal sit-down instead of a quick snack. The mats looked like colorful inkblots, rectangular and tissue paper-thin. "Please keep your hands away from the table for a moment," said Larry.

He shriek-whistle-clicked to a control panel hanging on the bulkhead. Half a second later, the place mats were gone and we each had a steaming tray of multi-colored something-or-other in front of us. I'm an expert at the fast microwave meal on Earth, but this was no comparison. I have to get one of these tables!

Doctor Bousteir touched the tray for a reality check. "That's marvelous!"

"It simplifies storage," said Larry, "and I have quite a varied menu." He fanned the stack of paper-thin meals.

"Should we say grace," I asked.

Larry looked confused. "Grace?"

"He said it. Let's eat!"

Neither the doc nor I could identify what was on the trays before us, but you couldn't argue with the presentation. It was definitely a good spread. There were green, red and yellow-purple vegetables, several condiment saucers with sweet, sour and spicy sauces, and a fairly large, sizzling steak. The potatoes were conspicuously missing, but the yellow-purple vegetable was whipped into a nice mound of mash with a dollop of what passed for gravy.

"This smells wonderful," said Doctor Bousteir.

"I think the Earth term is ambience. Would you also like some ambience with your meal," asked Larry. He gave a sharp whistle and the silver walls turned into a completely surrounding seascape with our table and benches situated on the high end of the beach. The water had a slight reddish-orange tinge and along with the sun, there were two moons in the sky, but it was definitely a tropical island scene. Gentle pink-foamed surf christened the wide, white beach. Shells in numerous configurations, including one that appeared to be a nearly perfect pyramid, dotted the sand near the water's edge. The most prominent tree closely resembled our coconut palms and most of the vegetation was green or deep purple. Thousands of strange flowers accented the foliage with a rainbow of colors. Birds were singing in the background, although one shrieked like a mournful banshee. Still, for Larry, that must be musical to a degree.

"Salt! That's salt air," said Doctor Bousteir. "And I can feel a light breeze."

"Is it too cold," asked Larry.

"No, it's lovely."

"Nice ambience, Larry! This beats a scented candle any day."

"Thank you, Tony. If you would prefer mountain scenery. . ."

"No, this is perfect," said my lovely, blanket-wrapped doctor.

My hunger reasserted itself. I put aside further discussion of the scenery and concentrated on my meal. The steak had a delicate texture, melting in your mouth like pudding. It tasted like chicken (trite, but true), lightly peppered and with a salty-lemon tang. Since I was starving, I decided not to ask about the origin of the steak until after I finished eating. Dr. Bousteir was apparently more curious than hungry. "This meat is delicious," she said. "What animals do you breed for food?"

"It's not an animal, Doctor. It's *shriek-whistle-shriek*, a waterborne fungus taken from our oceans. It grows very quickly and is easily harvested."

"Fungus," I gagged on a mouthful that had been tasty just a second before.

"Yes. We have sixteen different varieties. They're similar to your mushrooms, but very high in protein and they grow significantly larger."

"Mushrooms. That doesn't sound too bad," I said. "How large did you say they grow?"

"In Earth measurements, an average size *shriek-whistle-shriek* would be about thirty-seven meters in diameter," said Larry. "A large one would be over sixty meters. But that's just an estimate. I can look up the exact size if you like."

"That's okay." I gave it another tentative taste.

"I think it tastes very similar to the hippo steak I once had in Kenya," said Dr. Bousteir.

"Hippo?" Did she have the same meal as I did? She had to mean chicken!

I force shoveled another bite. "This tastes like hippo to you?"

"Similar. But, hippo steak is a little sweeter, like horse."

Horse! Fungus, hippo, horse—my appetite was quickly disappearing. Make that gone. "Damn! I was so hungry."

"Are you sensitive about what you eat, Tony," Larry asked.

"That's fairly common among humans," said Dr. Bousteir. "If you're not culturally adapted to certain foods, you may have difficulty eating them. For example, in many parts of the world, insects make up a significant portion of our dietary protein."

"Insects!" This time, I did quietly gag.

"Of course," she continued, "but in other areas, they are considered inedible. Also, many people cannot eat certain foods because their mind is focused on the image of what it used to be. It's especially common if that image has a personal context. For example, dog is served daily in many countries, but in other areas dogs are dearly loved pets. In the latter culture, you would consider dog to be inedible."

The dog did it! I pushed my platter aside. Larry and the doc continued eating while they discussed human psychology as it relates to the ingestion and digestion of the plant and animal kingdoms. Larry seemed particularly interested in what he termed my psychologically induced traumatic indigestion.

Thanks, Larry.

New rule: Never eat with scientists unless you steer the topic of conversation or they're both mute.

"Just send us both back to Doc's office or we'll end up without clothes."

"It will be my pleasure," said Larry.

"He's getting pretty good at human manners, isn't he, Doc?"

Doctor Bousteir had completely overcome her shock and was busily studying every detail of the ship that was within sight. "Pardon?"

"His manners. Larry has human manners, don't you think?"

"He's an excellent host." She was examining a panel with various colored crystal indicators. I couldn't tell whether she made any sense of the equipment. It certainly meant nothing to me.

"Would you like to go together on your return trip," asked Larry.

"Could we!" Doctor Bustier blurted out the exclamation, then blushed from the roots of her hair to the cleavage-nestled tuck of her makeshift toga. Though trying not to, she glanced at me several times. "What I meant to say was that returning together would be okay."

"Just okay, Doc? I'm the one standing here naked and you're embarrassed?"

She didn't answer.

"I understand your feelings, Doctor," said Larry. "The communion of two beings during transfer can be a uniquely satisfying experience."

"How does that work exactly," I asked. "Are our molecules feeling each other up or what?"

Doctor Bousteir flinched at my candid description. Larry's little hairy bounced to the four corners of his forehead.

Doc suddenly perked up. "He's not confused. He's laughing."

"Laughing?"

"His little hairy bit," she said. "It's bouncing around. He's laughing at you."

"No, he's not."

"Yes, he is. He's laughing at you. And he understands male humor."

"Are you laughing at me, Larry?"

"In answer to your first question, your molecules in the form of bundled energy packets remain separate during the transfer. However, your *shriek-whistle-whistle-shriek*, though bound to those molecular bundles, is not confined by them and can commune with another entity's *shriek-whistle-whistle-shriek* while contained in the transfer beam. In my culture, it's considered quite stimulating."

"Answer the second question. Are you laughing at me, Larry?"

He smiled and shriek-whistle-clicked as he said goodbye. Doctor Bousteir and I dissolved together into the beam.

Since my lovely doctor and I shared everything—literally everything—in transport, I now knew Dr. Bousteir's first name was Laura. I knew it like my own.

Moments seemed eternal, but we soon found ourselves back in Laura's office. Our second transport was wondrously more intense than the first. Our mingled consciousness had somehow learned what to look for and how to relax, making this trip even more electrically emotive. Soul mates never had a more exquisite meaning.

I also knew that meeting me for the first time had also given Laura's nervous system a jolt. Her memory of our first meeting was very vivid and easy for me to read/feel while we were in the transport beam. Maybe there is such a thing as love at first sight. Or maybe we just had the perfect chemistry. I didn't care what the explanation is. I'm with Laura and I'm happy.

After the usual final flicker of light, we stood facing each other, whole and painfully separate, with our eyes locked for a long moment before realizing we were both still naked.

Thank you, Larry!

"He didn't put us back in our clothes," she said.

"No." For once, I was glad I couldn't think of anything clever or witty to say.

Her kiss was warm, sweet and passionate, her breath nectar. My arms folded around her. Laura fit perfectly in my arms. More than that was this manifest feeling that she belonged there, as if my arms had no purpose but to hold her. Still standing in the exact spot where we'd landed, we kissed and caressed each other. Each fiery breath became more frenzied, frantic, needy.

Laura and I commit a breach of doctor-patient professional ethics on her couch.

Larry is now my best friend for all eternity.

Later, we lay entangled in a comfortable cuddle. I discovered that my lovely Laura had learned as much about me during our transit as I had learned of her. Laura pushed up on one elbow, her face hovering close to mine. Her gaze seemed to caress my face, then she smiled broadly, suddenly amused.

"Dr. Busty?" she inquired.

Oops.

Larry Learns Healthy Living

"Eat your greens, drink in moderation, and for you, Larry, I recommend a weekly colonoscopy."

Larry Learns Covert Ops
"The CIA, the NSA, basically the entire intelligence community learned covert tactics by watching men who are sleeping with two women at the same time."

Larry Learns the Female Psyche
"Women reject men for a remarkable number of reasons, some of which are very subtle. Perhaps a woman is PMS-ing when she meets a man who is breathing."

Larry Learns White Collar Crime
"It's the name we give to corporate executives who steal three billion dollars, get caught, pay a five million dollar fine to the government, then buy an island on the Riviera where they spend their remaining days worrying about their ruined reputation."

Larry Learns Evolution
"The scientific community tends to focus on the revolutionary moments in man's development. For example, when our earliest ancestors came down from the trees and began walking upright, the male and female of our species would occasionally meet face-to-face. Once it was discovered that women have faces. . ."

13

GET ME OUT OF HERE

I love waking up with that feeling that I've never slept better in my life. On such days, everything seems brand new and anything is possible. It really doesn't matter that I'm locked in an asylum. Today, I can conquer the world.

Perhaps you remember a philosophy generally expressed as *Carpe diem*, seize the day. It's a quote from the Roman poet Horace, who apparently seized one too many days and is now dead. His quote tells us that every single day is one of those magnificent days when all things are possible if each of us would just get moving and make our day productive.

What a bunch of crap!

On an average day, most people work in a job they hate simply to live indoors and eat every day. The words most commonly used to describe these jobs are mindless, unfulfilling, boring, tedious, monotonous, tiring, annoying, irksome and generally horrifyingly dull. Dragging your tired body out of bed each morning to pump some caffeine and face this reality is in itself a major accomplishment and the only thing likely to seize is your own frazzled nervous system.

Between nine and five, you pray that you won't be laid off in the next round of corporate cutbacks. Sometime after lunch, you realize that afternoon naps are wasted on children when it's their parents who need them most. At two minutes to five, you get handed another batch of paperwork that no one will ever read again after you fill in the blanks. Often, you'll wait till tomorrow morning to file such paperwork because you can't face one more thing today without screaming.

Leaving work almost at a run, you then inch along home on the poorly named expressway. Once again, traffic is bumper-to-bumper. Breaking the law, you find yourself on your cell phone trying to reschedule your dental appointment so that it doesn't conflict with something else mindless. And by the way, you missed the exit for the dry cleaners.

When you finally get through to your exorbitantly priced dentist, your bucket plan of cell phone minutes runs dry and the phone company charges you a fortune for each minute that the equally bored dental receptionist puts you on hold. Then you get rear-ended by an immigrant from Freak-istan, who can't speak English and thinks his expired insurance card is still valid.

By the time you finally leave the rush hour traffic behind and arrive again at Home Sweet Home, you're exhausted, aggravated and ready to kick the dog's ass for dancing so happily. You then find the dog dances so merrily to celebrate chewing your new goose down pillows into a blizzard of blowing feathers.

You four-legged, little turd!

Seize this day, if you can!

How I wish life was as simple as our ancient philosophers propose, *Carpe diem*. In the real world, the majority of people fall under another famous and more appropriate quote about leading lives of quiet desperation.

However. . .

Everyone has those occasional, truly marvelous days like I'm having today, the rarest of days, when you wake up smiling and energized before the alarm clock rings. The sun shines just for you. The air is crisper and sweeter. Your morning shower is just the right temperature on the first adjustment. Your hair falls into place by itself. Your clothing fits and looks better, and your spouse, if you have one, notices. At breakfast, coffee never tasted so good and the dog brings you the morning paper instead of peeing on it.

Aha! Seize this freakin' day! Do it now!

By that, of course, I mean that you should call in sick. Go to the beach. Go fishing. Find a museum full of wonders. Put new sheets on the bed and jump in with an accommodating nymphomaniac gymnast.

If you're at all rational, you'll do anything but face your mind numbing tedious employ, or risk anything else that will ruin your bright and cheery mood.

I'm very fortunate. I have no need to call in sick. At the moment, I'm already hospitalized.

Today, I'm going to *Carpe* this magnificent, magnificent day!

Yesterday, Laura and I ran out of time in her office, so I wasn't able to bring up the subject of my freedom. However, I was now supremely anxious to be immediately released from Sunny Park, the Happy Ward, and anything else ordered by the Superior Court of the State of New York.

I now have a witness, an ever so beautiful witness, who can testify that I am indeed sane. If I see an alien and there really is an alien present, my sled still has its skids. Now, it should just be a matter of filling in the proper blanks on the proper forms and I will once again be allowed to romp and play among the "normal" people.

One important caveat: I have to keep reminding myself to refer to Laura as Dr. Bousteir if anyone is listening. I don't want to cause trouble for her here at the hospital.

Mo checked the schedule for me. My next therapy session is at two o'clock. Six hours to go till my appointment.

I was ravenous at breakfast. I ate three eggs scrambled, four sausage links, a lightly toasted, blueberry English muffin, orange juice and coffee. It was wonderful. Everything tasted incredibly good and I went back for seconds on the eggs and sausage. Considering this is institutional food, my request for seconds was greeted with a bit of shock, but I enjoyed that, too.

While finishing my coffee, I planned my day. I knew that I needed to keep my mind occupied—and off my beautiful doctor—or I would drive myself crazy long before two o'clock. I had to stay busy. For the rest of the morning I immersed myself in the Happy Ward's thrilling amusements.

To be honest, the thrill was gone five minutes into my first day on the ward, but I'm willing to pretend that life here isn't trite, repetitive, monotonous, humdrum, cloned daily, tedious-us-us, routine, sleep-inducing, and did I mention repetitive?

Imagination, please don't fail me now.

I again played chess with Carl and his modified chess pieces. He managed to capture a particularly nice winged Pegasus quality on his modified knights today. I had to object however when he tried to glue feathers to my ears. I told him that he could modify all the kings, queens, knights and bishops that he wants, but modifying one's opponent is pushing the limits of civility. My ears did not need reengineering. Fortunately, Mo stopped by and once again, took Carl's glue away. It was obvious that he was getting the feathers from the persistent flocks of pigeons and geese on the hospital grounds, but the nursing staff still hasn't discovered the source of his glue supply.

"Where did you get the tube of glue, Carl," asked Mo. "You know you're not supposed to glue feathers on everything." Mo patiently asked three times about the source of the glue in the same firm but gentle tone that he always used for reprimands. Carl ignored him by intently studying the pawns on the chessboard. Likely, he was working out future modifications in his head.

In a whispered aside, Carl told me that historically the general public has always misunderstood truly great engineering geniuses. Before letting us go back to our chess game, Mo examined Carl's hands to be certain this truly great engineering genius hadn't glued his fingers together again.

Resuming our game, Carl whipped my butt even more easily now that all his pieces could fly. He was especially proud of his newest invention, a king that flew off the board when placed in check. Having learned this phenomenal new strategy, I tried to fly my checked king to safety. Carl produced a pair of child's safety scissors and snipped his wings. "Still in check," Carl announced.

A little after eleven o'clock, I had to delay the start of my table tennis rematch with Monty so that Anna could measure me for another sweater. I convinced Monty that he should let Anna make one for him also. He was adamantly against the idea until I explained that the mystical yarn Anna used had special qualities that would help prevent anyone from stealing his soul.

"Really," asked Monty.

"It's a fact, but don't ask Anna about it. She's afraid if she talks too much about the mystical yarn, some of the magic might wear off."

"I understand completely," Monty whispered, his tone deadly serious, "I won't say a word."

"I knew I could count on you, Monty. What color sweater would you like?"

"Green, with white stripes to match the table. And, do you think she could put a little net on the front?"

Unfortunately, Anna was out of table tennis green. Since Monty couldn't decide on another color, he put in an order for a mixed dozen. Anna was ecstatic and ran off to begin knitting my sweater and Monty's large order. It was good to see her happy.

Monty and I were now free to begin our daily championship game. While still missing a ball, Monty again destroyed me with his lethal overhand smash. Once again, I lost five out of five matches, however Monty counted it as four and one-half losses since he had insisted that he use both paddles for one game in order to show me his lethal overhand smash was ambidextrous. I defended my side bravely with my bare hand and was defeated when I foolishly crawled up on the table to rush the net.

In record time, Anna finished my sweater, pearl gray with peppermint twist sleeves. It was a beauty. I thought about asking her to add two more sleeves and a pocket so I could use it as a glove, but I wouldn't risk hurting her feelings. Instead, I swallowed my sarcastic streak and raved about her fine needlework. This was beyond doubt the best sweater she'd ever knitted!

Anna invited me to play a game of checkers. I lost again and she was a gracious winner. She hoped I would win our next game, and added a nicely sincere compliment. "Tony, did you know you're the only one here that plays checkers by the rules?"

"Really?"

"It's true," she said. "Monty wants to play with a paddle and Carl wants to glue feathers on my checkers so they can fly. And, you wouldn't believe how some of the others want to play!"

"Maybe they never learned properly," I offered.

"Maybe. Personally, I think some of them are just nuts." She placed the checkers neatly back in the box and slipped me a second sweater under the table for being such a good loser. This one was a rosy pink turtleneck with extra-long sleeves. Anna explained the long sleeves would allow me to roll them into turtle-wrists to match the turtleneck. Anna was very innovative.

Carl's wife, Tina, arrived with her daily platter of exotically flavored, leaden muffins. Today's offering was a mild strawberry-onion-turnip-pumpkin flavor, but I was in a great mood and had no reason to ruin it by eating one.

Anna politely took a muffin to have later with her tea. Carl took the one with the smuggled tube of glue inside. Monty took the remainder to practice his lethal overhand smash. The nursing staff hid in the office until the last muffin was gone. They then quickly reappeared to act disappointed that they had missed the treat. Tina promised to bring more tomorrow and asked if we wanted to try her newest flavor, jalapeño-mandarin orange-cranberry-broccoli.

Oh joy!

Saving most of today's muffin batch for later practice of his lethal overhand smash, Monty squirreled several muffins away in unique places, under chairs, behind the fire extinguisher, and on top of his head. He attempted to hide one on top of my head, but decided that I moved too much to be a good hiding place. He stashed the last muffin under a sofa cushion.

Monty always thanked Tina and Carl profusely for the muffins. He was very polite and he never overhand smashed Tina's muffins into the nurses' station until after she left. Normally, you'd think this would quickly become annoying, but the staff really didn't mind ducking muffins and cleaning up. They would rather sweep up splattered crumbs than risk eating one of those muffins.

Self-preservation is a very strong instinct.

Chess, table tennis and two sweaters, it was another great morning, Happy Ward style.

Lunch was very similar to the slop they served yesterday, but on this most beautiful of days, it was gourmet slop. (Some delusions are good for you.) However, the dessert was no delusion. They served an outstanding New York cheesecake topped with blueberry compote. Kudos once again for the baker!

As usual Mo accompanied me to my appointment with my lovely Dr. Bousteir and as we strolled through the corridors, I gained new insights into the ever-present sideshows. I realized the deft movements of Martin, our brushless painter, were incredibly similar to someone conducting an orchestra. He was playing music with invisible brushes and imaginary watercolors. I wonder if Mrs. Renardo was singing to his music. There was also a new addition, a scraggly-looking young fellow who stood rigid as a Buckingham Palace doorman while holding Martin's invisible palette for him.

Nurse Tammy ambushed Mo just outside one of the storage closets. I leaned against the wall and pretended to be interested in the ceiling.

"I was off yesterday. I missed seeing you," she said.

"Off, good time. . . uh, good to take. . . take time. . . off. . . time off, I mean."

I was so proud of Mo! He managed to get through the entire, nearly coherent sentence without having a stroke.

"I like your new haircut."

"I cut it. . . cut yesterday."

"It looks nice."

Whether for change of pace or simple novelty, Nurse Tammy wasn't wearing her usual scrubs today. Instead she dressed as a traditional nurse. In her retro white uniform, white shoes and little RN cap, I gotta tell you, Nurse Tammy could force dead men to leer.

Looking at her, I mentally ran through the list of time-honored clichés that every male child over the age of twelve knows by heart: hottie, babe, knockout, fox, a solid ten, hasn't got a single pimple on her ass, oh my God, and Lord have mercy!

I lost interest in my lurid little list when I noticed Mo fumbling for someplace to put his hands. Apparently, they no longer fit well on the end of his arms. He fidgeted and looked everywhere but in Nurse Tammy's direction. Finally, he settled for jamming his hands into his belt near the small of his back and intently studying a spot on the wall above her head. I was closer to the spot. Someone had mashed a fly next to one of the paintings.

Mo probably didn't need to know that right now.

"There's a new restaurant opening across the street from the main entrance." Nurse Tammy flashed a wide smile. "Maybe we should see what they have for lunch."

"I've ate. . . eaten, uh, eaten already. But, uh. . . uh, thanks."

"Maybe tomorrow?"

"I've already eaten," Mo stammered.

"Tomorrow, silly."

"Oh, tomorrow. . . I usually eat the patients. . . er, with the patients. . . the cafeteria, in the cafeteria. . . with patients. They like me. The patients, I mean. They're. . . they like that. . . me. . . to eat with them."

Tammy smiled sunshine at him. "Mo, it's nice to be dedicated, but you have to take some time for yourself."

Sweet Jesus, this woman was patient!

Mo squinted his eyes. His jaw hung a little slack. He was working hard trying to figure out what to stammer next. I couldn't take any more. I held open the door to the storage closet and courteously offered a wave to usher them inside. "Would you two like some privacy?"

They each tried to find an appropriate response to my question. Nurse Tammy tried laughing out loud. Mo tried apoplexy.

After we escaped from the totally-delicious clutches of Nurse Tammy, I again tried to get Mo interested in discussing her raging crush and his continually flustered responses. "For crying out loud, Mo, she wore that nurse's uniform to get your attention."

"No, nurses are allowed to wear uniform anytime they want."

"Uniforms from when, the 1950's? Did you see her little hat?"

Mo didn't answer.

"I don't understand you. She likes you and you obviously like her. You can't even talk when she's around."

"I can talk."

"You're not a recent immigrant, Mo. You don't have to speak broken English."

"Let's change the subject, Tony."

I could have let him off the hook, but somehow that didn't seem fair to either Mo or the universe. This was like watching my little brother flounder at the Soph Hop. I had to say something.

Besides, Mo had done a lot to make my involuntary stay at Sunny Park as comfortable as possible. The least I could do is spare him a few minutes to play Cupid. The meek will not inherit the earth if they're too meek to risk contact with members of the opposite sex. Sons and daughters are usually necessary for an inheritance, and if current biological theories are correct, it's tough to procreate by yourself.

"Mo, I'm your friend. I'll change the subject when you stop lying to me."

He stopped walking and faced me. "What lie? I didn't lie to you!"

"You lied to me and you're lying to yourself. You like her. You want to ask her out and you just don't have the balls." It suddenly occurred to me as I confronted him that Mo could tear me into little pieces without breaking a sweat.

Maybe I do belong in an asylum.

"We work together," said Mo.

"You work in the same building. You do not work together."

"It's the same thing, Tony."

"No, it's not. You don't work on the same wards or with the same patients and you only see each other by accident." I decided not to mention that Nurse Tammy probably contrived most of those accidents.

Mo started down the corridor again. "I'll think about it."

"Have lunch with her at that new restaurant."

"I'll think about it."

"What do you think about Nurse Tammy," I asked. "Tell me the truth."

"She's nice."

"Nice?"

"She looks good, too," he said.

"Just good? Mo, most men would sell their soul to get a smile from a woman like Nurse Tammy. She's a walking wet dream!"

"She's very pretty."

"Fair enough, you think she's pretty and she's nice. Ask her out, Mo. Just once."

"I have to think about it."

This was going nowhere. Matchmaking is a tough business. I should go back to the Dow and the NASDAQ. I was starting to think I should just stay out of it, but decided that I would simply have to think of a more indirect (or devious) way to save Mo from himself.

As we arrived at the door to Laura's office, I stopped in the middle of the corridor and gave it one last shot. "Mo, she likes you and wants to spend time with you. She's not asking you to get married and have babies. (Yet.) She just wants to go out for lunch. If you're going to be so mean. . ."

"Mean!"

That might work.

I could tell from his tone of voice. Mo would never accept seeing himself as a mean person. "Nice guys don't ignore other people," I said.

"I'm not ignoring her."

"Then, buy the poor girl a sandwich. How can a little lunch hurt? For crying out loud, you won't have to eat it naked!"

Unless you're lucky.

Maybe Mo would think it over. Maybe he wouldn't. The truth is nice guys really do finish last in a lot of circumstances, but no one likes to see that happen. I walked into the outer office, not giving Mo time to respond.

"Ms. Emily," I formally addressed Cerberus, "You look just lovely today. Have you lost weight?"

She peered at me over the top of her bifocals. "I've gained two pounds and if you ever mention my weight again, I'll lose your paperwork. You'll be locked up here till the next millennium."

"I'm so glad you're having a good day." I pointed at the clock on her desk. "I'm on time, I believe."

She waved me into the inner office as she returned to the mounds of paper on her desk. Mo escorted me to the door and pulled it closed behind me as he left.

Laura!

I had no more need for chess, table tennis, sweaters or matchmaking. The distractions that had helped me pass the long morning and midday disappeared when I once again saw my love. My beautiful doctor, my Laura was sitting at her desk though not working as usual on her notes. She'd also been anxiously awaiting our afternoon session.

Practical advice for those who seek wisdom: When a woman practically jumps over a desk to kiss you, stand there, shut up, and be kissed.

Frustration can be dangerous. It's a precursor to anger.

"I don't believe this!" I paced in front of the couch, hoping to calm myself, but it wasn't helping.

"It makes perfect sense," said Laura. "The symptoms of many illnesses don't manifest themselves on a timetable. You have to stay for the full thirty-day evaluation ordered by the judge. It's all perfectly legal. There's no way around it."

Taking my hand, Laura gentled me into sitting beside her. She did her best to console me, but I couldn't help being angry at a mindless bureaucratic system that was stealing a month of my life without cause. Another thirteen days of flying chess and there was a very real chance that I would indeed become a candidate for permanent residency among the citizens of Nutdom. "How can you expect me to accept this without a fight? You know I'm not crazy. Larry exists. You saw him. You spoke to him. You ate his fungus!"

"I know," she said softly. "But, how am I going to explain that and keep my license to practice medicine? I can't say there really is an alien zapping people up to his spaceship. They'll make me a patient instead of letting me treat them."

"There has to be a way," I said.

"I haven't been able to think of one." Laura caressed my cheek, helping to calm my agitation.

"What if you diagnose me with something that can be easily treated with medication? Then, you can give me some sugar pills and let me leave."

She shook her head, a definite negative. "I can't falsify records and prescriptions. It's unethical and illegal. There again, I could lose my license. It wouldn't help you either. It could endanger your future employment. Despite everyone's noble intentions, there's still a lot of stigma attached to mental illness and no one wants a mentally unstable stockbroker handling their account."

"I'm not going to advertise my stay here," I said.

"I know, but people talk. Also, you'd be at risk later in life. What if someone wants to sue for control of your estate when you're eighty? A documented history of mental illness would make a good case against you."

"You're overreaching. Besides, I hadn't planned on living that long. I'll risk it."

"There's no need." My lovely doctor gave me a comforting squeeze. "In a couple weeks, I can say that I've observed your behavior as ordered by the court and I've concluded you experienced a transient incident brought on by job-related stress. You'll be certified sane and no one will question your records or my diagnosis."

"Damn, Larry!" I vented my frustration.

"We never would have met without Larry."

"So, I'm ambivalent. Haven't you ever wanted to kill someone you like?"

"We'll get through this," she said, giving me another blood warming hug and laying her head on my shoulder.

I loved the smell of her hair. My lovely doctor actually made institutional incarceration somehow enticing. Reality slowly crept in, dissolving my budding anger. Another few weeks spent with Laura would be easily, even enjoyably survivable. I might even see more of her here in the hospital. If I were on the outside, would I be able to see her every day? We both had busy careers. Maybe I should think of my enforced stay as a few extra weeks' vacation.

Begrudgingly, I resigned myself to serving my full sentence. If there's no escape, I might as well try to enjoy it. Laura leaned up for a kiss. As our lips touched, I realized Sunny Park was a great place and getting better all the time.

You can pretty much rationalize anything. Amazing isn't it.

Cuddle time!

"I think you're just keeping me here for the full thirty days because you want your lover on 24-hour call?"

Laura's mischievous grin rivaled the most grandiose Cheshire Cat. "I don't need a court order or a diagnosis to keep you here."

She wasn't lying.

Oh God, that feels good!

I was able to sit up immediately on Larry's cold table. I'll have to thank him for disabling the restraints. Flopping around like a wounded fish isn't something that I'm going to miss.

After leaving Laura's office, my ability to rationalize vanished as incarceration induced depression dropped on me like a falling anvil. I was locked up at Sunny Park without a chance of parole or early release, and this situation was entirely Larry's fault.

I tried telling myself that I wasn't really angry with Larry. It was more a feeling of generalized irritation. Larry was merely an annoying but minor rash that wasn't going away anytime soon. Unfortunately, there is no soothing lotion to cure aliens.

One of life's little quirks: somehow we all become experts at lying to ourselves, but it doesn't always work.

In truth, I'm not irritated, annoyed, or just a little put out. I'm furious!

Another truth: I plan to unload on Larry this trip—fire, brimstone and bile. That scrawny little alien bastard screwed me and he deserves my righteous wrath!

Sunny Park isn't living. It's my prison, plain and simple.

On the outside among the legally sane, I could use my lovely doctor's name, Laura, in public. We could go where we pleased and see each other as much as we liked. We could build a life together. On the outside, I have my career, my friends, my Jacuzzi, beer and football. I'm almost never depressed. On the outside, I have a life.

As I mentally listed the advantages of once more being a free man, I realized that quietly resigning myself to my sterile little night-lit room at Sunny Park is impossible. Rationalization is useless. My anger is reasonable and fully defensible.

Larry entered a minute later.

"Good evening, Tony."

"Not really. Everything's messed up today."

"Really? Would you like to talk about it?"

"You talk. I'll rant."

I dove in, explaining my situation with the hospital and the court order and how my frustration had flushed my really great day down the toilet. I told him how Laura and I had to sneak around like a couple of teenagers, which at times was a lot of fun, but I didn't mention the fun parts.

I told him about crappy institutional food, three-inch sweaters, losing table tennis without a ball, garbage flavored leaden muffins and having someone try to glue feather on my ears. I told him about trying and failing to sleep with a night light, then being pulled up to his ship in the middle of what little sleep I did manage.

"Dammit, I can't even watch a Giants game!"

Lastly, I told him that the only reason I was crazy to begin with was because no sane person believes in aliens, especially Superior Court judges of the State of New York.

While my tone of voice may have implied that Larry was responsible for all the ills of the universe, I have to give myself credit for controlling the content of my brazen, howling outburst. I didn't blame Larry for slow traffic lights or burnt toast. What I lay on Larry was his sins and his sins alone.

There's a fine art to ranting. You have to be just belligerent enough to keep your audience interested, but not enough for them to take offense and walk away insulted. It's a delicate balance. It's like saying, *Screw you, but just a little bit*.

On this day, I definitely had Larry's attention, but he seemed surprisingly calm. "If you're stuck at the hospital," said Larry, "perhaps it will help if you find a constructive use for your time."

"Don't interrupt! I'm not done bitching, and before we move on to new business, we didn't finish our discussion last time, remember? You were laughing at me, Larry. Laughing at me!"

His little hairy jiggled merrily. "I have to admit that's true."

"So, I'm just part of the local entertainment to you."

"I originally brought you up to my ship as a research subject," he replied. "I believe examining and interrogating a native subject from Earth will provide greater depth to my work. However, long research projects can be lonely, Tony, and I find your stories very entertaining. My meetings with you are a refreshing break from work, and your continuous stream of lies is most humorous."

"You ruined my life for laughs, is that it?"

Finally, a little impact!

Larry paused, looking hurt. "Don't be upset with me, Tony. This is my first mission. I'm alone here. I have no one to converse with regularly, very little entertainment and. . ."

Larry now sounded like a defensive child. He was just a young student after all, and I admit that part of me wanted to respond with an appropriately protective posture. It's human nature to protect the young, even if they are from another planet. It's embarrassing to admit, but I was just too angry.

"Quit whining! You ruined my life because you don't have a shrieking-whistling-clicking-friggin' TV. How do you justify that?"

"I can't, so I compensated you instead," said Larry.

"Yeah! With what?" I roared.

"I allowed you and Dr. Bousteir to transport together."

Ooh! Nice save!

For a few moments, I didn't know what to say. Then, I had to ask, "You knew she was coming? It wasn't an accident?"

"Of course not. That is the only time I have transported you with someone else present and fully aware. Probabilities predicted that you would enjoy bringing her with you. I simply disabled the safeties and brought you both up together. Since you love her, I thought it most appropriate. Communion in transport is quite stimulating for two beings who care for each other."

"But I told you it was just an infatuation."

"When I scanned you the other day, my analyzer disagreed with you. I did question you about it, remember? While you seemed to know the difference, as you understand it, between love and infatuation, you did not seem able to resolve your own feelings regarding Dr. Bousteir. My scan clearly indicated it was love."

"But, I've only known her for a few days," I said.

"You've been looking for her for many years, have you not?"

He was right. I had been looking.

No, Laura was much more than I could have hoped or dreamed. I felt it in her soul. She wasn't just an idealized picture in my head. She was much more. We fit perfectly together on a level I couldn't possibly explain. I knew she felt the same, but how could Larry and his scanner have known that?

"What about her feelings," I asked.

"Dr. Bousteir was conflicted about you for several days before the transport. She made reference to love at first sight and also categorized her feelings as infatuation. You must have noticed that she was particularly careful to keep her responses very clinical when speaking with you."

"I noticed."

"She was going to turn your case over to another doctor because of her feelings. I didn't think you would like that."

"I wouldn't have." My curiosity was still killing me. "Did you somehow bring her up to the ship without her knowing it or did you scan her feelings from orbit?"

"I read her notes."

"From orbit!"

"Yes."

"What else did she say about me," I asked.

"Tony, please, Dr. Bousteir's notes are private."

"You read them!"

Larry seemed offended. "I read them as part of my research, not for personal gain."

"Just give me some hints."

"That would be unethical."

"Come on, Larry! Kidnapping is okay, but talking about someone's notes isn't ethical? Where did you get your ethics?"

"We're taught them in school. We learn from our *shriek-whistle-shriek* at home. And of course, there are numerous philosophical texts that provide insight into..."

Despite his advanced intelligence, Larry had yet to master the rhetorical question.

Since I've mentioned it several times to Larry, Mo and Laura (That doesn't sound quite right, does it?), I feel I should explain my being a New York Giants fan.

I grew up in Philadelphia. I now live in New York. However, shouldn't I carry my loyalty to the Philadelphia Eagles, the team of my youth, with me? Does the location of my residence really matter? Am I being disloyal by rooting for the home team in New York, the city where I now, but relatively newly reside?

Frankly, there are good arguments on both sides of this issue. There's a lot of warm and fuzzy nostalgia in rooting for the Eagles. On the other hand, rooting for the Giants there's a shot at Super Bowl tickets in my lifetime.

It's a judgement call.

~~*

The following afternoon, Laura and I lay cuddled on the couch in her office. Granted, if it came to light that she was involved in a relationship with a patient, it could cause her a great deal of trouble, but we felt quite safe with both a heavy-duty lock on the door and an extra-heavy Ms. Emily guarding that door. The former only latched from the inside and the latter never allowed anyone to interrupt a therapy session unless the building was on fire, so our privacy was practically guaranteed. There are very few people brave enough to argue with Ms. Emily, leastwise none that lived.

"Larry suggests I find a constructive use for my time." I said with a great deal of charm since at the moment I was also finding a very constructive use for my hands.

"Good advice. What do you think you'd like to do?" Laura asked.

I kissed her deeply.

"Besides that," she said.

"I don't know yet. I'll think of something."

With almost no effort, I thought of quite a few things to keep myself occupied. First, I talked my lovely doctor into granting me access to a computer terminal that was wired for the Internet. I planned on doing some trading on my personal account. Without a doubt, profitable incarceration beats regular incarceration, and it didn't really require much effort to persuade Laura to grant me computer access.

"Can I?"

"Sure."

She's such a tough sell.

I also planned several day trips. However, remembering the old adage about it being easier to beg forgiveness than to ask permission, I didn't mention planning any unauthorized excursions to Laura during our sessions.

On my next great escape, I wouldn't make the mistake of stopping in at the bar across the street. I would find someplace where I could watch the entire Giant's game. What's the worst thing that can happen if I'm caught? They lock me up. Since that's already my situation, there's no downside.

I hope.

Even with my plans, I still have tons of free time in between my "therapy" sessions with Laura. Since Sunny Park has yet to find a new, and perhaps braver, Arts and Crafts instructor, I've decided to develop my own amusements.

Okay, I've decided to stop lying to Larry, at least, most of the time. But in fairness to posterity, I really should document just a few more.

Larry Learns Modern Dance
"You put your right foot in; you put your right foot out…"

Larry Learns Safe Sex
"It's easy to protect yourself if you just follow some basic rules. Leave the lights on. Hide your wallet. Never keep your vibrator and your Taser in the same drawer. . ."

Larry Learns Prescription Marijuana
"We'll role play so you'll understand. I'll be the doctor. First, tell me that you have a lot of anxiety. . . .Okay, now show me the cash and wink."

Larry Learns the Olympics
"It's held once every four years as an international competition for undetectable steroid manufacturers."

Larry Learns Where to Pickup Women
"Church is a great place to meet women. They're always dressed attractively, always wearing makeup, and always smile when you greet them. It's like Hooters with kneeling."

PART TWO

LARRY AMONG THE PROBABLE LOSERS

14

LIFE AFTER DEPILATORY

The alien transport beam has become a rapidly growing addiction for my lovely Laura and I. It's far, far beyond freakin' wonderful! It's my Laura, all of her being. Sex doesn't compare. Laura's body and soul mixes with me totally. Her spirit mingles with mine; our very essence caresses each other, sharing, playing and loving. Thought and emotion surge through us in wave after wave, an interplay of consciousness, life, ego and understanding. Our desires and our demons fly freely, without fear. Throughout this entire experience, we are mother's womb comfortable as we coalesce in blissful unity. Laura and I become a true gestalt, effortlessly bonding all that we are or hope to become.

If you can't grasp the concept, don't feel bad. Until I experienced it, I wouldn't have thought it possible either.

Try picking up a good thesaurus. Look up *ecstasy* and closely examine all the words listed. Now, imagine experiencing all of them at the same time. This would be only a poor approximation of sharing Larry's transport beam with Laura.

As long as I live, I'll never feel alone again.

Since this experience is so powerfully, intensely, and divinely personal, if Laura asks, I didn't mention the transport beam.

On our next spaceship visit, Laura talked Larry into making a more detailed study of humankind, up close and personal.

Over another exotic lunch, with the foothills of a magnificent, snow-topped mountain range selected for ambience, Larry and Laura repeated their debate about collecting data at a distance. I thought I was an expert at arguing until I watched these two in action. Their debate varied from firmly, and sometimes loudly, prosecuted challenges to quiet forays with subtly shaded nuance. They thrust and parried with moves that would have honored the most gifted master epeeist.

epee n. - a dueling sword used in fencing with the tip blunted since stabbing your opponent is considered poor sportsmanship

epeeist n. - in fencing: a skilled athlete who prances with a sword because his friends laughed at him when he tried ballet

Laura finally trapped Larry with an extremely simple point: "Wouldn't you agree that removing distance from the equation must make your observations more accurate?"

Obviously, Larry had to agree, but he quickly explained the guidelines that Shriek-whistle-click students must follow when dealing with primitive alien cultures. (I know it's confusing, but in this case humanity is the alien culture. Primitive is just an arbitrary insult.) However as a student abroad, Larry was directed to stay in orbit, which makes perfect sense when dealing with any genuinely alien culture. Think of all of the unforeseen dangers that might befall a novice visitor to planet Earth. For example, right here in New York, a novice might think walking on the sidewalk is safe if he was unfamiliar with our taxi drivers.

Despite Larry's student regulations, Laura wasn't about to give up easily. "Surely it's different if you are invited and have two willing guides to steer you away from danger. The governing body at your university, I don't know what it's called. . ."

"*Shriek-whistle-(really burst your eardrums)WHISTLE.*"

"If you say so," Laura continued, "but if Tony and I keep you away from any danger, you will be able to safely observe the routine behavior of the human race firsthand. That would make your survey much more accurate. You're directing body couldn't possibly object to that."

"I am not granted the liberty of interpreting the guidelines," said Larry. "I simply must follow them."

While they argued, Laura ate with a genuine relish for alien cuisine. She particularly seemed to like the little wrinkled orange vegetable, a raisin look-alike that tasted of salt and hickory. Between bites, she pressed her attack. "What do your guidelines say about invitations to visit from resident aliens?"

"There is no guideline concerning invitations to visit from a culture as primitive as yours," Larry replied. "As far as I know, and I've studied the records from previous trips extensively, we've never received such an invitation. Communications with primitive cultures. . ."

"Can't we stick with *developing* rather than *primitive*," I asked. "It sounds a little better."

"If you wish."

"If there is no guideline," continued my lovely doctor, "then obviously, it's your decision."

I won't bore you with any more of the give and take they exchanged. I pretty much sat there quietly eating my fungus. What can I say? Hunger finally won out over disturbing mental pictures. And, it really is quite tasty!

In the end, Larry was going to capitulate. He just didn't know it yet. The outcome had nothing to do with first hand observation being preferable in scientific endeavors. Saying no to Laura is just damn near impossible. Especially when she looks so damn cute toga-wrapped in that blanket!

If she drops that toga, I know I'd give her anything.

My thoughts returned to my meal as I busily stuffed my mouth with today's dessert, a peanut butter and chocolate fudge flavored, blue-greenish, pureed something-or-other. Pudding, maybe.

Meanwhile, Laura apparently won a strong point in their debate. She graced Larry with her most devious smile and said, "Gotcha!"

I pretended I'd been paying attention as I jumped in with, "Hold on a minute. It's not that easy. We have to find some way to do this without getting him into trouble."

"I can bring him into the hospital as an unpaid assistant," Laura offered. "I'll introduce him as a visiting graduate student. They'll never check his references as long as he's not drawing a salary."

"The hospital won't do him much good. He's here to evaluate normal human society. If there is such a thing."

"I treat normal people, too. I have marriage counseling, group sessions for job related stress and I teach a seminar on differential diagnosis at Columbia University on Thursday evenings. He'll have lots of contact with normal people.

"At Columbia? Really?"

Laura doesn't wear glasses, but she has a cute way of tilting her head forward, as if looking at you over a pair of bifocals. It's her look of amused disapproval. She continued without giving my wisecrack further recognition, "The hospital is perfect and it won't hurt Larry to have contact with most of the in-patients. Studying abnormal behavior can give you some unique insights into the normal."

"It might work," I said.

"It will work. I'll keep him away from the violent patients. He won't get hurt."

"I'm more worried about him getting caught. Can't you see the headlines: *Prominent Psychiatrist Has Alien Assistant?*"

"They'd never print it," retorted Laura. "The *Times* will never change to a tabloid format."

I admit, I was also getting caught up in the idea. It's that same juvenile thrill you get when you pull a good practical joke on someone. There's the anticipation during the planning; the careful maneuvering of the victim into the trap, and finally, the satisfaction of watching them fall. Avoiding payback is also part of the fun, but in this case, there would be no payback. Laura and I were going to pull one over on the entire hospital, perhaps, the entire city. We were going to sneak an alien right into the midst of New York society. Then again, why stop at New York?

"After I get released, we could travel a bit, too," I said. "Larry might like to see some other parts of the world."

"Belgium!" Laura exclaimed. "I've always wanted to see Belgium and France—Paris. And Ireland!"

I pulled her close to me for an excited kiss. "We'll see them all. We'll see the whole world if you like."

"I'll talk to personnel and make arrangements for some time off," she said, hugging me warmly. "It shouldn't be a problem. I have fourteen weeks of vacation time accrued."

"It'll be wonderful!" We shared another kiss, lost in private reverie.

"Ahem." Larry cleared his throat, reminding us he was still at the table.

"Sorry, Larry," I said sheepishly as Laura and I broke our clinch. "I think we forgot that you have a choice in all this. Do you want to see our planet?"

He gave the idea another moment of consideration. "First hand observation of a developing alien culture, especially one so factionalized, would be most intriguing."

Scientists are great people. I have tremendous respect for their accomplishments. However, their focus can be a little overbearing. They have to dissect the olive and biopsy the gin before drinking a nicely dry martini.

"Skip the analysis," I said. "What do you want to do?"

There are an incredible number of details that need to be handled in order to successfully pass off an alien as human. Laura and I gave Larry a long, detailed briefing on what he should expect to see at the hospital.

We gave him some background on being a graduate student, Earth-style. We told him a bit about campus life at Columbia.

"You really store your students in big buildings while they wait to go to classes," Larry asked.

"Not exactly," I explained. "Dormitories have separate rooms, normally with two students per room. Generally, they don't have the same amenities that you would find in a decent industrial warehouse, but they have other benefits. The student cafeteria will serve you three platters a day of what is very loosely called food, and just to be safe, most campuses have a student union building nearby where you can find vending machines with six-year-old cheese and crackers next to the condoms and hair gel."

"Stop that," said Laura. "He might think you're serious."

"I am serious. I ate a ton of those cheese and crackers."

"Dorm rooms are not storage, Larry. They're living quarters that are generally a little more functional than comfortable. Dormitories are designed as a place for the students to study, so they're not much for esthetics, no frills. And the bathing and toilet facilities are usually communal."

"I understand." He still looked puzzled. "What are cheese and crackers?"

"This is going to be a lot harder than we thought," I said.

Common sense should have dictated that we scrap our plan, but whether fearless or stupid, we carried on. I thought momentarily that it would be easier to slip Larry in as a patient. We wouldn't have to worry about his behavior if everyone thought he was a mental patient, but Larry had no documentation and no personal history. The paperwork would be a major problem.

"Place of birth?"

"Shriek-whistle-click."

I don't think that will work.

Granted, no one knew who Monty was either, but that is quasi-explainable since he was a vagrant brought in by the police. The staff never questioned his paperwork. It was an official police matter. Some lonely clerk, tucked away in the sub-basement of police headquarter is probably assigned to locate Monty's identification. I doubt if it's their highest priority. I also doubt we could get the police to do Larry the same favor.

Laura handled the depilatory for Larry's forehead. She expertly applied some goop that ate away his hairy bit, then several coats of soothing aloe to calm any irritation. When she finished, Larry looked like a perfectly normal, slightly balding, undernourished, geeky, nerdy, please-don't-let-him-date-my-sister human being.

My next job was handling Larry's wardrobe. I was supposed to give him some of my clothing from the hospital and let him make alterations. Instead, I arranged another escape from the Happy Ward in order to take him shopping. It was easy. I just took advantage of yet another of the great quirk of humankind: no one ever sees or questions the janitorial staff. Borrowing a pair of coveralls, I walked straight out through the kitchen carrying a full can of garbage. One of the cooks even held the door for me. Larry met me outside the kitchen exit.

Aliens are punctual, in case you were wondering.

I ditched my borrowed coveralls behind some discarded boxes. Larry was pretty much stuck with his until I could get him some "Earth normal" clothing.

For this great escape, I used VISA's 24-hour card replacement service to arrange new plastic and we broke in my new card at a nearby 7-11's ATM. Before leaving the convenience store, I introduced Larry to the thirty-two ounce Pepsi. We sipped and belched our way through the soft drinks while waiting for a taxi. The cab driver didn't question Larry's coveralls with the built-in shoes and we didn't question his turban or the dot on his forehead. It was an unspoken agreement.

Macy's was our first stop and our first priority once inside the store was to find the restroom and recycle our oversized soft drinks. The restrooms in department stores are always hidden in the farthest corner of the store. In order to use the facilities, you have to march past aisle after aisle of crap you don't need but just might buy on impulse. The store's marketing department has incorporated every aspect of your life into the firm's sales strategy. That includes your full bladder. I figure they came up with the idea during a brainstorming session while they were all sitting around drinking thirty-two ounce Pepsis from 7-11.

Surprisingly, Larry wasn't the least bit frightened by his Earthly surroundings. He was fascinated by everything. It was difficult to keep him focused on shopping. Normally, I walk in, get what I want and leave. I find shopping and especially browsing aisle after aisle to be incredibly boring. Larry however wanted to see everything in the store. He looked at, touched, smelled and occasionally tasted every item he could reach. I realized how incredibly excited he must be. This was not only his first trip to Earth; he was also shopping a major department store with someone else's plastic.

As Larry ran from counter to counter, I trailed along behind, steering him away from things that would create a scene or get him arrested, such as, his attempt to enter the ladies' dressing room.

"You can't go in there, Larry?"

"Why not?"

"It's a ladies' dressing room."

"I've only met Dr. Bousteir, Tony. I think I'd like to meet more of your females."

"You'll meet plenty of them, but women prefer to meet you for the first time with their clothes on. It's called modesty."

"I know that word. It means unassuming in one's abilities; moderate or small."

"Not in this context."

"It means something else?"

"Yes, it means shut up and follow me."

It wasn't just the merchandise Larry was interested in seeing. He watched the other shoppers with intense curiosity, occasionally collecting some curious stares in return, and evidently, Shriek-whistle-click world does not have store mannequins. We wasted a good ten minutes running around Macy's clothing departments to examine the different varieties of dummies. Larry noticed a row of armless female mannequins in an avant-garde fashion display. One of Macy's window dressers is obviously still in art school, searching for a unique form of artistic expression, which he or she found by replacing traditional human forms with plaster amputees in hideous makeup. Larry took copious notes.

I also found the perfume counter was especially captivating for Larry. He sampled more than fifty bottles. "These products are intended to make your females more attractive," he asked.

"I guess you could say that."

"This one smells like flowers. Why is it called toilet water?"

"The word *toilet* doesn't just refer to a plumbing fixture. It's also defined as the process of attending to one's appearance, bathing, shaving, plucking, waxing, etc. All of the things a woman does to. . ."

"Waxing!" Larry lit up with recognition. "I've seen this on one of your TV broadcasts. 'Kruplemeyer's Armor Coat, an ultra-high gloss paste wax that goes on smooth and easy, but dries with that hard as nails protective finish.' A woman in her underwear was rubbing it on a large, red car. She seemed to be enjoying it immensely, but I don't remember the car having a toilet."

Welcome to Earth, Larry!

I picked up a bottle of perfume from among the clustered offerings on the counter. "Have you tried this one yet?"

Larry spritzed and sniffed his way through a dozen more atomizers. After spending so much time with us, the helpful young salesgirl was disappointed when we only wanted to purchase a single small bottle of aftershave, so I talked Larry into picking out a nice bottle of perfume for his wife, *(God awful loud) SHRIEK-whistle-whistle-whistle.* He chose a woodsy scent called *Bivouac*, guaranteed to appeal to women with an outdoor lifestyle and female military personnel who don't ask and don't tell.

We then took several rides up and down the escalator to satisfy Larry's fascination with stairs that move.

I couldn't handle anymore department store exploration, so we finally got down to shopping for Larry's Earth wardrobe. We picked out underwear, socks, handkerchiefs and two pair of Italian leather oxfords, one brown, one black. Since I didn't want Larry stripping out of his coveralls in the middle of the shoe department in order to measure his feet, I figured that we'd have to guess at the size. However, Macy's uses a standard Brannock Device to measure their customer's shoe size. Larry took one look at the scale, converted to Earth units in his head and ordered a 9-C. When he tried the shoes on later that day, they fit perfectly.

How does he do stuff like that?

Next, we picked up two pairs of slacks and a couple sports shirts. I wanted Larry to have something for casual situations. After paying for our purchases and giving him a surreptitious lesson in tying his shoes, Larry changed into his Earth-bound attire in the men's dressing room. He actually looked pretty good!

We stuffed his coveralls into a Macy's shopping bag and headed for the exit with a brief stop in sporting goods along the way. Larry wanted to see a football.

"Your people seem to have a peculiar fascination with this object."

I handed him a football. "You bet. That's some prime pigskin there, Larry."

"It's made of animal skin?"

"That's right," I said. "So are the shoes you're wearing."

Larry grimaced in disgust. "That's barbaric!"

"Come on! You're people must have worn animal skins at one time."

"It's true. Our archeologists believe that we wore animal skin in *The Ancient Age*. My people also used something like your automobile for personal transportation."

"Really?"

"Yes. At one time, we had millions of them flying around, polluting our air. It's not something we're proud of."

Flying?

Nevermind.

For dressy occasions, should he attend any, and for his visits to the hospital, Larry would need a couple of suits. Grabbing another taxi, I took Larry to my favorite Jewish tailor, Hirshfeld's. If Larry was looking for a uniquely human experience, this was it.

Hirshfeld's is buried amidst various corporate, legal and advertising agency offices on the sixteenth floor of a high rise building on Avenue of the Americas. Despite, or perhaps, because of their unusual location, Hirshfeld's is a booming business. Ozni Hirshfeld, the owner, is well past seventy, but alongside his three sons, he still works a full day, six days a week.

Ozni is one of those grand elderly gentlemen who appeal to the entire population of the world. Everyone who talks with him for more than thirty seconds loves Ozni.

He is also the only one I know who can laugh with an Israeli accent. His mischievous smile and easy charm win friends instantly. Ozni remembers every customer by name and likely remembers the name of the first customer he served more than sixty years ago. He also remembers to ask about your business or family, also by name. His memory is simply phenomenal!

Hirshfeld's makes clothing as a truly artistic expression. Wool, cotton and silk are Ozni's medium. Presidents and kings seek out Ozni when it's time for a new suit. As a result, so does everyone else who can afford his artistic prices and wants to be "in" in New York. The fashion section of the *New York Times* reported that seventy-two percent of the men who ranked in the top ten on best dressed lists during the last three decades owned at least one Hirshfeld suit.

Naturally, one does not simply walk into Hirshfeld's. The day prior to my escape from Sunny Park, it had taken numerous phone calls and several hefty favors to negotiate an appointment for us without the usual four to six week wait. Most of my favors were used in tracking down someone with an appointment. My neighbor's brother's accountant's attorney let us use his time slot. In return, I promised to do a complete review of his portfolio and managed to wedge him in on the IPO of a new tech stock that has tremendous upside potential. Last minute Hirshfeld appointments don't come cheap. I figure if this stock takes off as expected, our appointment will be worth about six to eight million dollars to my neighbor's brother's accountant's attorney's portfolio.

Believe it or not, Hirshfeld is worth it.

Arriving early at the tailor shop, we were warmly greeted by the Hirshfeld staff. Larry was anxious to practice the introductions I'd taught him. "I am very pleased to meet you," he said.

Larry was absolutely delighted when Hirshfeld's receptionist was very pleased to meet him in return, as he had been with the taxi driver, the building's doorman, the fellow running the newsstand in the lobby, the elevator operator and several passengers on the elevator. Larry was pleased to meet everybody. And to the credit of the human race, each of them was pleased to meet Larry in return.

While we waited, we sipped strong, sweet Middle Eastern coffee, a very aromatic blend that Ozni specially imports for his shop. The aftertaste is a little heady, but still very pleasant. Larry found the coffee similar to a drink on his home world, but I managed to stop him before he shrieked, whistled and clicked its name aloud in the reception area. "English only," I whispered. "It'll be very difficult to explain your whistles and clicks if someone overhears you."

"No problem, Tony. I speak excellent English."

"This is New York. Anything close will do."

Leading Larry over to a reception area display, we looked over several bolts of the newest European wool fabrics and I offered a quick overview of the source of Earth-bound clothing. "Wool is made from fur, sheared from an animal called a sheep. Cotton is manufactured from fibers gathered from cotton plants. Silk is collected from cocoons spun by Chinese worms, and polyester is a synthetic material specifically developed to clothe insurance salesmen."

Larry began quietly making notes on his handheld recorder. Mainly, he wanted to know what insurance was and why it required a salesman, but the receptionist politely called us to the counter interrupting his questions. The youngest Hirshfeld son, barely forty, led us into the fitting room. Ozni, himself, measured Larry for his new suit.

"Tony, it is so nice to see you again." Ozni met me with a beaming smile, hugging me as if greeting a long lost brother.

"Nice to see you too, Ozni," I replied. "This is a friend of mine, Larry. I told him you could fix him up with a couple of new suits, shirts, ties, the works."

Ozni turned on the Israeli charm. "My entire staff is at your service, sir. We'd be most happy to help you, Mr. . . ."

Damn! We forgot a last name for Larry!

"Xenomorph. Larry Xenomorph," I improvised almost without thinking.

"Isn't that an Armenian name," asked Ozni.

"There's no fooling you, Ozni," I said.

"When you've been in this business as long as I have, you learn a thing or two."

I ushered Larry up onto the small pedestal in front of three, angled, full-length mirrors and Ozni began measuring while recommending some nice fabrics that would work well with Larry's pale skin and dark brown hair coloring.

Ozni is amazingly spry for a seventy-year-old. While whipping the tape measure up, down and around Larry's torso and making copious notes, Ozni continued his running commentary, explaining his philosophy of tastefully elegant tailoring in the heavy Israeli accent he'd carefully maintained during his many years in America. "Armani is crap! Everyone should wear Hirshfeld. You're not properly dressed if you're not wearing Hirshfeld."

"I don't know Armani," said Larry.

Ozni reached his age-spotted hand up to pat Larry's cheek. "Good boy! Such a very good boy!"

"Gender is neither good nor bad," replied Larry.

"Oh, really," replied Ozni. "You wear one of my suits around some nice, beautiful young ladies. You will see, it's good to be a boy!"

The other highlight of our visit was discovering that Larry could jump nearly as high as he is tall, which he did when Ozni reached for his crotch while trying to measure his inseam. Ozni was flabbergasted. I was hysterical. Thank goodness for the high ceilings in these older New York buildings. Almost choking with laughter, I smoothed things over. "It's okay, Larry. He's just trying to measure your inseam, the length of your leg. He has to make your pants the right length."

"Did you see what he did," exclaimed Ozni. "He jumped almost six feet straight up!"

"Oh, that's nothing. He's a contender for the next Olympic high jump team. With a running start, his record is well over eight feet." I have no idea how high a record high jump is, but Ozni seemed to buy it.

"An athlete," said Ozni. "Such a good boy!"

When Larry finally stepped down from the small dais, Ozni helped him pick appropriate fabrics for the suits. Larry wasn't concerned much with color or striping, but seemed to have a preference for the texture of lightweight wool. He also chose some nice dress shirts and neckties to match his suits. The shirts were an excellent quality linen, again Larry chose them based on texture, and Ozni recommended solid colors, white, aqua blue and something that was just shy of being peach to match the fabrics selected for Larry's suits.

We also chose neckties based on Ozni's recommendations. Larry didn't know much (or anything) about neckties, *such odd decorations*, so he appreciated Ozni's advice. It's tough to fault the advice of a septuagenarian tailor who started working in the family business at age eight or nine. "These are very tasteful," said Ozni. "Just the right mix of style and power."

"I bow to your expertise," said Larry, and of course, he did.

Ozni was most honored and returned the bow with a huge smile.

Larry learned to tie a necktie after being shown only once, but he felt obligated to mention that it is inherently unsafe to knot a piece of colored rope around one's neck.

Who can you argue with that?

I paid Ozni's cashier the customary extortion for twenty-four hour service so that tomorrow, Larry could be tasteful and elegant in two new Hirshfeld suits.

As always when leaving the store, a laughing Israeli voice had the last word. "You will see, my nice, new friend, Mr. Larry Xenomorph," called Ozni from the back room, "a Hirshfeld suit is a better investment than even Tony can make for you."

I had planned on going directly back to the hospital, but Larry expressed an interest in seeing where I worked.

Why not?

I was already AWOL from the hospital and they can't hang you twice for the same crime. Besides, it'd been way too long since I'd been on the trading floor. I missed the buzz, the excitement and the high stakes conflict of testosterone-saturated egos. I missed the smell of $$$$$.

I asked the cabby to turn around and head for Wall Street. Frankly, I was rather curious to see Larry's reaction to the boisterous commotion of the exchange floor.

The most common first impression newcomers have of the New York Stock Exchange is that they are witnessing chaos. Everyone is shouting, hustling and running. A thousand traders are all yelling at once trying to be heard over the bidder next to them. Lights flash, bells ring, tickers scroll and terminals jump from screen to screen of data, adding more auditory and visual anarchy to the constant roar of the crowd. A patchwork carpet of trash and trading slips covers the floor. It will be swept away today and replaced again tomorrow. If there is method to the madness, it's well concealed from most outsiders.

One of my university professors once told me that if you sit quietly and watch the floor of the exchange carefully, you will find an elegant dance being performed, a dance of money. That sounds good in a classroom, but it's pure bull. The truth is exactly what you see. The floor of the exchange is barely organized chaos with everybody grubbing for another dollar. There's nothing else like it. It's great!

"Everyone seems very excited," said Larry.

"They are excited," I responded. "This is the economic heart of the United States. People make and lose fortunes here every day."

"Yes, of course, they are trying to get money."

"The term we use is *make money*, not *get money*. Investors from all over the world are trading on this exchange, right here, right now," I said.

"I should like to try this." He was catching the excitement of the floor.

"Larry, you can't just walk in and two minutes later, throw down your money. You'll lose it. You have to study the market."

He pointed to the overhead, scrolling ticker. "The figures up there are correct?" Larry asked.

"Yes, but there's more to it. The key to sound investment is careful research. You have to examine a company's price\earnings ratio, their asset management, their board of directors, production, marketing strategies, future contracts and their competitive position in the marketplace. Find out who their competitors are and if they have an edge. Is the company gaining or losing market share? Do they have a solid research and development team in place? Do they have new products coming onto the market? Is their advertising properly targeted for their consumers?

"Then there's mood. The market has moods, reacting to political and economic news, government policy changes, and just plain naked fear. It's not as easy as it looks. There's a lot you should know before investing you're hard earned money."

"I didn't earn it," Larry said, pulling a lump of gold the size of my fist from his pocket. "I made it this morning."

"Put that away!"

"This is valuable here, isn't it?"

"Yes, it's valuable," I replied. "That also means that it can be easily stolen."

"You mean someone would take something that wasn't their property? They do that here?"

"This is New York, Larry."

I figured a little extemporaneous instruction on the market might help dissuade him from tossing away his lump of gold. We found an open terminal and I began with the basics of trading, starting with simplistic overviews of stocks, bonds, commodities and options. I explained as patiently as I could and tried my best not to laugh at his questions. It was like teaching a small child to read, but within a few minutes, Larry was reading on his own. He scanned the various indices on the monitor and was extrapolating movements on several key industrials and two high tech stocks. After one or two leaps onto dead end tangents, he started making sense (if there is any) of our system of economics.

"There is currency being traded also," he asked.

"Yes, you can exchange one currency for another."

"And mutual funds are a large group of investors acting as one."

"Yes."

"Large mutual funds," he continued, "can have a significant impact on the market when they make large purchases."

"They can." That was a pretty good insight for a novice. Larry was definitely a quick study.

"Okay, I'm ready."

I couldn't control myself any longer, I had to laugh. "Take it easy. This is your first day. Maybe you should just look around a bit."

"No, I would like to trade." He looked up at the ticker.

"It's okay with me as long as you understand that you're just gambling with your money."

"It's not a gamble, Tony. It's a mathematical certainty that I will make money."

"That's what everyone who walks through those doors thinks," I said. "Most of them go home broke. Mathematics isn't everything, Larry. Remember what I said about markets having moods, panics and swings in sometimes-insane directions. There's a psychology, sociology and politics to money that can't always be predicted. You have to feel it. It has nothing to do with mathematics."

"Your mathematics is very primitive. All of those factors can be easily calculated," he said as he sat down at the terminal.

Since I couldn't talk him out of it, we began by opening a day trader account for him with Greedy & Grabby. He used my address and social security number. I gave him ten thousand dollars from my money market account to get started. Larry insisted that I take the lump of gold in exchange.

"See, you're already starting off with a losing trade, Larry. This is probably worth twice that much."

"I believe your expression is that you may keep the change."

"Gee thanks." I pocketed the lump of gold and tried not to feel like his waiter.

Reaching into his pocket, Larry retrieved a small, dull silver disk about the size of a fingernail and stuck it on the side of the terminal.

"What's that?"

"It is a remote interface for some equipment on my ship," he said.

"You're going to use your ship's computer to out-think our computer?"

"Not exactly." He pulled another small disk from his pocket and placed it on his left temple. It stuck in place, looking like a large silver mole.

"Now, you're interfacing with the computer."

"Not exactly."

"Stop being cryptic, Larry. Tell me what you're doing."

"I'm trading monetary instruments, Tony."

"I should warn you, a lot of people have tried to out-compute the market. Most of them went belly up."

"Is that bad?"

"Belly up means they lost all their money."

"I promise you," he said with genuine sincerity, "I will not go belly up."

He began playing the terminal's keyboard like a grand piano. The best executive secretaries I've seen at G & G can't type as fast as Larry does. He had to be inputting nearly two hundreds words a minute without the slightest falter or hesitation. If appearances count, he sure looked like he knew what he was doing. Still, I was amused at the way he was going to throw away ten thousand dollars. It would be a good lesson in humility for him and I began mentally practicing a soothing speech to soften the blow when he inevitably crashed.

I continued to laugh when he made money on his first trade. I chuckled in amusement on the second and third. By the fourth, I was trying to figure out what he was doing. From there on out I was seriously confused and asking him a lot of questions. Larry finally asked me to hold my questions for just a few minutes, as he was quite busy. The speed of his trades accelerated at a blinding pace.

Call it bragging if you must, but I'm really very good at what I do. Still, Larry was losing me. I tried my best to keep up, but his fingers flew over the keyboard. The monitor of his terminal was constantly scrolling. I couldn't begin to follow everything he was doing. I don't think any human could.

Almost an hour later, Larry was up three hundred sixty-four million dollars and beginning to draw a serious crowd. I dragged him away, pulling the silver whatever-it-was from the side of the terminal. We waded through the crowd, heading for the main entrance. I didn't stop even after we were out the front door. We dodged several pigeons, a slew of pedestrians and a hot dog vendor as I pulled him to a reasonably quiet spot fifty yards down the street. "Christ, Larry!

"I think I understand money now, Tony," he interrupted. "It's very exciting and exhilarating to start with something small and make it big. It's like building something out of nothing."

"Larry, you can't do this. You have to give that money back."

"Why?"

"Why! You don't have a real social security number. You don't have a legitimate address. You have no documentation at all. You really are an illegal alien, Larry. You don't exist here."

"But your monetary instruments, the stocks and bonds, they exist."

"You don't understand. The Securities and Exchange Commission, the government here, is going to take a very close look at anyone making three hundred million dollars in an hour."

"Three hundred sixty-four."

"Fine, three hundred sixty-four. But they're going to come sniffing around and you can't afford that kind of scrutiny. Just take my word for it."

Larry shuffled his feet a little. I shouldn't have raised my voice. I keep forgetting that he's a student, fairly young and inexperienced in alien terms. In human terms, he doesn't have a clue. Larry had no point of reference to explain our world. He truly was like a small, lost child, confused and perhaps just a bit frightened.

Or, so I thought.

"I'm sorry, Tony. I'm really sorry."

"Hey, it's okay. We'll just go back in there and lose the money. Then we don't have to worry about the SEC or any other government agency finding out you're an alien. They'll chalk it up as a fluke and no harm done."

"No, I mean I didn't know your government would be involved or I wouldn't have done it."

"Larry, it's okay. It's fixable." He wasn't listening to me.

"You've got to believe me. If I'd known you would get in trouble with your directing body, I would never have put all those stocks in your name."

I had started to soften my voice and shuffle my feet a little to mirror Larry's movements, hoping to make him feel more comfortable. It took me several seconds to process what he said.

"You put three hundred sixty-four million dollars' worth of securities in my name!"

My voice became shrill till I lost it completely and I don't know if my feet were still shuffling or not. I couldn't feel them. I couldn't feel my whole body.

You know that dark, black blanket that folds over you just before you pass out. It's really warm, isn't it?

~~*

By the way. . .

If you're ever in New York and need a hot dog vendor who carries smelling salts, he's the one wearing the New York Giants ball cap while tending the unlicensed Nathan's cart with the orange and white umbrella just outside the stock exchange's main entrance. His name is Majdi, but he also answers to, "Let me have one with the works."

The hot dogs are excellent. While I recovered, Larry ate two of them.

15

But I Like Being Filthy Rich

I have a real name. I have a legitimate address. I have a genuine social security number. I also have three hundred sixty-four million dollars!

I've never kissed a man on the lips before and still haven't, but I damn near kissed Larry. Of course, I went over all of his transactions just to make certain there was nothing fraudulent in the mix. And while I still have no idea how he did it, everything appears to be perfectly legal.

When we arrived back at the hospital, we covertly made our way to my room and Larry tried to explain his performance, "It's really quite simple. From direct observation, I determined that the markets flow in quantifiable and non-quantifiable directions. You demarcate the quantifiable and reduce the non-quantifiable to probabilities based on available data, including the historic trends, which were available in your computer. Add in factors known to be constant, then simply adjust the balance for unforeseen influences. It's nearly impossible to be wrong."

Does that sound like a load of crap, or what?

I opened two bottles of beer from the twelve-pack I'd smuggled in from the bar across the street and handed him a cold one. "Everyone I know, including myself, has been wrong at one time or another, and we've all had to pay for the privilege. And what you said makes no sense at all. Unforeseen influences would be non-quantifiable."

"Not true." Larry smelled the beer, trying to decide if it was safe to drink.

"It's just a beer, Larry. It's made from grain and has a bit of alcohol in the mix."

He gave it another sniff. "It smells wonderful."

"Try tasting it. That's wonderful, too."

Larry took a cautious sip and decided I was correct. He drained the bottle in a single, long pull.

"Slow down there, bud. I wasn't kidding about the alcohol content."

"It's very good. Can I have more?"

Larry drank his second bottle more slowly as we continued to discuss his method of kicking butt on Wall Street. Even with a master's degree in finance and twelve years' experience as an active trader, his explanations made absolutely no sense to me. I didn't understand his perceptions of the market and I couldn't follow his otherworldly mathematics. Maybe that's because I didn't have one of those silver, fingernail disks stuck on my temple. Frankly, I don't care at this point. I've got the money!

"In future," I said, "we have to stick to things you can do without drawing so much attention to yourself."

"That may be difficult," he said, starting to sound a little manic. "I can do anything!"

"I don't think you fully appreciate the problem, Larry."

"Sure I do," he shouted. "I'm better at everything than anyone on this primitive planet. I'm the best. I can do anything!"

I suddenly realized that Larry's metabolism may not process alcohol in quite the same way as humans. Mr. Can-Do-Anything swallowed the last gulp from his second bottle of beer, fell out of his chair, threw up on my floor and passed out.

He may be right about being the best on the planet. I've never seen anyone do it better.

Some things are just difficult to explain to women.

"First, Larry made me rich. Then, I passed out, but the famous hotdog guy had smelling salts and Larry liked them a lot, with mustard. Then we got back to the hospital and Larry passed out because he's the best at everything except drinking beer."

"How many beers have you had," asked Laura.

"With or without the bourbon?" I caught a disapproving look. "Larry and I were celebrating," I explained.

After giving Laura a sweet, drunken kiss, I went back on hand and knee to continue scrubbing the floor where Larry had gotten sick. I'd long since cleaned up Larry and laid him out on my bed, and I'd lost count, but I think I was up to the sixth or seventh cleaning of the floor. I wonder if I was becoming alien germ phobic. Larry snored softly while I scrubbed and detailed his first full day on Earth to Laura.

"Three hundred and sixty-four million dollars!" My lovely doctor was even beautiful with her mouth hanging open.

"Plus the seventeen million I already had. That's, uh, um. . . I'll figure it out tomorrow. I need another beer." As an afterthought, "And here, this is for you."

I handed Laura the lump of gold.

"Is this gold?"

"Yeah, Larry made it on his ship. We'll get it made into a nice necklace, a bracelet or something later." I handed Laura a beer also. "We can afford it. I've got three hundred sixty-four million dollars!"

"Three hundred and sixty-four million dollars!" She said again, trying to comprehend suddenly having a boyfriend, who was one of the wealthiest men in the country. She stared at the bed where Larry was sleeping off his two bottles of beer. "You'll have to get him a really nice gift."

"I don't want to die here."

"You're not going to die, Larry. It's just a hangover." Laura put another compress on his forehead.

"I'm never drinking that stuff again."

"Everyone says that. Put the sunglasses back on. It helps with the light sensitivity."

"Stop yelling at me!"

"You're going to be fine," Laura whispered.

"I'm not going to die?"

"You're not going to die. Believe me, I'm a fully qualified physician."

"On a miserably primitive planet."

"Fine. I'm a witch doctor," she conceded, "but I still know how to treat a hangover."

"I don't want to die on this primitive planet," he moaned.

I was sleeping off my own celebrating in another room so I missed most of Larry's hangover. Laura didn't know enough about his physiology to risk medicating his pounding head, especially after the way he'd reacted to simple alcohol. She did everything possible to make him comfortable without prescribing anything stronger than TLC, and somehow managed to get him to keep down some food. Happily, Larry survived.

When I woke up, I had sincere doubts that I would live through my own hangover. Fortunately, I had the benefit of heavy doses of analgesics and a blistering hot shower. I know, they recommend cold showers for alcohol-related disabilities (P.C.), but steamy hot works for me, along with a minor dose of the dog that bit me.

My recovery also required numerous caring hugs and kisses from Laura, but that's simply a bonus.

On the Happy Ward, in public so to speak, it's becoming more difficult to address Laura or even think of her as Dr. Bousteir. It really takes conscious effort on my part. There's just no intimacy in formal titles.

My ever so lovely, incredibly patient Dr. Bousteir nursed both Larry and I through our self-inflicted pain, vomiting and whining, while covering up for us as best she could with Mo and Nurse Cassilio's help. Laura is the one who should receive a really nice gift, maybe, a personal yacht or a nice island in the Caribbean. I'll think of something.

Once Larry and I were both sober and stable, Laura called us to her office and explained how much trouble we had caused her. Covering up my second escape and our somewhat less than secret shenanigans here at the hospital was no easy task. We'd jeopardized her career and Larry's safety, which is the one thing she'd promised we would look after. "And, you brought alcohol onto a mental ward! Don't you know how dangerous that can be! There's also the little matter of Larry being an alien. If that had gotten out while you two were drunk and gallivanting about the hospital."

"Gallivanting? We never left my room," I protested.

"I have the floor at the moment!"

Yes, ma'am!

Laura dressed us down for several minutes. She never raised her voice loud enough to be heard outside her office, but the quietness of her tone may actually have been more effective. Justifiably, she was really angry.

Larry was fascinated to witness a genuine Earth female tirade. So fascinated in fact that for a while, he didn't realize that he was also being chastised. When he did realize, he seemed to enjoy it even more.

I sat quietly and listened, considering her lecture part of the price the human male must occasionally pay for a good drunk.

"My name is Rudiger—Sebastian Rudiger."

"My name is Bond—James Bond," I replied.

Mr. Rudiger was from the Securities and Exchange Commission. It surprised me that they responded so rapidly. Normally, the government functions so slowly it's amazing that anything gets done, but when you don't want them involved in something, they turn up on your doorstep before you can finish the thought. It was at least some comfort that they hadn't shown up with handcuffs.

From what Mr. Rudiger told me, they tracked me to the hospital through my department head at G&G. Intent on seeing me today, Rudiger bullied his way past the hospital staff by going directly to my best buddy, Arnold Pelekinako, Sunny Park Hospital's administrator. I can just picture Arnold drooling at the thought of them dragging me away to the federal penitentiary.

According to Mr. Rudiger, the SEC had screened all of the transactions that Larry executed the previous day and couldn't find any irregularities. "Still, we do have some questions we'd like to ask you," he said.

"Shoot."

"How did you do it?"

"I had help from a visiting alien," I replied. "His spaceship is in orbit over New York right this minute."

Rudiger went deathly quiet for a good five seconds. Then, he vented his bureaucratic outrage, "All we're asking for is a little cooperation in this investigation, Mr. . . ."

"Sterling, my name is Tony Sterling. It's not really Bond."

"If you don't want to cooperate in this investigation. . ."

"What are you investigating," I asked, interrupting him again.

"Your transactions on March fifth. According to our records, your account made over seventy-eight thousand trades in less than an hour and you didn't take a single loss. Not one."

"That's true. I had a pretty good day," I said

"I'd say so! You started a new account with ten thousand dollars and made three hundred sixty-four million dollars in fifty-three minutes of trading."

"Is that illegal?"

"Well, no, it's not."

"Were any SEC regulations violated?"

"Not that we can determine." Rudiger's attempts to sound threatening collapsed completely.

"So what are you investigating," I asked.

Mr. Rudiger squared his shoulders, trying to regain an intimidating presence. "We'd like to know how you did it."

"So would I. Let me know if you find out."

Later—much later—that night, I stared up at the ceiling. I'm rarely unable to sleep, but my life had changed so radially in such a short time. Racing thoughts bounced around in my head like bumper cars. I'm a mental patient who now had love, wealth, and hopefully, I would soon be declared sane once again.

Crazy!

16

Alien Without References Seeks
Temporary Position

Laura is one of those exceptional people who can get angry, vent, accept your apology and move on with her life. Once the argument is over, it's over. It's a very sensible way of handling anger. It leaves so much more time for hugs.

"I never saw anyone react that way to two bottles of beer," Laura commented as she snuggled a little closer to me on the couch in her office. "Larry's metabolism is radically different from ours somehow. I should run a few blood tests while he's here. There's a lot I could learn."

"You can't send alien blood to a lab," I said.

"I'll run the tests myself. I'll take a sample when he comes in later today."

I kissed the top of her head. Her hair smelled wonderful. Conversation wasn't really on my mind; I was losing myself in the feel of her body pressed against me. Still, I tried to keep the small talk going. Women seem to like that for some unknown reason. "I'm going to resign from G&G tomorrow."

"What will you do?"

"Drink beer and chase women."

She playfully slapped my thigh. I gave an appropriately playful flinch in return. "If you can believe it," I continued, "I thought I might go into archeology. It's been my hobby since high school. I've always been fascinated by ancient cultures."

"Why did you go to work in the stock market?"

"The same reason most people don't end up working in their ideal choice for a career, money. Archeologists are always living from grant to grant. Most end up teaching instead of exploring. It's a tough field to make a living." I massaged the length of her thigh, wondering briefly if it was for her benefit or mine. "Don't get me wrong. I really like working the market. I enjoy the hell out of it, but it was always meant to be temporary. As soon as I had enough money to do as I pleased, my plan was to move on."

Laura jumped up, one of her personal traits. When she was excited about something she bounced. If she were prone, she bounced to a sitting position. If she were sitting, she bounced to her feet. Something told me there was some cheerleader history in her background.

A short skirt and pom-poms! Oh, yes!

"That's so marvelous! To be able to do what you really want," she said.

"At least I won't have to starve while I'm digging up ancient burial sites." I gently pulled her closer to me again, kissing the velvet nape of her neck.

"You're going to make wonderful discoveries. I can feel it."

"Discovery is only half the battle. You have to figure out what actually happened, how people lived and why they lived that way. Sometimes, it takes a lot of creative thinking."

"That's not a problem," said Laura. "You're very creative."

"Thank you." I gave her a squeeze.

"Sarcastic as hell, but creative."

I gave her another squeeze. "Thanks again, I think."

"Well, archeology is definitely a better career choice than professional wise ass."

"I don't know, I think I've done a pretty good job so far.

"You forget," she said, "I've shared shriek-whistle-whatever with you in Larry's beam. I know who you really are behind all of your masks."

"And, who is that?"

"The man I love."

Laura kissed me so deliciously that I didn't want to break away for mere air to breathe. "When will Larry be coming back?"

"About two."

I eased her back down to lie with me on the couch. "Then we have lots of time."

Those long, warm, wet kisses I'd been consistently craving were now mine whenever we were together. Kissing was different with Laura. It was much more satisfying than with anyone I'd kissed before her. Love was definitely part of that feeling, but there was more. Something I couldn't define very well. Her lips fit perfectly to mine. She fit perfectly in my arms. Laura fit perfectly in my life. I'd never felt more comfortable with a woman, and yet, my need for her was never sated. "I love you, too," I said.

She kissed me again. "Hush," she said. "We don't want to scandalize the neighbors."

"Screw the neighbors."

"Well, if you don't mind waiting your turn."

Both my laugh and our plans were unexpectedly cancelled by a voice from the other side of the room, "Am I early?"

We looked over to see that Larry had appeared in the corner of the office. He was wearing his new Hirshfeld and beautifully polished oxfords.

Damn! Why couldn't he have waited just a while longer?

Overly conscious that Laura and I were both naked, I greeted Larry with a little wave and, "Larry, I think it's time for a talk on knocking."

Ms. Emily wanted to know how Larry had managed to sneak past her. Laura convinced her that he had arrived during Ms. Emily's lunch hour and had been in the inner office for several sessions. "He's a post-doc from Columbia here to observe for a few days," said Laura. "He's spent too much time in academia and needs some hands-on hospital experience. Larry Xenomorph, this is Ms. Emily."

"Pleased to meet you," said Larry.

"Me, too." Ms. Emily eyed him somewhat suspiciously. Larry had gotten past her guard into the inner sanctum; a mortal sin if ever there was one. "That's a rather unusual name you've got," she said.

"I'm sorry," said Larry, looking at me. "I understood that Larry was quite common."

Ms. Emily followed Larry's gaze to me. "Like Dr. Bousteir said, he's spent way too much time in academia."

As planned, Laura introduced Larry to the hospital staff as a visiting graduate student. He cut a very professional figure thanks to Ozni's expertise. While he and Laura were making rounds and attending therapy sessions, I found other business to keep me occupied. I started with a phone call.

"Wilford, this is Tony. I need a favor."

"Bummer. How's it feel to need?"

I know it's difficult to believe, but Wilford actually thinks that's humorous. "I have a better question for you. How would you like to give me a couple hours of your time in exchange for me personally devoting myself to making sure your portfolio grows into a seven figure account?"

Even more difficult to believe, Wilford was quiet for several moments. Finally, his quaking voice came over the receiver. "I'm there. Whatever you need. In fact, I'm free tomorrow afternoon."

"Make it next Thursday morning. Now, how much do you know about computer controlled elevators?"

I wasn't able to see much of Larry during the day. He spent most of his time in Laura's office or accompanying her as she made her rounds at the hospital. She did her best to keep him out of trouble, although Larry did manage an occasional slip as he adjusted to humanity. Laura kept me informed of his progress, and whenever she couldn't bring him along to staff meetings and such, Larry spent his time "observing" in the Happy Ward where I could keep an eye on him without being too obvious.

To be honest, I didn't put much effort into stopping Larry from making mistakes. After all, making mistakes is part of the human experience. I intervened only if I thought he was about to do or say something that would expose his alien identity. For the most part, I sat back and watched, allowing Larry to collect his data while I amused myself collecting a bit of my own.

Actually, Larry was pretty good at being human. His curiosity was insatiable. He examined every item in the hospital, large and small. There was almost a toddler-like innocence to his exploration of Earth, especially with his tendency to take the English language as literal, which required occasional intervention. Remember the old expression, *out of the mouths of babes*, used to explain the incredible things said by young children that have the ring of truth, an unusual insight, or are just plain funny. Larry's neophyte mistakes were very similar.

A few of my personal favorites:

In the corridor, walking past Mrs. Renardo as she tuned up for her ear-splitting opera:
Mrs. Renardo (singing): Shrieeeeeeeek!
Larry: Why, thank you. That's very kind of you to say.

While playing a game of chess with Carl:
Larry: The rules I read last night didn't mention scissors.

While being measured for a sweater by Anna:

Larry: I promise not to jump to the ceiling when you reach for my genitals.

Talking to Carl's wife, Tina:

Tina: It's a lemon-maple-rhubarb muffin. Homemade.

Larry: Why is that fly landing on everything but your muffins?

Passing Mo in the corridor as he is once again ambushed by Nurse Tammy:

Larry: It appears that female wants to mate with Mo despite his speech impediment?

Me: It's not a speech impediment; he's just nervous.

Larry: Are they going to mate now? Can we watch?

To a server in the cafeteria line:

Larry: Yes, I've heard of beef. It s from an animal called a cow. Which one of you killed it?

After Laura and Larry sat in on a graduate level physics lecture while visiting Columbia University's campus, he related to me the following:

Larry: And then, the physics professor writes the answer on the board as lambda four the velocity of the fractional mass cubed! Haaargh!

(Thirty seconds of uncontrolled alien laughter.)

Dr. Bousteir: I'm sure it was very funny, Larry.

Larry: It was, Doctor, most amusing. And Tony, I got to try the vending machine's six year-old cheese and crackers!

Meeting the hospital administrator, the infamous Arnold Pelekinako:

Larry: I've been looking forward to meeting you. Everyone talks about you and I've never met a putz before.

Reading *Cosmo* on the Happy Ward:

Monty: Turn to page sixty-seven. They have a fashion layout with some really great-looking babes in lingerie.

Larry: I see. They appear to be very beautiful women. Which one has the cottage cheese thighs?

Fortunately, odd behavior doesn't stand out on a mental ward. Larry fit right in.

Laura pulled me aside in the Happy Ward, looking around carefully to be certain no one would overhear. "I finished running a few tests on Larry's blood."

"What did you find out?" I was as curious as she was.

"He's not anemic, despite how he looks. I've never seen such robust blood. His immune system, I've never seen anything like it. I don't think he's capable of getting sick, at least, not the way we understand it."

"What did you do with the blood?"

"I returned it to him," she said. "That was the deal I made with him. I also had to give him all of the printouts from the tests and delete everything that was on disk. He can't risk leaving any traces of his alien nature behind."

"Well, allowing you to run your tests certainly shows that he trusts you."

"I know, that was nice." Laura had a far-off stare for a moment, a look of uncertainty.

"Is there more? What else did you learn?"

"Not enough. I wish he could let me run some more tests," she said. "I don't think his blood is that way naturally."

"Not surprising. Shriek-whistle-click World's medicine has to be light years more advanced than ours."

"You're missing the point," said Laura. "His blood, it's. . . If Larry were human, he'd be considered a superman."

"Larry? You're kidding!"

"I'm not. Biologically, he's much stronger than any human."

I could see that Laura wanted to discuss her discovery with her colleagues. She desperately needed to talk with learned men who understood the mysteries of biology, calculated everything to five or more decimal places and had their own dictionary of convoluted terminology. Laura wanted her questions answered, and I didn't have the background to understand even the most basic blood test that she'd run in the lab. I was only good for moral support. "Talk to Larry. He'll answer your questions if he can."

"I already tried that," she said. "He's afraid of interfering with our natural development. He's already out on limb letting me run the few tests that I've run so far. I don't think he'll let me run any more."

"You're frustrated."

"Incredibly!"

"Well, at least you have the satisfaction of one major discovery," I said.

"What's that?"

"Aside from me, you're the only one on planet Earth who knows that Superman is a short, skinny guy with a custom tailored suit and a hairy bit."

She laughed. "And kryptonite is imported beer!"

Larry spent the next ten days or so collecting data and making friends at the hospital. He appears to enjoy human contact to a degree that, in all honesty, I wish we as a species could emulate. The nurses dote on him and he surprised the hell out of me with an as yet undiscovered talent, Larry was a flirt!

He told every female on staff how beautiful they were. He complimented hairstyles, makeup, accents and womanly charm. I was nearby when he told Nurse Cassilio, "It takes a very special woman to make scrubs look that good."

Nurse Cassilio smiled incessantly whenever he was on the ward, exhibiting symptoms of a classic teen crush and flirting in return. This led to a follow-up conversation between Larry and I.

"She had a cramp in her shoulders, that's why I was rubbing them."

"Okay," I asked, "then why did she rub your shoulders in return?"

With Larry's pale skin, he blushes terribly when embarrassed.

"Earth cramps must be contagious," he answered and winked at me.

Aliens wink?

Finally, I had to ask. "Your social skills are not exactly Earth-normal, in fact, they're pretty funny at times. But you never seem to make mistakes when you're flirting. How do you do that?"

"I pretend I'm talking to my mate."

I took that to be definitive proof that Larry is indeed the smartest man on Earth!

Laura was also impressed with Larry's professional behavior. She told me he's very conscientious about not interrupting during the patient's therapy sessions. He waits until after the session to ask questions, which he's patiently lists on his recorder. Larry also offers comments and insights that, despite their alien perspective, Laura often found quite useful.

While interacting with the patients on the Happy Ward, Larry eagerly engages them in conversation. He's interested in hearing everyone's full and complete and don't-leave-out-any-minor-details life history. Larry listens as they talk for hours. The patients love his visits. It wasn't long until they were competing for his time.

I discovered later that Larry had studied each of the patient's charts, and he was careful not to question them directly about whatever trauma had brought them to Sunny Park.

I thought everything was going wonderfully until Larry pulled me up to his ship a few days before my expected release from this wonderful institution. It was the middle of the night again, but as usual, I wasn't sleeping well anyway.

Larry seemed agitated and I wondered if the long hours were wearing him down. I've never seen him resting. Come to think of it, I'd never bothered to ask if he required sleep. I just assumed that he did.

"My species requires less sleep than yours," he said. "We can operate at full potential for several days without rest."

"My days or your days," I asked.

"Several days in either case. It's normal for us." Larry was unconsciously fidgeting with his recorder and pacing about the compartment.

"What's on your mind," I asked.

"It's been most interesting working with Laura."

"Well, I imagine psychiatry is an interesting field."

"I've met interesting people, too."

"Good," I replied, wishing he would just spit out whatever was bothering him.

"Not just the patients," Larry continued, "the staff at the hospital is very nice. They've been very helpful, teaching me how the hospital operates."

"They're good at their jobs."

He set his recorder aside. "Their work is pointless," he blurted out finally.

"Pointless?"

"They give the patients drugs or use talking sessions."

"Therapy sessions."

"Yes, therapy sessions," he repeated. "They use them to teach the patient skills to cope with their illness."

"The staff is supposed to help the patients. That's the whole purpose of Sunny Park being a hospital."

He picked up his recorder again, clutching it with both hands in a white-knuckle grasp. "They don't know what they're doing!"

"How can you say that, Larry? Sunny Park is one of the best hospitals in the country. Their staff is easily ranked with the very best professionals in the world."

I watched as Larry's grip on his recorder eased. He began mindlessly flipping it end-over-end from one hand to the other. Possibly, he'd spent too much time with Monty and his paddle.

"There's nothing wrong with the hospital staff, Tony. They're wonderful people; I know that. They just don't understand what causes mental illness. How can anyone cure what they don't understand?"

"Our medical community is primitive. Is that the problem?"

"Not exactly." Larry stopped fidgeting with his recorder, setting it down on a side table. "Your world is undeveloped. I expected to find primitive methods, but I didn't expect. . . The patients are suffering terribly, but I'm not permitted to help. I see them suffering and I feel. . ."

Larry couldn't seem to finish his thoughts.

"We call it empathy," I said, touched by this broad stroke of humanity in an alien heart. "It means to understand the feelings of another."

"I know Carl could be a fantastic engineer if he were healthy," said Larry. "Monty is capable of being anything he likes, except he's terrified of the world. His paranoia and uncontrollable anxiety are the only thing preventing him from being a real champion. And Anna, poor Anna. . ."

Instead of cultural insight, Larry's stay at the hospital had led to genuine distress. In part, this was my fault. Laura and I had overlooked one very important factor in bringing Larry down to meet the people at Sunny Park. Observing from orbit allowed Larry a critically important emotional buffer. Removing distance from the equation removed that buffer, and it's impossible for a sane, feeling human being (or alien) to remain completely 100% objective when face-to-face with genuine suffering.

Sunny Park's patients were no longer mere statistics. Larry spoke to them. He knew their names. He'd touched their hand, and personally witnessed their pain.

Not being a doctor by profession, Larry did not have the training necessary to help compartmentalize his feelings. He had no professional detachment and was suffering along with Carl, Monty and Anna.

"Your people must occasionally run into mental illness," I said.

"We cured it long ago. It's basic biochemistry."

"The cause of mental illness is entirely physical?"

"No, of course not."

He began pacing a circular path around my table while he talked. It was annoying having to swivel, constantly looking over my shoulders to see him.

"Mental illness has many causes," said Larry. "There's disease, injury and genetics, but there are also environmental factors to consider. Stress, trauma, shock, poor emotional training or a harsh environment, these factors can all cause mental illness, but curing the physical aspects, resetting the biochemistry, is primary."

Larry finally stopped pacing and continued, "With a healthy brain and metabolism, teaching the patient to understand and cope is very simple. The counseling required is generally a day or two at most. Some severe illnesses may require additional education. A few also need the patient's family members to undergo treatment. Regardless, it's minor once the chemistry is in proper balance. Just give them a healthy brain and the proper tools and the patients usually cure themselves over time."

"And you believe you can cure the physical abnormalities? The chemistry?"

"Pshaw!"

Pshaw? Who the hell uses pshaw anymore?

Larry continued disdainfully. "With a brain as primitive as yours, I could easily cure all of them!"

"And while you're at it, please give the chimp a banana!"

I shouldn't have been insulted. Assuming the human race survives, evolution would eventually take us to the same level as Larry's people. We may even surpass them. Who knows?

"I'm sorry," I said.

"I wasn't trying to be offensive," he responded.

"I know." The cold table was starting to bother my butt. I tried to rationalize my irritation, obviously caused by yet another midnight transit, by blaming it on my half-frozen tush. It didn't work. I wasn't offering Larry what this situation really required, empathy, just as I'd defined it for him moments ago. In truth, I wasn't being a very good friend, but I resolved to correct that and tried to draw him back into conversation. "How exactly would you cure a mentally ill brain?"

"I have a full medical suite onboard. I could cure the entire hospital in a matter of seconds."

"Seconds! You don't need to operate or give them medication."

"It's a simple biochemical manipulation. Once the *shriek-shriek-click-click* has the normal functions of human physiology in the database, you simply scan for abnormalities and repair them. A *shriek-warble* could do it."

He lost me for a second. I'd never heard Larry warble before.

"Larry, there's nothing wrong with feeling the way you do. It's perfectly normal to want to help someone who is suffering."

He whistled at the wall. It bulged, forming a comfortable looking lounge chair and Larry flopped down into the chair, dejected. "I told you, I'm not permitted to help them."

"Why not?"

"I can't give your species technology that is thousands of years ahead of their development. The results could be disastrous."

He feared giving the human race a real Pandora's Box.

I imagined being a modern doctor transported back to the Middle Ages and witnessing the ravages of bubonic plague and small pox. You have the cure in your possession, but are only permitted to watch as those around you suffer and die. It was a distressing thought.

Laura would know how to help. "Let's talk to Laura," I suggested.

Larry slumped further into his chair. "I can't."

"Why not?"

"I like Laura. How can I tell her that she really is a primitive?"

I didn't have any other ideas. There was nothing I could say at the moment that would lift Larry's troubled mood. In human terms, he was capable of performing miracles. But then, shouldn't that mean he was also capable of curing his own distress?

Miracles!

"Larry, did I mention that Thursday is my last day confined at Sunny Park?"

"No."

"Smile, buddy. Thursday is going to be a great day. Just take my word for it."

Back in my room, I reflected on the strangeness of our discussion. Larry really was a student. He was a young man seeking his place in the world, or in his case, the universe.

Larry was more advanced than any human in our history, but he was still a young, developing mind and soul. Yet, his people had sent him to Earth with a database as a mentor. Apparently, no matter how advanced an alien race may be they still screw up like the rest of us.

I wonder if we should take comfort in that.

17

Everybody Wins on Thursday

I awoke early on my last day at Sunny Park. After a quick shower, I dressed and made my way out to the Happy Ward. The only other patients up and about were Monty, who always arose with the sun, and the fellow a few doors down who needed to crow at it every morning. Monty was just finishing his morning practice session for his lethal overhand smash.

Nurse Cassilio was working a double shift again today. She gave me a little knowing smile and wave from the nurses' station.

More on that later.

Breakfast was a king's feast. I tried the Spanish omelet, excellent with crisp vegetables and several dashes of my favorite hot sauce. The baker produced some wonderful corn muffins, still warm from the oven, and the strong, black coffee was sweet without the need for sugar. Everything tastes better when buttered with the prospect of freedom.

Wait! I'm starting to enjoy hospital food. Get me out of here!

"You're getting out today. I told you that you'd make it."

I turned to find Mo grinning at me. "And, I told you I wasn't crazy," I said. "But, you've done a great job all the same."

Mo was always happy when returning one of his charges to normal society. Picking up one of the warm corn muffins, he wrapped it in a napkin. "Do you still believe in aliens," he asked.

"Of course! I have an appointment with one later today."

"Good." He somehow managed an even broader grin. "Just don't mention that to any judges and you'll be fine."

"Do you want some butter for that muffin? You should eat it while it's still warm."

"I'm saving it for later," he said. "I'll eat it when Tina brings in the muffins for Carl. I want her to think someone on the staff likes her baking. It's important to Carl."

"You never think about anyone but your patients, do you, Mo?"

"Sure I do. I get to eat the corn muffin, right?"

As soon as she arrived, Laura ordered the paperwork for my release started. I stopped into her office, but missed her since she'd run down to the cafeteria for morning coffee. Ms. Emily was typing up the proper discharge forms for me, although this was not one of her regular duties.

"I'm only doing this as a favor to Dr. Bousteir," said Ms. Emily.

"Come on! You'll do anything to get rid of me."

"True," she agreed.

I turned up the charm. "I know the real truth, Ms. Emily. You just want me out of here because you're afraid you'll finally give into temptation and run away with me."

Ms. Emily shifted her bulk in my direction, catching my eye with a rigidly serious stare. "My husband barely survived our honeymoon. You'd be on life support in under two minutes."

Whoa!

I ran into Laura in the corridor, already overflowing with morning traffic. Just seeing her walk in my direction caused my heart to beat a little faster. It's amazingly difficult to act reserved when all you want to do is grab your love for the clinch and kiss of the century. "Good morning, Dr. Bousteir," I said, conscious of so many people around us.

"Good morning, Tony. You're getting out today." Her lovely green eyes communicated an entirely different message that the numerous passing pedestrians would, I hope, not be able to read.

I love you, too.

"Come to my office about ten, I'll have your paperwork completed," she continued.

"Can we make it noon?" I asked. "I'm afraid I have plans for this morning."

"Plans?"

"Goodbyes, that type of thing," I explained.

"I see."

"And, I want to thank you for all your help." I extended my hand and we executed a very professional doctor-patient handshake. The passing staff members and patients would not understand this either. My need to touch her was uncontrollable.

"Noon," I whispered.

"You're sure this will work?"

"Of course, it will work. It's not rocket science. It's a freaking elevator." Wilford put the finishing touches on his program. "Is two hours enough?"

"That should be plenty."

Wilford has the interpersonal skills of a surly cadaver when dealing with people, but when dealing with computers, he's smooth, graceful and diplomatic. Whether or not his forays into the binary world were entirely legal was another matter. However, I wasn't concerned because I was answering a higher and nobler call to duty. Wilford wasn't concerned because he'd earlier toked two fat ones in the parking lot.

It was fascinating to watch him work. It took Wilford less than a minute to hack into the hospital's computer system. He uploaded his program and told the system to standby to execute on command. "You're all set. The elevator is in place and the program is hanging in cache memory, ready to go." He pointed at the keyboard. "Just hit Control-Alt-Y, then the enter key. The program will run itself and the execution will be nearly instantaneous. There won't be any delays."

"Perfect. Trigger the program when I signal you," I said.

My co-conspirators were already in place. Nurse Cassilio was catching up on her morning chart entries at the nurses' station when I came up to the counter. "We're ready."

Broadly grinning, she reached for the wall mounted telephone. Moments later, the receiving phone was answered in Physical Therapy on the fifth floor. "Mo, we need an extra hand on the Happy Ward," said Nurse Cassilio. "Can you come down for a few minutes?"

With these seemingly innocuous words, my coconspirators and I put my plan into operation.

It was a very simple progression:

1. Mo gets on the elevator, which just happens to be patiently waiting for him on the fifth floor.
2. Monty yells down the stairwell to Carl on the fourth floor.
3. Carl signals Nurse Tammy, who pushes the elevator call button.
4. Nurse Tammy joins Mo on the elevator when it stops on four.
5. Carl yells down the stairwell to Anna on the first floor.
6. Anna signals me.
7. I signal Wilford.
8. Wilford's program jams the appropriate elevator between floors and disables the alarms.

It was Nurse Tammy's day off and the entire nursing staff arranged to cover for Mo during his two hours trapped on the elevator, so no patients would be neglected. Anyone looking for Mo would be handled, put off, or sent on a wild goose chase.

There was still a slight chance that someone would notice the non-working elevator, but elevator repairmen have a miserable response time, and even if they do show up, Wilford has assured me that they won't be able to find, much less undo his program before the two-hour clock runs out. After two hours, our highly illegal program will resume normal elevator operation, delete itself and be completely untraceable.

Wilford does really nice work.

There are only two real dangers. First, the hospital administrator may somehow find out that we planned this little conspiracy and have a bureaucratic fit. But then, irritating Arnold is not something that concerns me much, or at all. Second, once he's free again, Mo may find out who trapped him on the elevator and kill all of us.

Monty, Carl and Anna all excitedly ran up to me. "We did it," said Anna.

"Are you sure this was a good idea," asked Carl.

"It was a great idea," I replied. "With everything he does for us, don't you think someone should help Mo in return? Just don't tell anyone."

"What do we say if they ask," wondered Anna.

"They won't ask."

"I can't lie," said Carl, "I'm an engineer."

"Relax," I said. "No one is going to ask you about a stalled elevator."

"What if they inject us with Sodium Pentothal," asked Monty.

"They won't inject you with anything."

"Besides, Sodium Pentothal is nothing compared to the drugs they have now," said Carl. "They can give you stuff that will make you tell them anything they want to hear."

Monty backed away in horror. "Damn CIA!"

"Oh, my," said Anna. "What if I'm truth drugged when my grandchildren come to visit. I don't want them to see me like that."

"No one is going to give you truth drugs," I said. "No one is going to ask about the elevator. Everyone will assume it's a simple equipment breakdown."

"I can fix that," said Carl. "I'm an engineer."

Next time, sane co-conspirators only.

I concluded my deal with Wilford before ushering him out through the reception area. I would look after his portfolio until it hit seven figures. He agreed not to interfere with my stock picks and that the money for his children's college would be placed in a separate trust. Wilford surprised me by discussing his plans for starting a new software firm with the money. I'd been certain he was going to retire to a tropical island where the primary cash crop was marijuana.

I tried to picture Wilford as a software mogul. Anything is possible.

Larry was waiting for me in my room when I got back. He was bent over, adjusting a large piece of equipment, which sat on the floor beside my desk. "I'm almost ready," he said.

The whatever-it-was machine had a dull silver finish. What a surprise! "Silver again. Doesn't your race have anything in another color," I asked. "A little red, green or blue?"

He stood up, but continued to hover over his equipment tweaking various controls. "For deep space missions, it's more *whistle-shriek* to produce everything in one color."

"Naturally." I wonder what the hell he said.

It was just after eleven. I hoped I had timed this correctly. I didn't want to be late for my appointment with Laura. "What do you need me to do," I asked.

"You cannot assist. You don't understand the equipment."

"I can always hold a screwdriver or something."

"That will not be necessary." Larry finished his adjustments. "I'm ready."

"You're sure you want to do this?"

"Yes." Larry stood tall and firm.

"You're not going to get in trouble when you get back home, are you?"

"No. An incident this isolated will not even be noticed. The entire *shriek-shriek-click-whistle* will be confined to the hospital. It will not even penetrate the exterior walls. My calculations were very precise."

"You're a good man, Larry."

"I am not a man, Tony. I'm an alien. Don't you remember?" He smiled at me and gave his equipment a shrieked command.

It was **BLUE!**

The deepest, bluest blue you can possibly imagine washed over us in a wave that swept floor to ceiling. Every other color of the spectrum momentarily faded into. . . .I guess I'd have to call it blueness; there's no other way to describe it. The wave was gone in an instant, making me question whether I had really seen it. I also questioned a brief, almost unnoticeable, tingling sensation on my skin; was that real or had I imagined it?

"Wow! Interesting. What's next?" I asked.

"Nothing," Larry replied. "We're done."

"What? That's it!"

"What did you expect?"

"I don't know. I didn't expect a blue flash. I thought it would be something spectacular, fireworks, or something, a little bugle corps fanfare. And I thought it would take more time."

"No, I'm done," said Larry. On command, his equipment disappeared in the light beam, streaming back to his ship. The human race was once again safe from advanced alien technology and Larry wouldn't have his butt in a wringer for leaving something behind when he returned to Shriek-whistle-click World. Only Larry and I were present in my room, so no one else even had a glimpse of the machine.

"Of course," said Larry, "the molecular realignment within the patient's brains will take several seconds to stabilize. Stabilizing their full body chemistry will take slightly longer."

"They won't be acting strangely, will they?"

"They're mental patients, Tony."

"Right, dumb question. What I meant was, will anyone notice?"

"I doubt it. It's only a few seconds, and once stabilized their brain function and body chemistry will be completely normal."

I led Larry out of my room onto the Happy Ward. Nothing seemed to have changed. Anna was still knitting. Monty was re-taping the grip on his paddle and Tina was delivering a new tray of muffins to Carl.

No one mentioned a blue flash, so the patients and staff must have had the same questioning reaction that I did. Was it real or just a trick of light and shadow that one occasionally experiences, a phantom perception?

Still, nothing seems to have changed on the Happy Ward.

Maybe whatever Larry did had some sort of time delay that he hadn't explained. Maybe it wouldn't work on humans.

"How will we know if it worked?"

"It worked," said Larry.

"But, how will we know?"

Just then, Carl stood up and gave Tina his personalized version of the clinch and kiss of the century. "Tina, you're my wife. I love you more than life itself, but your muffins taste like crap!"

18

BELIEVE EVEN IF IT
WAS IN THE NEWSPAPERS

Larry was no longer anxious about his incognito visits to the hospital. He's feeling much better.

So am I.

So is everybody.

I'm sure you've read about it by now. Banner headlines such as *Miracle Cure at Hospital, Sunny Park Miracle* and *Doctors Baffled* capped the front-page stories on newspapers around the world. TV news crews crowded the hospital parking lot, overflowing out onto the street. The Internet caught fire, abuzz with breaking news, interviews, blogs and chat. A remarkably high percentage of social network member pages, video\audio posts and e-newsletters quoted knowledgeable, reliable sources of the "real" story, such as *JohnJohnHandsome996, SlapHappyInIdaho842*, or *AnotherEgocentricMoron388*.

Theories multiplied like manic rabbits, but no one could definitively explain how the entire patient population of Sunny Park Hospital's mental health wing could be cured at the same time without calling it a miracle.

Almost no one.

As soon as the news began circulating at the hospital, Laura knew immediately who was responsible. She caught up with Larry and me on the Happy Ward. "Are you crazy?" (Which is not usually a question your psychiatrist asks.) "What do you think you're doing?"

I've always found the truth to be an excellent defense. "Practicing medicine without a license," I said.

"You can't do this," she whispered.

"Why not?"

"Well, it's. . . It's. . . You just can't do this."

"We already did," I said.

"But. . ."

Since we were not alone, I had to take the usual precautions not to be overheard or act too familiar. Still, I gently touched her arm. "Laura," I said quietly, so only she and Larry could hear. "They're cured. Just be happy for everybody."

"I am. I'm happy; I really am. It's just such a shock," she said.

"A good shock, I hope," said Larry.

"You are a genuine wonder," she replied, wrinkling Larry's Hirshfeld suit as she gave him a killer hug and a buss on the cheek. I laughed as Larry's blush traveled upward, right past his missing hairy bit to the edge of his hairline.

There was never any need for Larry or I to beg forgiveness for our quackery. I knew Laura would be pleased. We'd shared shriek-whistle-whatever together in Larry's light beam. I knew in my soul that she loved miracles.

"Thank you, doctor," Larry said when Laura released him from her hug.

Monty joined us, rushing up with great excitement. He asked Laura if he could contact Mikhail Valeskow, the premier table tennis coach in New York. Monty wanted to try out for the Olympic team Valeskow was organizing!

Anna wanted to see her husband, Roy, and her son, Roy, Jr. She had faced the tragedy that befell her family and her thoughts now were of the living, who would need her support in overcoming their grief. Anna had a family to tend once again and was eager to get started. "And I want to cook tonight. Roy always likes dinner on time. That man is ruled by his stomach!"

Politically correct or not, women like Anna are born to nest, but such thoughts were unimportant at the moment. Anna was smiling for the first time in years.

Miracle!

Her smile was warm and cheery and loving. What could possibly be better?

I looked around for Carl. He and Tina had slipped right past me and he was hanging on the payphone outside the Happy Ward's swinging doors. "I'll take anything to start, entry level, production line inspection, anything, it doesn't matter," he said.

Carl was speaking with his old boss, asking if there were any engineering positions open. Tina hung onto his arm, trying to hear the other side of the phone conversation and doing little cheerful hops in the air when she heard good news.

All of the corridor regulars were crowding the discharge desk asking to be released. Mrs. Renardo was no longer singing. Martin was no longer painting. Winston Churchill had rediscovered that his real name was Jim Constant and he was anxious to get back to his jewelry business. The teenage Bonnie had abandoned her toilet brushes in the janitor's closet and wanted to see her parents. Everybody wanted to return to his or her life on the outside, and they wanted to get started now. Right now!

The Happy Ward burst into a happy party. The volume was turned up on the sound system. Doctors and nurses were dancing with the patients and each other. Everyone was singing to the music, whether they knew the lyrics or not. Laughter erupted spontaneously from every corner of the room. The payphone in the corridor soon had a line of patients waiting to call home with the good news.

Larry's miracle was without doubt the most joyous occasion I have ever witnessed. If we'd had champagne, we would have bathed in it.

"Where's Mo," asked Nurse Cassilio as she danced past me, leading Monty in what was very likely the first dance of his life.

I checked the large industrial wall clock.

Where had the time gone?

The two hours timed into Wilford's elevator program was nearly up. The elevator should be opening any second. "We have to meet Mo. Let's get to the elevator."

"The elevator?" Laura was not one of the great elevator caper's coconspirators. "What did you do to the elevator?"

"Nothing. I just have a feeling Mo's on his way down." I hoped my please-don't-hit-me smile made up for the white lie.

Laura shook her head in amused disbelief. She instinctively understood that I'd done something else marvelous, or perhaps, mischievous. When the light comes on behind her eyes, it's amazing. Not that her eyes aren't beautiful all the time. They truly are, but that extra sparkle of delight is knee-buckling awesome.

"What did you do this time, Tony?"

"Me! What makes you think I did anything?"

I was saved when the elevator *dinged*, announcing its arrival.

As the doors opened, Mo and Nurse Tammy were wrapped tighter than a vending machine sandwich. Nurse Tammy's thin frame practically disappeared into Mo's huge arms. From the intensity of their kiss, I sincerely doubt they were in the mood for company. For several seconds, the couple remained unaware that they had drawn an audience.

"Uh-hum," I loudly cleared my throat, and everyone broke into cheers and applause. Suddenly without privacy, Mo and Tammy turned to face the sea of grinning faces gathered outside the elevator. Without a word of acknowledgement, Mo reached over and hit the door close button.

Mo has style!

Giving Mo and Nurse Tammy a reasonable shot at happily ever after was the last item on my To-do list for the day. I now had time to address other important issues. "I'm done here," I told Laura. "Any chance you have a key to the front door?"

"Come with me." She was still chuckling quietly. "I'm sure your discharge papers are ready by now."

"Great!" I lowered my voice to a whisper. "Can I call you Laura in public now?"

After a month at Sunny Park, I looked forward to going home with nearly rabid anticipation. I wanted to sip cold beer and drown myself in a good book for several wonderfully solitary hours. I wanted to go to my gym and sweat till I dropped. I wanted to sleep in my own gloriously cozy bed without a night light. I wanted to eat on my schedule and cut my meat with a sharp knife. I wanted to sit in my recliner, a chair designed for comfort instead of easy cleaning. I wanted my life back!

I had no idea someone else was using it.

I arrived home to find the court appointed conservator living in my apartment, drinking my champagne, eating my imported caviar and humping a blonde that, fortunately for him, wasn't mine.

Have you ever had the feeling that there are some doors that you shouldn't have opened?

We had one of those wildly uncomfortable, embarrassing chats with multiple mentions of butts being kicked and lawsuits being filed. He and the blonde got dressed and left rather hurriedly. After she found out the Park Avenue apartment, the champagne and the caviar belonged to me, the blonde slipped me her phone number on the way out the door.

And they say Wall Street has no ethics!

I think it's fair to say that my uninvited guest had miscounted the days and did not expect me home until tomorrow.

The conservator phoned me later to apologize a second time. He was worried the Superior Court judge would find out about his "little indiscretion" as he called it. He offered to pay for everything he'd used and have a maid service clean the apartment. I almost felt sorry for the poor sap. I told him that I had cooled off and was no longer angry. In what should be an Academy Award nominated performance, I played the nice, understanding buddy and promised not to tell the judge. "Any guy still breathing who had a shot at that blonde would have done the same thing."

"I knew you'd understand," he replied.

I assured him I did. At the end of our conversation, I let him slide on paying any damages, but just to be fair, I gave him three hot stock tips that, in no time flat, should bankrupt his portfolio.

Okay, maybe I'm not completely over my anger.

Regardless, I'm home. My maid service has cleaned up and changed my sheets. I'm feeling "normal" once again, and now you'll have to excuse me, my delicious, delectable, devastatingly beautiful Laura has just arrived. We have plans.

The following month, the Happy Ward patients and staff got together for a picnic on Sunny Park's south lawn to celebrate our group recovery and subsequent release back into the real world. This was supposed to be the first of many reunions, but somehow I knew it would be our last gathering. The picnic, arranged by Mo and Nurse Tammy, was the perfect opportunity to wish all my fellow patients a good life and good luck as they once again entered the realm of the "normal" people. To mark the occasion, I purchased some thoughtful gifts.

I said goodbye to Anna with a large selection of various colored yarns. She loved it and immediately began choosing which yarn to earmark for various knitting projects. Her poor husband, Roy carried the box of yarn around the lawn all afternoon. Anna also brought a gift for me, an angel food cake, home baked. "It's laced with shredded milk chocolate," she said. Then, whispering, "I'm sure you'll like it better than one of Tina's muffins." She playfully laughed aloud, a wonderfully joyous laugh. Anna was whole again.

On the marvelous news front, Roy, Jr. and his wife announced the forthcoming arrival of a new grandchild. I imagine baby booties will figure heavily in Anna's future knitting projects. She also promised to send me a sweater, real-life size, for my birthday every year.

I said goodbye to Carl with a box of genuine Canadian goose feathers and a tube of glue, which prompted a laugh from everyone, including Carl. Buried in the goose feathers were several of the latest, thick as a brick reference books for engineering. I hoped they would come in handy since Carl was back at his old job. His boss had told him, "What's the big deal? You were out sick and now you're back."

It's nice to know that there are still some enlightened, thinking, compassionate people around.

Carl's latest family sedan design (sans feathers) was chosen by his company's design board to be next year's production model. How Carl completed his winning design in only one month is a mystery. I guess he really is a genius.

With the hefty bonus for his new design, Carl and Tina plan a trip to Europe this spring. I also discovered that Carl has a sense of humor. He promised to send me Tina's recipe for Gag-muffins.

Tina, a genuine sweetheart, explained that she only made the exotic muffins because Carl had *engineered* the recipes during his illness. She didn't like the awful flavor combinations any more than the rest of us. "I'm pretty sure Carl's favorite, sesame-chocolate-rhubarb-oregano, is the reason they raised the terror alert last August," Tina told us.

Today, Tina brought some significantly saner chocolate chip muffins, but just to be safe, I'm still choosing a slice of Anna's angel food cake for dessert.

I said goodbye to Monty with a custom-gripped pair of table tennis paddles with '*Your Dead Meat!*' stenciled on the side facing his opponent. In return, he promised that if anyone ever stole my soul, he would get it back for me.

"You don't still believe in soul stealing, do you?"

Monty flipped his new paddle over his shoulder and caught it left-handed behind his back. "No, but the only other gift I could give you at the moment would be to let you beat me at table tennis. I've seen you play," he said sincerely. "Frankly, I don't think I could take the humiliation."

We laughed together and shared some of the beer that we'd managed to sneak onto hospital property. The Olympics are more than two years away at this point, but when they arrive, I'll make a point of following the table tennis matches.

No, I can't leave it there.

Monty would win gold in the Olympic single's competition. The commentators for the event all tagged his overhand smash as "lethal." Monty's interview after the Olympic match showed his fabulous new confidence in himself. "I may be an ugly dwarf, but I'm bringing home the gold," he yelled to the crowd.

On a side note, Monty's newfound confidence led to another benefit besides the usual commercial endorsements, etc. Wearing Olympic gold, he was introduced into some fairly lofty social circles, which then became loftier and loftier! Monty ended up attending parties in New York's social stratosphere where his extreme ugliness became chic and he turned into a wildly successful babe magnet! There's a great video of him on the web with a devastating redhead on one arm and an equally devastating blonde on the other.

Go figure.

I also learned Monty's last name, Kristoff—Monty Kristoff, which sounds very much like a sandwich selection from the menu at Schweitzler's Delicatessen. However, the important news is that Monty is no longer afraid of someone using his last name as a weapon against him. He proudly wore it on his nametag at the Olympics.

Good luck to you, professional athlete Monty Kristoff.

I said goodbye to the nursing staff with fresh, long-stem red roses for the ladies and some excellent Havana cigars for the gents. Nurse Cassilio is currently lusting after a recently hired X-ray technician and kept after me to stall the elevator for her and her new crush. As she's another genuine sweetheart, I couldn't turn down Nurse Cassilio. I gave her Wilford's phone number.

No doubt, Laura will let me know how that works out.

I said goodbye to the hospital's pastry chef by offering him a ludicrous amount of money to bake for any future entertaining that Laura and I might plan. He accepted our offer.

I said goodbye to our beloved hospital administrator, Arnold Pelekinako, with a twenty-five pound gob of mashed potatoes and gravy. The staff roared with laughter. Arnold wasn't amused. What can I say? It's tough to shop for stodgy bureaucrats, but everyone at the picnic enjoyed eating his tasty gift.

I told Arnold that I held no hard feelings about being locked in a padded cell and wished him well. Arnold either returned the sentiment or merely grunted out of habit; I'm not sure which, but I'll assume that he's forgiven me after seeing himself repeatedly interviewed about the *Miracle Cure* on CNN, NBC, ABC, CBS, etc. Arnold is not the least bit camera shy! In fact, he's an outright publicity slut.

However, I did get the feeling that I'm not completely off the hook. Arnold is still suspicious that I had something to do with the miracle on the Happy Ward.

"Are you kidding? I don't have a medical degree."

"You take care, Tony," said Arnold as he headed back to the food laden picnic tables.

Don't believe for a second that Arnold is softening or somehow turning into a nice guy. He's still a prig who yells at the patients and staff at Sunny Park, buffaloing his way through life. (You didn't think Larry could cure everything, did you?) However, I will give Arnold credit for knowing how to be polite at a social gathering, and I resisted my urge to stain his new tie.

I said goodbye to Ms. Emily with a two week, all expenses paid vacation at a luxurious, pamper-you-till-you-fit-in-your-jeans fat farm, one that I understand is frequented by more than a few movie stars. A trip to a fat farm as a gift may sound a little cruel, but it wasn't. I checked with Laura and the other staff members and found out that Ms. Emily had always dreamed of going but could never afford it. I now have pots of money and seem to end up liking the strangest people, ergo, two ridiculously overpriced weeks at the fat farm was a reasonable choice for Ms. Emily. Call it a spa if you're touchy. In any case, Ms. Emily actually kissed me. I've got witnesses.

Ms. Emily also introduced me to her husband, Bill. She may have been telling me the truth about her love life on that last day in her office. This guy looks tired.

I said goodbye to Mo and Nurse Tammy by convincing Larry to let them co-mingle their *shriek-whistle-whistle-shriek* in his light beam. Larry pulled them up while they were asleep, kept them in the beam for a few minutes and sent them back to bed. They're convinced that they shared a wonderful dream together and are more in love than ever. Of course, nourishing their souls is not a particularly solid gift. To have something in hand at the picnic, I also gave them tickets to box seats at the latest, hottest, kill-for-a-seat-if-you-have-to Broadway musical and a pass for two to the immediately following after party, practically guaranteed to flaunt wall-to-wall celebrities. I only managed to get the tickets by calling in a few favors from influential clients, but Mo and Tammy are worth it.

I've also introduced them to the new Broadway musical's phenomenal and very recently discovered superstar vocalist, who assures me the show is fabulous. Who knew Mrs. Renardo could really sing?

In case you're still wondering, Mo now speaks coherently around Tammy. He's never been long-winded, so most of his sentences are still short and to the point, such as at a quiet little suburban church on a sunny April afternoon when he said, "I do."

At least monthly, Laura and I still get together with Mo and Tammy for a beer, a dinner or a show. Maybe someday, I'll explain Larry's light beam to them. Regardless, I'm making it a point not to lose touch with Mo. It's people like Mo who are the real hope for humanity, and off duty, he loves both good beer and football, which I believe all rational men consider a prerequisite for male bonding, or some other psychobabble. However, Mo is destined to become my lifelong friend.

The female side of this couple's friendship also works extremely well. Laura and Tammy talk on the phone together almost as much as they shop together. I also have the feeling that "Let's do lunch" is a euphemism for "It's so much easier to gossip about our husbands with full glasses of wine."

Who's next?

With the return of my nerves of steel and a little professional massaging, Wilford's portfolio made tremendous gains on the current high-flying market. I released some of the money early, even though we haven't hit seven figures quite yet. Wilford used the money to start a new software company, Pit Bull Data Security. You must have seen their ads:

If you're not using Pit Bull, your data security is just plain bull.

Wilford is currently the most sought after ex-hacker in the computer industry. His wife, Pinken Pretty (I know you still don't believe me, but I swear on a stack that's her real, she-went-to-court-and-made-it-legal, read-it-yourself-on-her-driver's-license name!) retired from the stage and opened a chic floral and herbal tea shop. Their children will both be going to Harvard and paying cash for the exorbitant tuition. Strange as it sounds and strange as Wilford and Pinken are, Laura and I also get together with them for an occasional drink. Like I said before, I often end up liking the strangest people.

I said goodbye to Dr. Laura Bousteir by changing her name to Mrs. Dr. Laura Bousteir-Sterling, or some reasonable equivalent that will look good on a business card.

Laura and I were married quietly by a municipal court judge two weeks after my release. Mo and Tammy stood up for us. Larry attended in one of his Hirshfeld suits. Of necessity, we have to keep it quiet for now with doctor-patient ethics, professional review boards and all the other bureaucratic bull that can make a nice young couple's life difficult. After a respectable year or so, Laura will announce her engagement at the hospital and we'll throw a regular wedding with all the frills. In the meantime, we make love; we ride Larry's light beam regularly, and make love some more.

I could get used to this. In fact, I have.

Laura is ludicrously busy with her career. Sunny Park has a new crop of patients. Unfortunately, our world produces a never-ending supply. When Laura talks to me about her patients, she gets incredibly excited over their progress. She and Mo share a common belief that with time, proper care and medical advances, all of their patients will eventually return to their families and again lead productive lives. Laura never loses faith.

As to me, I resigned from G&G as planned. Well, not exactly as I'd planned.

"Hi, remember me? I am out of here!"

In reality, I was significantly more polite and politic. I never burn bridges. One never knows in this life when you might have to retreat, and bridges left unburned are always easier to re-cross.

I moved on from G&G with firm handshakes, good wishes and several requests to keep in touch. However, the latter may be a bit difficult as I pursue my new career choice.

Currently, I'm working hard on a second degree in archeology at Columbia. If things go as planned this coming summer, I will be flying to my new digs (pun intended) at a desert site in Arizona, where a road excavation crew accidentally uncovered a Neolithic American Indian settlement. There are also hopes of uncovering the oldest intact tribal burial site in North America. (Naturally, representatives from the local tribal council will be on hand to ensure the graves are treated with proper respect.) However, archeology is no longer merely an interest or a hobby and I'm loving every on-my-knees-in-the-dirt minute of it. I can now claim literally to be the biggest kid in the sandbox.

I'll be working with a team from UCLA and the proposed dig will be funded by a grant from the Tony Sterling Foundation.

I'm paying myself! Can you believe it?

To date, I spend most of my time in classrooms or the library, and as yet, I can't say that I've made any phenomenal new discoveries that will rock the foundations of the archeological community. This is a new career for me after all. I have to give myself time to study and learn. In a few years, I'll work on phenomenal new discoveries. Larry gave me some advanced alien orbital scans that tell me exactly where to look.

No, that's not cheating! Okay, maybe a little.

I still follow the stock market everyday. Occasionally, I stop in at the exchange to catch some of the old excitement and say hello to some of my fellow sharks. "Remember me, the naked guy?"

Every evening I go home to Laura, my lovely, lovely Laura, which is why I can honestly say without the slightest reservation that my incarceration at Sunny Park was time well spent. At the time, I only wanted my life back, but now I have a freakin' fabulous life that's better than I could possibly have dreamed.

Thank you, Larry Xenomorph.

Larry!

Take a moment to catch your breath and I'll update you on Larry.

Laura and I were seated in the kitchen area of Larry's ship, snacking on alien chips and dip. The chips were flat, rectangular and perfectly smooth, almost shiny. They tasted of barley and salt, and since I was enjoying them, I didn't want to know what they were really made from.

The dips were a smorgasbord of color and flavor. The yellow dip was spicy hot, clearing your sinuses faster than any Chinese mustard. In an odd twist, the lime green dip was bland vegetarian and the pea green dip tasted sweet and citrus fruity. The red was pickle vinegar tangy, the orange slightly fishy, and the blue a take your breath away menthol. There was only one dip I refused. After Laura gagged and spit out the purple dip in her napkin, I was afraid to attempt it. As a general rule, I try to avoid eating things that may, once again, send me to the emergency room.

Naturally, Laura was somewhat embarrassed about spitting at the table and apologized profusely, but Larry was the perfect host. He simply told her not to be the least bit concerned and led the conversation off in a new direction. English royalty could not have shown more poise.

The evening's projected ambience was truly awe-inspiring, yet strangely comforting. We ate while seated on the floor of a massive, high-vaulted underground cavern. The soaring walls and lofty ceiling were encrusted with bioluminescent flora, similar to moss or lichens. The softly colored glow from the plants constantly shifted, flowing in cryptic patterns. It was surprisingly soothing to watch. "This my favorite place to visit on my planet," said Larry.

"I can see why," said Laura. "I feel so relaxed here. I could almost fall asleep."

"Would you like to lie down?"

"No," she laughed. "I will fall asleep!"

Larry scooped a large dollop of the purple dip onto a chip. Laura was amazed that he ate it with so much relish. "It tastes like raw sewage," she whispered to me.

"It's considered a delicacy on my planet," said Larry. It's no stranger than your scrambled eggs, which I find most revolting."

"You keep forgetting about his sensitive ears," I reminded Laura.

"I'm sorry," she said.

"Don't be. I'm not offended." Larry helped himself to some more of the purple. "It's just one more good story to tell when I get home. I'll be leaving very soon. My research here is nearly complete. In fact, I'm fairly certain I'll be leaving tomorrow."

Neither Laura nor I had any response. It's as if we were stunned that *our alien* wanted to leave us. We had long forgotten the fearful shock of first meeting Larry. During his brief stay, he had crept into our hearts, or perhaps stormed the walls. Regardless, we both loved him. He was a child, filled with wonder at store mannequins. He was a wise mentor, guiding the two of us into that leap of faith necessary for those who will risk love. He was a miracle worker who dared using forbidden technology to ease the pain and anguish of suffering souls.

Larry was our best friend.

"When I get home, I'm going to lobby the *whistle-click-click* to change the status of your planet. My research is fairly conclusive and I no longer think you are destined to destroy yourselves."

"Are you telling me, the human race is no longer classified as probable losers?" I forget if it was Laura or I who asked.

The burr that was re-growing into Larry's hairy bit jiggled. "I told you that was a poor translation."

"What changed your mind about us," asked Laura.

"Many things," he said thoughtfully. "But, the most convincing was your hospital administrator."

"Arnold Pelekinako!" I blurted out my raw disbelief. "He's a freakin' moron!"

"Exactly," said Larry. "None of you like him or wish to emulate him despite his high rank at the hospital. It gives me hope that, in the future, there will be fewer freakin' morons in the leadership positions of Earth organizations."

"There's always hope, Larry," I said.

"I'm afraid the *whistle-click-click* may be difficult to convince. I certainly could use some help. Would you two like to come along for a visit to my world?"

I'm rarely speechless. To be honest, I don't think I've ever been described that way, but for a moment, Laura and I were both stunned silent. Larry was offering us the chance to explore an alien planet, to meet and interact with an alien race, to see sights beyond our imagination. We could literally go where no man has gone before! NASA astronauts would likely kill for such an opportunity. I know people who would walk the journey if they could.

Laura was as excited as I, but her eyes were full of questions. Could we really fly off into space with Larry?

"Won't you get in trouble with your governing body? I finally asked.

"I looked it up," said Larry. "There's actually a precedent from an expedition many years ago. A student, much like myself, brought back two Banderlinks and he was actually commended for original thinking."

"Banderlinks?"

"They're a sentient species that looks somewhat similar to Earth's Chihuahua, but hairless with opposable thumbs and a prehensile tail. Physically, they're a little slimy, but they're a very personable species. They have a lively pre-industrial society and a most interesting social structure. Their farms raise a mouse-like creature, which they call—Larry then made a noise that sounded like someone stepped on the Chihuahua—which translates literally as *snacks*."

Laura grasped my hand, giving it a little squeeze. Her soft touch communicated overwhelming disappointment. Obviously, we couldn't go to Shriek-whistle-click world. Our responsibilities here on Earth simply wouldn't allow such a trip.

"I would really love to visit your world, Larry, but I can't leave my patients," said Laura. "I have a full day of appointments scheduled tomorrow. Mental patients need consistent therapy to make progress. I can't cancel on them."

"And I'm due back at Columbia," I added. "Not only do I have classes scheduled, but I also have to complete my doctorate before I'm too old to crawl through the steaming jungles of Ecuador. It's sort of a professional requirement. Archeologists have to discover ancient ruins before they become one."

Larry sighed. "Stop thinking of time as so linear. I'll pick you up at lunchtime, we'll spend a few months on *Shriek-whistle-click* and I'll bring you back to the exact time and place to make your afternoon appointments, Laura, and for you to attend your classes, Tony. You'll even have time to shower and change."

"You can do that?" I asked.

"A *shriek-warble* could do it! Would you like some more chips, Tony?"

"No, thank you." I squeezed Laura's hand and she gave me a glorious smile and a little nod of agreement. "What time do we leave?"

Shriek-whistle-click!

Free excerpt - also by Jay Cole:

SEXUAL EVOLUTION

A Naughty Comedy of Social Madness

Note: DST – Direct Synaptic Transference is not a toy or a video game, but a direct feed into the human brain. Technology has finally duplicated sex and society has indeed gone MAD!! Almost all marriages are now arranged by the Federal Marriage Bureau.

~~*

Panic Attacks Are Good for You

After throwing six dresses, three pants outfits, and several of the less formal business suits across her bed, she sat on the end of it, and raged a steady flow of tears through her waterproof eye makeup.

I'm no good at this. That's why I haven't been able to get a date with anyone decent.

Two of Carley's friends had managed a date outside of the Marriage Bureau's arrangements, but she had never been that lucky. Once, she thought one of the traders at work was hitting on her, but wasn't sure. She ignored him. If she'd been wrong about his intentions, she would have been humiliated at work. It wasn't worth the risk. He wouldn't have been much of a catch anyway. She'd never found short and paunchy to be attractive.

Is that a prejudice?

As she sat on the end of the bed, she saw the cheongsam dress that she'd worn to last year's Halloween party at work. She'd returned the huge Oriental wig that came with the costume, but the dress had a small stain on the hem and the rental shop wouldn't take it back. The black satin-blend was covered with intricate Chinese designs and writing, all in gold. Skin tight and slit up to the hip on the side, she'd caused the entire office to choke on their prim and proper when she'd walked into the party. After their initial reaction, everyone laughed with her except Phyllis, a secretary who resented all of the men eyeing Carley's thigh every time she moved in the dress. It was hell trying to sit down in the damn thing. She was certain that at any moment, the seams were going to let go and the entire dress would drop like a curtain leaving her with nothing but panties, a smile and that ridiculously huge wig. She pulled the dress from her closet and held it in front of her in the mirror.

Why not? This whole thing's a joke anyway.

Carley dried her eyes, careful not to smudge her smudge-proof eyeliner. Hanging her bra on the closet doorknob, she wedged herself into the dress. The stain on the hem was barely noticeable. That costume shop had ripped her off. The dress was still tight as the head of a snare drum, perhaps more so. She'd put on a few pounds since the party. It accentuated the small bulge of her stomach. Not terribly, but just enough so that she couldn't pride herself on a perfectly flat tummy anymore. She noted in the mirror that it was also tighter over her butt than it had been.

I'm not going to think about it!

Looking at herself full length, she laughed aloud, almost wishing that she'd kept the wig.

Almost.

Carley walked the block to the boulevard, knowing from previous experience that trying to drive in this getup was a pain. Upon seeing how heavy the traffic was becoming, she knew that would have been a pain, too.

"Taxi!"

What makes it so God-awful difficult is that courage and stupidity are often so similar.

Capt. Parnell Washington, USN
History of Warfare Instructor
US Naval Academy

Carley carefully slid her way out of the taxi under the Pakistani driver's conspicuous leer. She had a sudden twinge of fear as she paid the fare, then dismissed it as she walked to the door of the Federal Marriage Bureau. Several male pedestrians stopped to stare. She felt great. If they didn't get the joke, that was their problem. She entered the bureau five minutes early for her appointment. The receptionist nearly did a spit-take with her coffee, and everyone in the waiting room stopped talking.

This is the best idea I've had in months!

~~*

Peter relaxed in the armchair, laid back, eyes closed. This was his fourth day interviewing women who didn't like him anymore than he liked them.

Federal Marriage Bureau . . . Federal Waste of Time. Why couldn't congress pass a law making the government leave the poor citizens alone?

Maybe they should make sperm banks mandatory? Women could still have a choice if they used different color test tubes. Maybe put a roulette wheel or a few slot machines in the waiting room to keep it interesting. Hit three cherries and your donor will be a Harvard MBA.

At least, I'm becoming accustomed to the overstuffed chairs.

Comfortable.

Could a sperm bank get a casino license? Maybe if they use American Indian sperm.

Comfortable.

Please let the next one be able to talk about something--anything-- that's not covered by People magazine.

Peter fell asleep.

~~*

The receptionist led Carley through the maze of cubicles as she checked her chart. They stopped at 37A and the receptionist knocked curtly on the cubicle's separation panel. "Mr. Kurloff, this is Ms. Harper."

Peter offered no response beyond regular breathing.

"I think he's asleep," said the receptionist.

Carley looked past her at Peter slumped in the chair. "That's okay. I'll handle it," she said.

Nodding, the receptionist ran back to the front desk, eager to escape from the crazy woman in the Oriental dress. Carley looked at her proposed victim.

Vengeance is mine, sayeth Carley.

She cupped her hands in a makeshift bullhorn, and screamed as loud as she could. "WAKE UP!"

Peter jumped, almost falling out of his armchair. A dozen heads popped above various cubicle partitions and out of the doors of the surrounding offices. Carley smiled at them and waved. The heads dropped out of sight, one by one.

Peter fought himself conscious, and stared at a tall brunette with a Chinese (?) dress that fit like a coat of paint. His eyes locked on a delicately tapered thigh, nearly fully revealed through the slit up the side. He rubbed his eyes and convinced himself that he was really awake before taking another look. She had shoulder length hair, very pretty girl-next-door features, average bust. The legs were definitely the hook.

Freakin' fabulous!

Realizing that Peter was looking at her bared thigh, Carley was momentarily self-conscious, but quickly regained control.

Revenge has no mercy.

"Do you prefer to attend all of these interviews unconscious, or is it just me?"

Peter wearily stood up. "I'm sorry. I guess I'm still not used to an early morning schedule."

"Does that mean you work nights, or you're unemployed?"

Did I really just say that?

The alarms in Peter's head were screaming louder than Carley's wakeup call. There must be a polite way to simply dodge this one. He'd probably have to see Ms. Bender to skip an interview.

Really nice legs!

"Can we start over," he finally asked. "I'll promise to stay awake if you promise not to go for the jugular before we've been properly introduced."

Carley hesitated, suddenly unsure how to respond.

Oh, shit! He's nice. Why did I have to pick today to do this?

She looked Peter over. He was six-one, very muscular in the shoulders, black hair, blue eyes, strong jaw, and a really mellow voice. He was handsome in a rough cowboy sort of way.

Who am I kidding? He's gorgeous!

The pause in their exchange became pregnant and had time to birth quintuplets, but Carley still couldn't think of anything to say. Her courage was rapidly fading into creeping uncertainty.

"That's a rather unusual dress," Peter said.

Carley responded impulsively. "I'm just so fed up with this entire Marriage Bureau farce. I figured this was the only chance I'd get to fuck with you."

I didn't say that! Tell me, I didn't say that!

Peter was momentarily stunned by her outburst. They both started laughing. Several heads rose above the partitions again to see what was going on. Neither cared. Their anxiety-fed laughter rolled into a giddy jag. Heads continued to pop up, then drop back behind the cubicle walls. Their tension drained, cascading from every pore as their laughter slowed and subsided. Peter checked his watch. "It's eleven o'clock. Want to catch an early lunch?"

Carley felt, more than heard, her disembodied voice say, "Sure."

I have a date!

Peter offered his arm. Carley hooked it firmly, and they steered through the cubicle maze toward the main entrance. Passing the receptionist's desk, Peter left a message for Ms. Bender to cancel the rest of his appointments. He'd call her. Then barely shy of running, they were out the front door and on the street, heading away from the dreaded Federal Marriage Bureau.

Free at last. Free at last. Thank God Almighty, free at last.

Reverend Martin Luther King, Jr.
American Hero

"There's a nice club two blocks from here, the Sports Spectacular. Do you like sports?"

"Not really," Carley replied, wondering if that was a relationship-killing question. Maybe she should hedge a bit more on the preliminaries, but Peter didn't seem to be put off by her answer.

"Do you like good food?"

"Calories and I are very old friends." Carley smiled.

"Close enough. What are you in the mood for?" Peter eyed her dress. "If I had to guess, I would say Chinese?"

Carley laughed again. She was still holding his arm. She gave it a little squeeze, confirming that Peter was real. Her confidence returned.

I have a date!

She now felt great! "How about a steak?"

"Medium rare, sautéed onions and mushrooms?"

"That sounds really good."

Peter pulled out his cell, and hit the speed dial. "Tran, two Prime Rib, medium rare with the works. You pick the sides. I'll be there in five minutes."

Carley couldn't hear the other side of the conversation.

"It all worked out. I'm happy," he said as he hung up. Peter looked at her again trying to find something to say. Should he try for clever? Witty? Straightforward and honest?

He settled on, "I'm Peter."

It's not true that, upon being introduced to a woman, a man will immediately try to picture her naked. By the time you get to the introduction, he's already done that.

Leilani Maka'alohi
Waikiki Beach Tour Guide
Shtick from her tour bus commentary

~~*

Ms. Bender looked a second time at the message the receptionist had handed to her. "You're kidding. They walked out together, those two?"

"Just this minute," said the receptionist. "You should have seen the dress she was wearing!"

Ms. Bender picked up the profile sheets for Peter Kurloff and Carley Harper. "You never know about long shots. The only thing they have in common is that they both like croissants for breakfast."

Two weeks later, Ms. Bender received and filed form J758A-348P, Declaration of Engagement with Intent to Begin Marriage Arbitration for Peter Kurloff and Carley Harper.

~~*

The meeting with the attorneys ended two hours later. The date of the wedding and Peter paying for the reception were the only issues resolved. Everything else remained on the long list that Peter and Carley looked over as they sat in a booth in the Baseball Room.

Philadelphia was playing Atlanta on the large flat-screen at the front of the room. The Phillies were at home and behind by two. Since the game was a replay, Peter knew Philadelphia would pull it out in the bottom of the seventh inning, a crushing home run with runners on first and third. The announcer's voice played over the speakers:

And the Braves take the field as we head into the fifth inning. The clouds are holding off. I think we'll be able to play this one out.

"You want to watch the game," Carley asked.

"No. It's a replay. Philly's gonna take this one. Great triple play next inning. Meyers is still stretched out over the mound, just recovering from his pitch when he snags a line drive and . . ."

"Peter!"

"Sorry." He paused searching for a good starting place. There didn't seem to be one. "I just didn't know getting married was going to cost more than buying my club."

Carley sipped a wine cooler. She knew they were out of fashion, but she liked the sweet, fruity taste and was able to nurse one for hours so that she wouldn't get tipsy. It was only twelve o'clock. She didn't normally drink this early, however today was a worthy exception. "You don't want to do this, do you?"

Strike one, low and to the outside.

"It doesn't matter what I want, does it," said Peter. "I have to get married, or get taxed into oblivion."

What a stupid err! I can't believe he dropped that ball!

Carley gulped her wine cooler. It was icy cold. Drinking too fast, she choked, nearly spitting a mouthful back into her glass before she recovered.

"Are you okay?"

"I'm fine." She cleared her throat several times. "You didn't answer my question."

It crossed Peter's mind that he should follow Carley's lead, choking on his draft, rather than answer that question. He tried to find words that wouldn't hurt her feelings, but it was always better to play it straight. "You deserve an honest answer. You probably won't like it, but it's better than a lie, isn't it?"

"I've always thought so."

"I have a really nice life here, Carley. I work twelve to fourteen hours a day, sometimes seven days a week for months, but I love every minute of it. I built this business from scratch, and pretty soon, I'll own it free and clear. Then, I plan to open another club and make that one a success." He sipped his beer. "Look around. This place is packed every day because I made Sports Spectacular into the best club on the strip. All my clubs are going to be top of the line. They're all going to be packed. I'm not trying to build an empire, but I have plans for building a good solid business, much bigger than I have now."

"What are you building it for? Your DST hostess?"

Strike two! A screaming curve, the kind that breaks two inches from your face!

"You want me to admit I use a DST. Okay, I admit it. I don't know anyone who doesn't use one. I work hard; I play hard when I have the chance. Maybe it's not perfection, but it's a damn good life."

Carley wasn't angry. Maybe she should be. She felt the need to cry, the pressure slowly building, tear ducts ready to let go. She refused to give in. At least he was being honest. That's supposed to be better than a lie.

It doesn't feel better.

"What about love," she asked.

"If you're talking about a personal life, kids and all that, I'm not sure what I really want. I think about it sometimes, but not often. I wonder with my workload if I have time for a family."

"I'm a good woman, Peter."

"I know that. You don't have to defend yourself."

"I am not defending myself! I'm stating a fact. I work long hours, too. And I have plans for my life. I've been working for four years for my promotion at Brighton-Marshack. I also plan to have children, with or without a husband. I just can't seem to give up on finding one yet. Maybe I'm deluding myself. I'll never be able to compete with that fucking machine."

"Why is DST always the issue? Do you want to go back to the days when fidelity meant everyone was sneaking around behind everyone else's back? Let's all be holy in church, and forget that yesterday the minister's wife and I copped a quickie in the backseat of the Chevy."

"It wasn't like that."

"How can you look at the divorce statistics and tell me it wasn't like that? Who's kidding themselves here? You either had to settle for adultery or serial monogamy. The perfect marriage that women want never existed."

Strike three! He is outta there!

Carley handed him her copy of the arbitration list. "You can keep this. I don't think I'll be needing it."
Peter watched her walk out.
"Damn it!"

Time for another batter.

"Will you shut up!" Peter realized that he'd yelled at the TV. Everyone in the Baseball Room turned to stare at him. He picked up the arbitration papers and headed for his office.

The relationship between sex and baseball is uniquely American. If you hit it off, you start with a run at first base. If she likes you, you steal second base and keep pushing to steal more bases. To win the game, you have to score. You never lose that desperate desire to drive in the winning run. When you finally do hit a home run, she evaluates your performance and assigns you to the Majors, the Minors, Little League or Pee Wee.

Otto Mauldin
Pitching Coach
Cincinnati Reds

Read ***Sexual Evolution*** TODAY at: http://amzn.to/1gkkW1A

~~*

Please review *Conversations with Larry Xenomorph?*

Let's be honest, most people enjoy a little groveling on occasion. So, this is another independent author on bended knee asking for a review.

Don't laugh. Using the same method, I ended up married.

I sincerely hope you enjoyed the book and will take a minute to tell others about your experience with Larry and company.

Many thanks,
Jay Cole

Post your review at: http://amzn.to/1eKYEnQ

~~*

About the Author

Jay Cole is a writer of immense talent and insight. He lives in Vermont on a maple syrup farm with his wife of thirty-two years, Maxine, their three lovely children, Number One, Number Two, and Number Three, and his dog, Worthless. Jay Cole personally wrote this biographical blurb, and he has absolutely no shame about lying like a rug.

. . . That about covers as much of my personal life as I'd like to post on the government's NSA servers.

(Relax, paranoia is just a hobby!)

My real story is one of laughter. As soon as I learned to read at about age five, I asked Santa for joke books. I wrote my first short story in fourth grade — not a homework assignment. The written word simply appeals to me, especially when it reveals the absurdities of life that so often spontaneously arise in our daily routines.

I've written magazine articles, novels and scripts, and a ton of standup comedy. My favorite genres include humor and comedy, romantic comedy, science fiction, and a bit of action adventure, but I have to say that humor and comedy top my list of preferences.

I've found that the humor in life is a vital resource that we all share. Everybody laughs, and isn't that truly marvelous!

Granted, it's often a little harder for some of us to laugh in the arena of romance and sex, but if you can't laugh joyously in bed, what are you doing there?

Nevermind. I don't really want to know.

www.ingramcontent.com/pod-product-compliance
Lightning Source LLC
Chambersburg PA
CBHW060929180626
46817CB00004B/1457